Suraiya Jafari

An American President

A Novel by

Cindy Moy

Suraiya Jafari: An American President by Cindy Moy

This is a work of fiction. Names, characters, businesses, places, events and incidents are either the products of the author's imagination or used in a fictitious manner. Any resemblance to actual persons, living or dead, or actual events is purely coincidental.

ISBN: 978-0615993997

Published by Plum River Publishing

The Office of President Suraiya Jafari

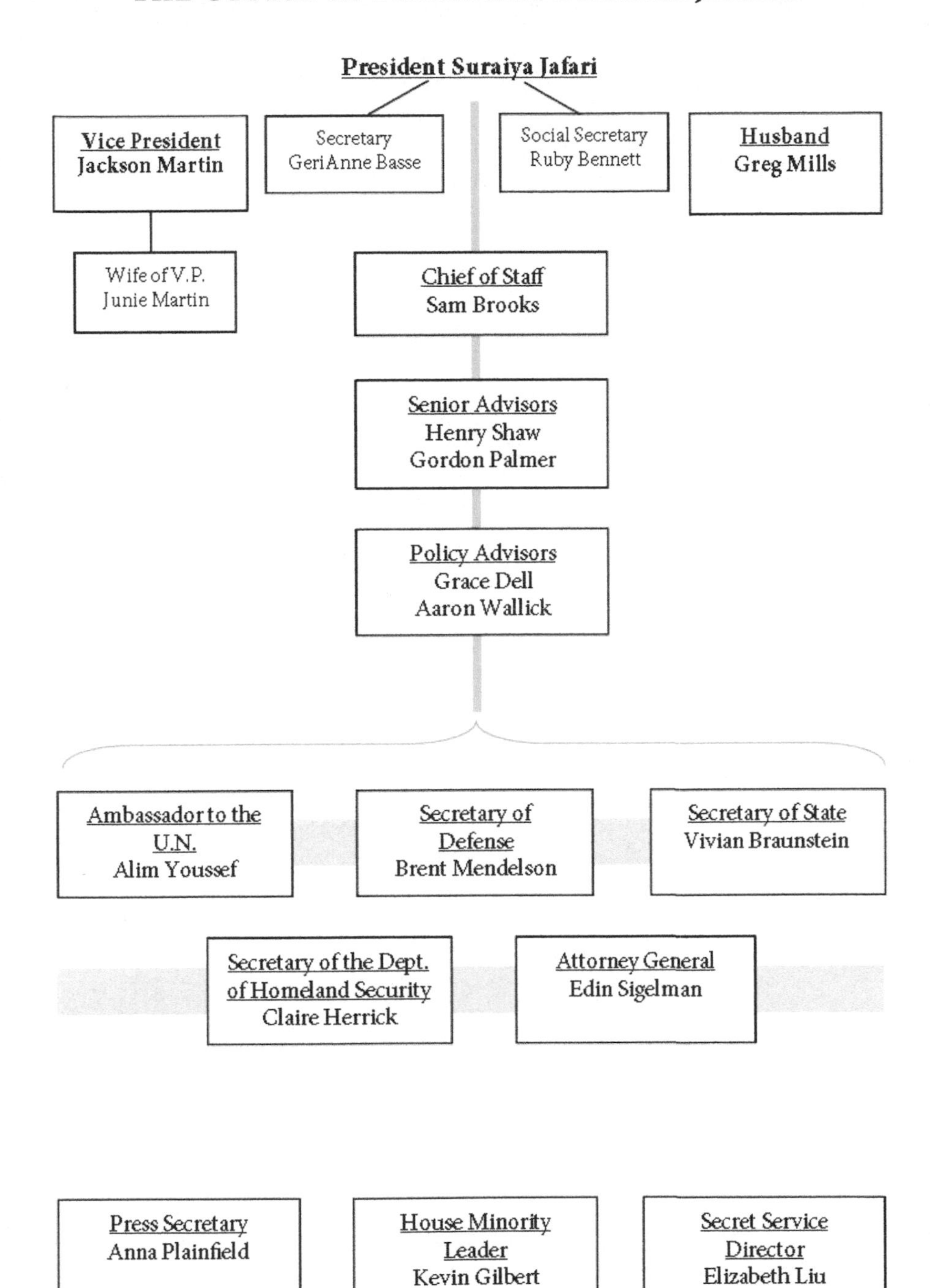

"The one truth that would help us begin to solve our ethical and political problems [is] that we are all more or less wrong, that we are all at fault, all limited and obstructed by our mixed motives, our self-deception, our greed, our self-righteousness, and our tendency to aggression and hypocrisy."

—Thomas Merton

Prologue

The late President Dennis Wilkins always said that a woman would become president over his dead body, and he was right. It would be significant even now, in 2050, for someone like me to become the American President. I fear my country's political climate has not changed all that much in the intervening years. Someone such as me has about as much chance of being elected to the presidency now as I did thirty years ago, which is nil.

My presidency was either an accident or the act of a supreme being. I'll leave that for you to decide. In 2023, I thought we had come far enough as a nation that my ascension to the White House would matter only as a notation in the history books.

I would prefer to be memorialized for how I handled the trials and tragedies—secession, a coup of the White House, the brink of a third world war.

More likely, I will be remembered for the asterisks behind my name in the presidential lineup: the first female, the first Indian-American, the first Muslim.

This is the story of how I, Suraiya Jafari, became the forty-sixth president of the United States of America. It is a story of chance, and of family, and of faith. It is the story of my life, and, more importantly, the life of my country.

—*Suraiya*

Chapter One

My predecessor, President Dennis Robert Wilkins, was elected by a landslide in 2016, defeating his Democratic opponent, Senator Lionel Peterson, by more than eighteen million votes. That's about sixty percent of the popular vote, a feat not seen since Richard Nixon's resounding defeat of George McGovern in 1972.

The President's landslide victory was due in no small part to the fact that the fifty-six-year-old Dennis, tall and fair-haired and athletic, just *looked* like a president. He had a movie stars' angular features. It was as though the Republicans ordered him directly from central casting. He was also, as my mother would say, charismatic as all get out, although his charm was lost on me. He and I could barely stand to be in the same room.

When people think of the President of the United States of America, no one thinks of someone who looks like me. They might imagine a black president or a female president, but they do not picture an Indian-American woman, barely five feet tall with black-framed glasses and her unruly hair pulled back into a severe bun. I look more like a librarian than the leader of the free world.

They especially do not picture a Muslim president, so imagine the surprise of the American people when they woke one day to find me in the White House. We were all, I as well as the rest of the populace, victims of surprise and hostage to the Constitution, guinea pigs to this great experiment called democracy.

Dennis's effectiveness as president was due in large part to Vice President Theodore Adelson, who was the real leadership muscle behind the duo. Few people know this, but it was Theodore who chose the Cabinet appointments and who made all important decisions. Theodore was the brains behind that operation. He had a way of telling Dennis what to do while making Dennis think that he had made the decisions on his own. That's why Theodore was known for being a hands-on vice president. He had to keep his eye on Dennis at all times. Theodore was the hand in the puppet's behind.

The Republican plan was for Dennis to be president for eight years, then Theodore for another eight years. Until the spring of 2023, it certainly seemed as though the plan was on track.

That year I was serving in the House of Representatives, representing Minnesota's Third Congressional District. Six years before, I was only the third Muslim to be elected to Congress. The other two Muslims in the House at that time were black, male, and Democrats.

I've often wondered why so many Muslims are Democrats rather than Republicans. Most Muslims I know are against abortion and gay marriage, which are solidly Republican stances. Maybe it's because so many Republicans are of the evangelical Christian variety. Even today, I don't think Christians realize they share the same religious forebearers as Muslims.

We believe in Abraham and Moses and, yes, even Jesus. We believe Jesus was born of a virgin and performed miracles and was a great prophet. We celebrated Christmas in our house, as do many Muslims in America, although I believe Mother did that so my brother Daris and I would fit in better with our Christian classmates.

We never went in for the Santa bit, though. I always found the idea of Santa creepy. Why do Christians insist on associating one of the holiest of days of their religion with a magical elf who spies on children and sneaks into houses at night? I've never been able to wrap my head around that.

Muslims part ways with Christians when it comes to believing that Jesus is the son of God and in the resurrection, but I always thought our shared reverence would be enough to overcome our differences. Maybe someday it will. For now, I only know that if Republicans stopped painting all Muslims with the terrorist label, it would be easier to recruit Muslims to our party.

When I launched my initial campaign for the House of Representatives, Congress had the most religiously diverse House in history. At any given time, there are 435 members of the House, plus six non-voting delegates from D.C. and the U.S. territories. Besides three Muslims, in 2016 there were thirty-one Jews, one Quaker, two Buddhists, and an atheist. That left 397 representatives who considered themselves Christian. I'm not one to tell tales, but suffice it to say, many of those so-called Christians failed some of the basic precepts of Christianity, especially the rules against adultery.

There were seventy-five women in the House, and out of the seventy-six representatives of color, there was not one person of Indian descent, although there were six congresspeople who fell into the category of "Asian."

So while it was not out of the question that a female Indian Muslim could be elected to Congress, it was definitely a long shot. To be honest, I don't think I could have been elected without the endorsement of my predecessor, John Carlson. He represented Minnesota for twelve years before he retired.

While I don't think Carlson was thrilled at endorsing a Muslim, the fact was that the Republican party was looking to diversify its candidate pool to pull in more votes, and with me winning the Republican primary for the congressional seat, he did not have much choice in the matter.

"At least you're not a real Muslim," Carlson said to me when he called to say I would get his endorsement.

"I'm not?"

"You don't wear a headscarf, so you're not really Muslim," he replied.

"Not all Muslim women wear the hijab," I said.

"You'll go farther in politics if you change your name and convert to Christianity. Consider going by 'Suri' and becoming

Catholic," Carlson said. "It's always good to appeal to the Catholic vote."

"I'm not going to pretend to believe in something in order to get votes," I replied tersely.

Carlson laughed. "Sure you will. What do you think politics is all about?"

I was sufficiently non-threatening to be palatable to the party. My parents were non-practicing Muslims. Technically, my dad was more of a humanist, but that label upset my mom, so Dad referred to himself as non-practicing.

My parents believed the basic tenets of Islam—service to others and social justice were the most important aspects of our religion—and raised my brother Daris and me to follow that path. I've never been entirely sure which parts of my upbringing were based in religion, culture, or merely habit.

My father, Rabee Jafari, was a professor at the Humphrey School of Public Affairs. He died of cancer during my second term in Congress. Physically he was a small man, barely five-foot-six with a slight build, but the strongest and wisest man I've ever met. I could have used his counsel many times both in Congress and the White House. There is not a day goes by that I do not miss him.

My mother, Cala, became a force of nature in her own right after we moved into the White House. As much as the world owes my mother, I owe her more. Mother was a woman strong in spirit and soft in nature, always smiling yet never hesitating to inform me of the clear guidelines on how virtuous young girls were to act.

She believed that cussing was a dirty habit for the uneducated, and was fond of substituting ice cream flavors for cursing. If Cala Jafari looked you in the eye and told you that you were full of spumoni, you knew you were in trouble.

It's natural for children to view their parents as nothing more than, well, parents, but how could I not have seen the role she would play in world events? Not once did I look at her and think, *This woman will change history.*

Chapter Two

My dad had three rules for me: tell the truth, work hard, and create good in this world. Those were the rules he lived by, and he expected me to do the same. My mother had dozens of rules, but the major ones were: do not talk to boys, dress modestly, be kind, respect your elders, tell the truth, do not curse, and never, ever get a tattoo.

My parents' rules were grounded in Islam, but they were never presented to us as religious in nature. My dad believed that each person needed to make a personal decision about what it meant to be a Muslim.

"Let your behavior speak for your religion," he would tell us.

He did not realize how difficult that would be for a child never taught the basic tenets of the faith. Or perhaps he did. I learned more about Islam in my World History class in junior high than I did from my parents. I had a vague idea of Islam, but details were sorely lacking. Most of my classmates assumed I was a Hindu.

"Where is your red dot?" a boy asked me in seventh grade.

"Red dot?"

"On your forehead. Indians are supposed to wear red dots on their foreheads," he informed me.

"You mean a bindi? Bindis are a Hindu symbol," I explained. "I'm Indian, but I'm not Hindu."

"What's the difference?"

To me there was a lot of difference, but I didn't know how to explain this to him, so I avoided him as much as I could. I wish I would have had the words to make him understand the intersection of race and religion and culture, but I did not, and I doubt that even today most people would understand.

Growing up, I was a brown kid in a mostly white neighborhood, and I tried my best to be invisible. My friends tended to be other Asians, but they were not Indian like me. They were Chinese or Hmong, and even among them, I was an oddity, what with my family being in America for generations and many of theirs arriving only in the last ten years.

Among the few Indians, too, I was different. They were Hindu, and their parents were immigrants. My mother tried to help me look for similarities more than differences, as she knew the difficulties I was facing. However, she, too, was struggling to find her place, always airing out the house so it would not smell like curry or incense.

"In India, houses are better ventilated, so the smell does not linger," she would say for the umpteenth time.

How would you know? I would wonder to myself. I understood her vigilance about the smell, always wanting to make sure that my clothes bore no odor of Indian spices, not wanting me to be set apart from my classmates.

My brown skin invited the oddest of comments from the kids sitting next to me in class, descendants of pale Europeans.

"You're so lucky to have your tan year-round," said one girl, who laid a beach towel on her front lawn and sunbathed as soon as the spring temperatures rose above sixty degrees.

I became inured to repeated questions of "Have you ever ridden a camel?" (No) and "Where are you from?" (I live one block over from you). My classmates took one look at me and thought they knew me, without even asking my name. Our differences divided us, and we were too young, too inexperienced in the world, to bridge that gap.

I used to wear my Girl Scout vest when I ran errands with my mom. It was a sign of my Americanness, and when non-Indians would give us the once-over at the store, their scowl would relax when their eyes found my green vest. It was a mark that we belonged. At one point I begged my mom to let me change my name to something I considered more American, such as Sarah, but she refused.

"I hate having to explain my name to people," I complained.

"Just because your name is different from your classmates doesn't mean you are any less American," she'd reply.

People often refer to me as the first Indian President, but my family has not lived in India for more than a hundred years. I was born in Minneapolis, as were both of my parents. Dad attended the local public school, while Mom attended an all-girls Catholic school.

"But Mom," I asked, "weren't your parents worried that you would burst into flames when you walked through the doors as a Muslim?"

Mom laughed. "The nearest mosque was 1500 miles away. St. Kate's was the only all-girls school available. They had to make some choices."

Now that I am older and wiser, I think that sums up life pretty well. We all have to make some choices, and as a Muslim in America, that means making do with the facilities at hand, and often the option most closely aligned with Islamic values are those of Christians. For example, it was difficult for my parents to find entertainment they considered wholesome enough for Daris and me when we were teenagers. One of the few things they would let us do is go to Christian music night at the Roller Garden, the local roller-skating rink. I don't know where all the Christian teenagers were on Christian music night, but all the Muslim kids were at the Roller Garden.

None of my grandparents were born in India either. All of my grandparents were born in Mozambique, Africa, where my great-grandparents were wealthy cashew traders. My great-great-grandfathers emigrated from Gujarat, India to Mozambique in the late 1800s to join other Gujaratis seeking their fortune in the cashew trade.

My great-grandfather Mahdavi was a cashew trader. He spotted my great-grandmother when she was working for her father, who ran a general supply store in Nampula, a northern province in Mozambique. According to Muslim custom, they were not allowed to speak to each other, and he approached her father to arrange a match.

"That's how it was done in those days," my grandmother Layla told me. "The parents chose your partner based on the common good of the family."

"But Grandma," I protested. "What about love?"

"Love is fleeting, *beta*. What lasts are shared values."

It all seemed so barbaric to me as a teenager. I understand it better now. Shared visions of the future smooth over many rough moments in a marriage.

Grandma Layla and Grandpa Ebi met in Mozambique as children and were wed as teenagers. My great-grandparents became concerned for the safety of their family and their business in 1947 when India was partitioned into two countries, India and Pakistan, under the Indian Independence Act. The Act ended the British colonization there, and meant that Indians suddenly had to choose between citizenship of the two countries, even those Indians in Mozambique.

My family chose to retain British citizenship while other Indians registered as Indian citizens, a move that would change the course of our family. There was growing tension between Portugal and India over the rule of Goa, a Portuguese colony at that time, for more than four hundred years. Goa is a state in western India, and after partition, India wanted it back, but Portugal declined to surrender it. Throughout the 1950s, my great-grandpa Mahdavi grew increasingly concerned about this tension between the countries.

My great-grandparents stayed in Africa and sent my grandparents to Britain, with instructions to continue on to America. They did as they were told, eventually setting up a cashew-importing business in Queens, New York, and finally settling in Minneapolis, where my mother was born. As my mother said when I told her I wanted to enter politics, "you might as well. One group of nuts is the same as the other."

My great-grandparents were imprisoned in the Portuguese internment camps in 1961, their fortune confiscated. They never made it out of the camps. Their children—my grandparents—were poor, but they were free. They never took anything for granted again, and they taught me to never take anything for granted either, and that included freedom.

When I was a sophomore in high school, the state American Legion held a contest, and my civics teacher gave extra credit to any student who entered. Extra credit was always an enticing prospect for the part of me that not only wanted to outperform the other students, but wanted to leave them in the dust. Students were invited to submit essays on the subject "What does it mean to be an American?" The winner received an all-expense-paid trip to Washington D.C. with forty-nine winners from the other states.

I poured my heart and soul into that essay. I wrote about Grandpa and Grandma Jafari coming to America as teenagers with nineteen dollars in their pocket, and how they put themselves through school and became doctors. I wrote about their struggles to adapt to American ways, and their determination to succeed. I wrote about their sacrifices in building a better life for their son (my dad), and how, in their later years, they gave back to the country they loved by volunteering at a medical clinic for the poor in the Phillips neighborhood of Minneapolis.

It was touching, if I do say so myself. I did not include the fact that my grandparents achieved affluence through sacrifice and hard work. Not cashew-trader wealthy, but certainly upper middle class. The interesting thing about America is that we all want to become rich, but we distrust and misalign those who are already there. I knew the key to winning the essay contest was to be the underdog. I also knew the only way I would get to go to Washington as a fifteen-year-old was as the winner of that contest.

The Legion announced me the winner, and in June I headed to the nation's capital—with my mother.

"You are not going halfway across the country without a chaperone," she insisted.

"But Mom, none of the other kids are going to be there with their parents," I protested.

"If the other kids jumped off a bridge, would you?" she demanded.

I continued to whine, to no avail.

"I'm smart enough to not jump off a bridge, Mom."

The Legion would only pay for one ticket, so my mom paid her own way, including an extra hotel room where she and I stayed, on a floor away from the other kids. It was humiliating. I refused to acknowledge her presence the entire trip, which was difficult, because none of the other kids wanted to be near me with Mom hanging about, so I had no one to talk to. She was right to be worried, of course. A number of those other kids spent their evenings getting high and hooking up.

More importantly, that trip was my first vision of American government in action. We visited the Congressional building to watch the Senate debate a bill—I don't recall which bill—and after listening to the rhetoric for awhile, I recall thinking, "I could do that." Even in my insecure teenage days, I could see that the Senators were mere human beings, as opposed to the superior intellectual beings I had presumed.

"Some of them didn't seem that bright," I told my dad when I returned home. He laughed.

"It is not about being smart," he told me. "It is about who is able to disappoint people at the rate they can stand while raising the most money."

That trip inspired an interest in public service, but I never intended to run for office. Politics seemed too dirty for a respectable person.

Chapter Three

Occasionally my parents would decide we were becoming too white. They would try to teach us more of what it meant to be Indian, although they were never quite sure what "being Indian" meant in America. Every Saturday the four of us would drive over to Izzy's Ice Cream parlor on Grand Avenue in St. Paul for avocado ice cream, which my parents told me was an Indian flavor. I have since learned it is African. This is what we mean when we say America is a melting pot. Even the ice cream flavors melt together.

One time Dad heard of an Indian-American comedian performing in Chicago, and took Daris to Illinois to see the show. Dad didn't think to find out if the comedian's material was suitable for a ten-year-old boy. The show turned out to feature all kinds of off-color humor about women and intimacy and bodily functions. Daris had a lot of questions after that show, but Dad refused to discuss it. Ever.

Masala chai, an Indian classic, was part of our everyday life. Mom was quite particular about her tea, creating her own chai masala by grinding together black pepper, white pepper, ginger, cinnamon, cardamom, cloves, and nutmeg. These spices would be put in a suacepan with whole milk, water, loose black tea leaves, and sugar, and brought to a boil, then steeped and strained before drinking. I've tried versions of masala chai from tea shops all over the world, and no one ever made this spiced tea better than my mother.

When I was all of fifteen years old, I qualified for a state program called the post-secondary enrollment option. Essentially, PSEO allowed me to take college generals in lieu of my last two years of high school, putting me on the fast track to graduate from college before I was nineteen.

Ambitious high schoolers loved PSEO because it put them in more challenging classes with more mature students. Parents loved PSEO because the state picked up the tuition for those two years. I was fine with leaving high school early. I never fit in there anyway. Other than playing badminton after school twice a week with a few of the other Asian kids, I spent most of my time outside of school reading in my room at home.

One day during my last year of high school, Mom and Dad were arguing about where I would go to college while Zee-TV USA blared in the background in Mom's latest attempt to instill a bit of Indian culture in our house. Zee-TV USA was a satellite station out of India that broadcast Indian programs in Hindi with English subtitles.

Mother wanted me to attend the University of Minnesota, so that I could live at home and ride to school with Dad every day. Dad wanted me to attend the University of North Dakota in Grand Forks, which straddles the Minnesota border. More importantly, UND offered tuition waivers for students of color, meaning that I could finish college there for free.

"Do you really want to send our baby to a place so desperate for students of color that they have to bribe them to attend?" demanded Mother.

"She's going to be surrounded by white people no matter where she goes," argued Dad. "She might as well go to a university that is dedicated to diversifying."

"What about your daughter? Do you think she wants to go to North Dakota?" retorted Mother.

Dad turned to me. "What about it, Suraiya. Are you willing to go to North Dakota?"

"If you want me to," I said. "But everyone will assume that I only got in to UND because I'm Indian."

"Hah! You see?" said Mother. "Do you want your daughter to be a token Asian?"

Dad rolled his eyes. "The waiver only applies if she gets accepted. She still has to meet all the qualifications."

"The other kids won't see it that way, Dad," I said quietly.

He looked at me, and I felt bad for the pang of pain that passed through his eyes. Dad always tried to protect me from racism and discrimination, but he could not protect me from the knowledge that the rules were different for kids who looked like me. If I went to UND, I would bear the stigma of affirmative action, and this was a burden he was loathe to put on my shoulders.

Mom won, and I attended the U of M, graduating in May of 2007 at the age of twenty with a degree in pre-law obtained under the close watch of my father, much to the disappointment of my grandparents Mahdavi and Jafari. They expected me to go to medical school. That September I started classes at Hamline University School of Law in St. Paul. I considered living on campus in the law dorm, but Mother nixed that idea.

"You need to spend your time studying, not cooking and doing laundry," she told me. Daris had gone to college by that time, choosing to go to Stanford University near San Francisco, a move that Dad later blamed for Daris's life choices.

Mom spent a lot of time with her friends playing bridge and doing yoga, and I think she was nervous about her and Dad being empty nesters. In Minnesota, when a Caucasian couple is tired of each other but don't want the hassle of a divorce they buy a lake cabin and one spouse spends most of the time there and the other spouse spends time in the city.

Indian families are not like that, even in the Midwest. They stay together. I was, in short, a buffer between my parents. While they had always gotten along just fine, they had little desire to transition from a child-centered relationship to a partner-centered one. Two years after I began law school, though, a partner-centered relationship is what they would have, whether they liked it or not.

Chapter Four

In September 2008, in my second year of law school, law firms and military recruiters set up booths in the atrium to recruit students for clerkships the following summer. Along with my friends, Grace Dell and Aaron Wallick, I made my way through the labyrinth.

Grace, who speaks Mandarin and Spanish and is the daughter of a white father and black mother, was a hot prospect for the monolith firms that preferred lawyers who could handle international business. She was one of the few people I knew back then who understood what it meant to walk the line between two cultures.

Aaron was a Minnesota farm boy who had spent the previous four years backpacking around the globe by himself. Tall and fair-skinned, with reddish curly hair, he was older than Grace and me by about seven years, with a laissez-faire attitude born of sleeping in roadside campgrounds in dodgy, sometimes dangerous places. Few things rattled Aaron.

Every firm I talked to acted excited to see me.

"We represent companies doing business in India," they would say. "We would love to talk to you more."

"I don't speak Hindi," I told them, and they lost interest in me, my brown skin no longer a desirable trait.

We stopped by the booth for the Navy Judge Advocate General's Corps, better known as JAG. JAG is basically the law firm for the military, with the Army, Navy, and Air Force each having its own branch. Aaron was interested in becoming a criminal defense attorney, and there was no better place to get trial experience than JAG.

I leafed through the glossy JAG brochure while Aaron chatted with the recruiter about what he called knife-and-fork school. In JAG, officers go to a regular law school, then to six weeks of knife-and-fork school to learn about military protocol. There is some physical training involved, but there is no basic training like there is for enlisted men and women.

"Are you interested in JAG?" the recruiter asked me.

I shook my head. "I don't think it's my thing," I replied.

"You should think about it. It might help your citizenship application," he informed me. I could feel Aaron tense beside me.

"I was born here," I answered. "My parents were born here."

He nodded. "Then this probably isn't for you," he said. "We don't see many of you in our ranks."

I stared at him.

"Excuse me?"

"No offense," he said, holding up his hands. "I just mean that you don't see a lot of Indians in the military."

"Do you see a lot of Americans in the military?" I asked hotly. "Because I'm an American."

"Come on, Suraiya," said Aaron, pulling me away toward the next booth, manned by a burly African-American Marine with a shaved head. The Marine recruiter, Staff Sergeant Del Embers, had watched the exchange with the JAG recruiter with bemused detachment.

Aaron nodded to SSgt. Embers as he nervously picked up the Marine Corps brochure. I stewed beside him, my arms folded across my chest.

"You interested in joining the Marines, kid?" he asked me.

"JAG isn't for me," I responded.

He shrugged. "The Marines don't have JAG. Marines are

Marines first, lawyers second. In JAG, lawyers are lawyers first. There's a difference."

"Do you have a knife-and-fork school?" I asked sarcastically.

Embers laughed. "Only if you survive boot camp. A third of every Officer Candidates class drops out. Then after law school there's The Basic School, and if you survive that, Naval Justice School. If you get through all that, kid, you can tell that JAG recruiter where to put his knife and fork."

Now it was my turn to laugh.

"Suraiya, you don't have to prove anything to anybody," said Aaron urgently. The military had never been part of my career plans, but Aaron was wrong. I did have something to prove, and I had a sudden urge to prove it to everyone.

When I finished filling out the paperwork with SSgt. Embers, he asked me if my parents would be upset about me joining the Marines.

"Furious," I told him. "I may just leave a note on the kitchen table and show up at boot camp where it's safer."

I gathered up my papers and jacket and prepared to go home to face the music.

"Hey kid," Embers called to me. I turned to face him. "Drop me a line. Let me know where you end up."

"Will do," I promised.

I waited to tell the news to my parents until that spring and listened quietly as Mother yelled the entire Baskin-Robbins menu at me. Dad refused to speak to me for weeks. I spent the summer between my second and third year of law school in Officer Candidates School at Quantico, Virginia.

I wrote imaginary emails and texts to SSgt. Embers the entire time I was there. When I was sitting in a field at three a.m. on watch duty, cradling my assault weapon, I would imagine an email that read *Dear SSgt. Embers, I hate you. I hate you so much. This is all your fault. Sincerely, Suraiya Jafari.*

It would have been rude to send such an email, and Cala Jafari would not tolerate such rudeness in her daughter, but I imagined that same email when I was on a thirteen-mile hike, loaded down with gear, with the other women in my platoon. I imagined that email when the drill sergeants were in my face, screaming orders at me. I imagined that email when I was crawling on my stomach through muck and mud while fake mortar shells exploded above my head.

Somewhere in those ten weeks of torture, I stopped imagining that email and started imagining my future as a Marine. For the first time in my life, I was part of something bigger than my family, and it felt good. I belonged somewhere.

The fall after OCS I returned to Minneapolis for my final year of law school, and after graduation in 2010 went back to Quantico for The Basic School, where they teach Marine officers eleven principles of leadership. To understand me, both as a person and as a president, you have to understand the principles:

- Be technically and tactically proficient
- Know yourself and seek self-improvement
- Know your Marines and look out for their welfare
- Keep your Marines informed
- Set the example
- Ensure the task is understood, supervised, and accomplished
- Train your Marines as a team
- Make sound and timely decisions
- Develop a sense of responsibility in your subordinates
- Employ your unit in accordance with its capabilities
- Seek responsibility and take responsibility for your actions

That is the code I still live by today. After I finished The Basic School, followed by Naval Justice School in Newport, Rhode Island, I finally sent SSgt. Embers the email I promised.

Thank you, was all I wrote. I did not expect a reply. I doubted he even remembered me, a single recruit from years before, but the following morning I found a message from SSgt. Embers in my inbox: *The only label you wear now is Marine.*

Chapter Five

In 2013, I was a lieutenant in the Marines, originally assigned to the Legal Operations Directorate of Combined Joint Interagency Task Force-435 in Parwan, a U.S. military base a few miles from Bagram Airfield. My job was to assist the commander in establishing the new rule of law in Afghanistan. The war in Afghanistan was winding down, twelve long years after the United States went after the terrorists that declared war on our country by using commercial aircraft as missiles, killing three thousand people on American soil in a well-orchestrated sucker punch on September 11, 2001.

This is not to say the Afghans had been freed from tyranny, but rather the Afghan government and military were sufficiently stabilized as to soon be able to continue to rebuild without American military intervention. The Obama administration was gearing up to bring the last of our troops home in 2014. To meet that deadline, the Afghan government had a lot of work to do and relied on American military to train not only its own police forces, but also its government leaders. That is where people like me were essential.

I didn't know how I would fit in when I landed in Afghanistan. Would the Afghans see me as less of a Muslim because I was

American? Would my fellow soldiers view me as less of an American because I was a Muslim?

I felt the same suspicion about the *Mujahideen*, the Afghan soldiers who fought alongside the Americans in the effort to oust the Taliban. They claimed to be on our side, but how could we be sure where their loyalties lay? The *Mujahideen* guarded our camp and we relied on them to protect us as we rid their country of extremists, while helping them to rebuild the Afghan infrastructure, including the rebuilding of schools and mosques.

Many of the *Mujahideen* spoke broken English, and from them I heard tales of atrocities committed by the Taliban against the Afghan men and women. By the time I arrived, conditions in Afghanistan were much improved, and the relationship between the Afghans and the Americans was cordial, if a bit wary.

The reaction of the *Mujahideen* when they met me was confusion. The Americanness of an Indian and a Muslim woman baffled them. There has been much written about the concurrent American wars in Afghanistan and Iraq, and while the Iraqi war was highly unpopular, both in Iraq and at home, the Afghan war was both necessary and welcomed by the Afghans. Freedom is not a uniquely American concept. It is desired the world over.

Still, we Americans had to protect ourselves from everyone: enemy combatants, suicide bombers, corrupt Afghan officers, and the drug cartels. The adrenaline from being constantly on guard was like wearing an intravenous drip of Red Bull.

The conditions were brutal. More than a thousand enemy combatants were detained at Parwan, making the base a frequent target for rocket attacks. Any personnel going into or out of the base could expect to be ambushed by improvised explosive devices and small-arms fire. The military may not have classified "lawyer" as a combat position, but we were all well aware that we could find ourselves in the middle of a firefight at any time of the day or night.

One day I was in a conference room built of plywood, explaining due process to a group of Afghan prosecutors and defense attorneys while sweat ran down my face and back, when a mortar exploded inside our compound. A vehicle was blown apart, shattering glass that rained against the thin plywood walls and sending a jagged edge of metal fender through the plywood above my head.

Add to the mental stress the physical stress. My helmet, flak vest, M-16 rifle, and M-9 pistol weighed seventy pounds altogether, plus my bag of legal files. Carrying that around in 140 degree heat was a tough load. In all my months in Afghanistan, I don't think I ever stopped sweating. To beat the heat I would get up at five o'clock in the morning and run laps around the inner compound. It was the only way to maintain the physical stamina deployment required.

It was not all bad. I was worried about how I would be treated by the Afghan men. In Afghanistan at that time, women had few rights. But I found the average men and women of Kabul generous and hospitable. Sure, some of the men refused to even acknowledge my presence, much less take counsel from me. Most of the men, though, were professional. They knew I had a job to do there and they were intent on doing theirs.

These men and I shared many meals in the justice centers—which were sometimes little more than canvas tents—sitting cross-legged on the floor, eating with our hands and discussing the future of their country. For some of them it was the first time they had spoken to a female outside of their family. For my part, I conceded to Afghan tradition and wore a headscarf.

Sometimes being female in a patriarchal society was a distinct advantage. Afghan women were not allowed to be in the presence of men to whom they were not related. If American servicemen were present, Afghan women refused to leave their houses. I was the only U.S. military personnel allowed to speak to female witnesses.

"I am Muslim too," I would tell them after pleasantries were exchanged through my translator, Dauod.

This small tidbit of information helped to put them at ease, and once relaxed, they would bombard me with questions about America. I helped at least a dozen women set up internet accounts. Two generations of Afghan women knew nothing but repression. That small connection with the world at-large led to a new view of the possibilities available to them outside Afghanistan. Now women are a driving force in rebuilding the country. It is long overdue.

Six weeks after I arrived at Parwan, two JAG officers and I were reassigned to be legal mentors to the officers in the fledgling Afghan military judicial system in Kabul. Our assignment was to educate the Afghan military legal teams on how to prosecute corruption within the military system using the U.S. Uniform Code of Military Justice, a task we soon learned was all but impossible as many of the most corrupt officers were the very officers we were mentoring. These officers would prosecute young soldiers for stealing food rations, all while the officers were trafficking in narcotics. We spent weeks ferreting out corrupt officers and bringing them to trial, only to watch the local Afghan judges succumb to political pressure and declare them not guilty. The word got out that military justice was an oxymoron when it came to high-ranking Afghan officers.

Three months into our deployment to Kabul, I received a report that a battalion commander was charging local villages a "protection fee." Villages that did not pay the bribe were subject to marauding bands of soldiers pouring into the villages, stealing what they could and raping anyone they could find, male or female, adult or child.

I started interviewing witnesses in the villages, which was no small task. Everywhere I went I was escorted by armed U.S. soldiers and Daoud. All military lawyers had these escorts. The constant threat of attack was part of the job, and our soldiers were scarier than anything seen in a horror movie. That's great for scaring off attackers, but not so good when trying to convince people to come forward against their own people.

One night, a young man, not more than fifteen, came to the base. He had heard that I was looking for witnesses to the latest attack, and his friends had convinced him to come forward. He would not enter the buildings for fear of being detained there. He was covered in sweat and dirt. Always in Afghanistan, there was the sweat and the dirt.

We met outside, in the shadows of the mess tent, my military escorts on alert. The young man was not the only one at risk. It was not unheard of for suicide bombers to masquerade as witnesses to get inside an American compound. Trust is a precious commodity in war. While I listened to the young man tell his story, I also listened for sounds of danger—footsteps nearby, the click of a trigger, a change in the insect pattern. Anything that would indicate this was all a setup.

"I am going to kill him," said the young man of the battalion commander, after telling me in broken English what he had endured at the hands of the commander's thugs.

"You don't need to do that. He will have to answer for what he has done," I reassured him.

"You cannot make him answer for his crimes," he said bitterly. "No one will listen to you."

"I will make them listen," I said, although I was unsure whether the commander would ever see the inside of a jail cell.

"If you do not, I will come back. I will kill him," said the young man, breaking down in sobs, then fleeing into the night.

By that point I wanted to kill the commander myself. My Afghan counterpart wanted nothing to do with the prosecution. I had to threaten to court martial him in order to get him to do his job. One of our undercover operatives sent word that a contract had been taken out on my life unless I dropped the charges. Two hundred bucks to kill me. That was how little my life was worth to them.

We presented seven days of evidence against the commander, most of it financial records that showed a standard of living far beyond the commander's pay grade. The young man could not be located and did not return to testify. The witnesses who did show up changed their testimony. The commander had many friends in the Afghan parliament and I received daily calls to drop the case. I refused.

After a two-week trial, the judge rendered his verdict: guilty of racketeering. The commander was sentenced to a mere two years in jail. I was livid, despite knowing that the commander receiving any jail time at all was a bit of a miracle.

When I was leaving the courtroom, throngs of journalists from around the world, as well as Afghan soldiers, were tapping away at their cell phones. The news was out: the law now applied to everyone.

As I entered the courtyard, clad in my helmet and flak jacket, I was surprised to see the young man who had been brave enough to come forward lurking at the edge of the crowd, and I surreptitiously made my way in his direction.

"Thank you," he said quietly as I passed.

"What will you do now?" I asked, not looking at him.

"Go to the mountains. I will not be able to return home."

I often think of that young man and wonder if he is safe. I got to return to the comfort and freedom of my barracks. I doubt he lived much past that day. The commander served fifty-two days in prison and was released. He was assigned to the position he had when he was arrested. Such results made it difficult to not feel impotent.

Chapter Six

Four months after being transferred to Kabul I was sent to Paktika province on the border with Pakistan. It was the most remote of the places I was stationed, and I was the lone female at the post. As the only female in Paktika, I was given private accommodations. The guys had to suffer it out in bunks in a tent. I had a trailer with a cot and a toilet. Not a bathroom; a toilet. When I stood in the middle of the trailer, I could touch both walls. The heat was stifling, and the small window did little to let in fresh air, but it was mine and mine alone, and I felt guilty for having privacy the males lacked.

Paktika is where the incident with a fallen soldier occurred that nearly got me court-martialed. The military Mortuary Affairs, the unit assigned to recover fallen soldiers, is highly trained in forensic disinterment and identification techniques. Recovering America's fallen requires the MA to scale cliffs and tiptoe among unexploded ordnance and mortar shells to reach battle sites. It is both physically and emotionally brutal. Mortuary Affairs has one of the most significant rates of post-traumatic stress disorder in all of the military.

The United States spends millions of dollars and hundreds of thousands of man-hours to search for the remains of our soldiers fallen in battle—whether that battle be in Iraq in 2012 or Sicily in 1945—to identify those remains, and to return the remains to the soldier's family.

Why do we do this? The official, clinical answer is so that we can accurately account for our people. So that we can examine the remains and know the exact cause of death, whether it be bullet, heart attack, or chemical weapon. To reassure those still fighting that their bodies will not fall into enemy hands should the same fate befall them.

But there are other, more personal reasons. Because the creed of the military is "no man left behind," and that includes those whose souls are departed. Because a soldier's family deserves to know for certain what befell their son or daughter. Because it is the right thing to do.

One December morning in 2014, a week before Daoud and I were sent to the Paktika province in Afghanistan, a patrol of six American soldiers went out on reconnaissance. Five came back; four alive and one dead, carried by the others. Pfc. Eric Forsberg had been the first to fall, with Sgt. Andrew Swanson falling second, as he tried to get to Forsberg's body. The four survivors sought cover and returned fire, driving back the enemy until they took off with Swanson's body in their vehicle. The enemy got to Forsberg's body before our guys could, and everyone in camp was angry and tense.

We all knew Forsberg was dead, but it is one thing to know that a comrade is gone for good, and another thing completely to put that person to rest. Until Forsberg was found, he was as good as living, and we were all on the lookout for any clue as to where he might be found.

Enemy combatants know that Americans are as protective of our dead as we are of our living and use it against us. They plant bombs on the bodies of dead American soldiers, knowing that we will risk our lives and those of our friends to recover our dead and return them to their families.

On Christmas Day 2014, when I was twenty-eight years old, I was driving to a remote village with my four-man unit and Daoud to interview the locals about drug trafficking in the area. I was not entirely surprised when a farmer flagged us down and approached me with a small bundle in his hands. Inside the dirty pouch made of sheepskin were the dog tags of Pfc. Forsberg, along with a photo of a smiling middle-aged couple and two teenagers who looked as though they would rather be getting their teeth drilled.

The driver of my unit, Pfc. Bussman, identified the photo as that of Forsberg with his parents and younger sister, taken for the church directory the year before, in Cedar Rapids, Iowa. The guys in my unit, already on alert as part their jobs, now grew even more agitated. Forsberg was their friend and they wanted him back, no matter what the cost. As an American and a fellow member of the military, I wanted him back just as much as they did. Even though Forsberg and I had never met, we were part of the same military "family."

"Where did you get this?" I asked the man through Daoud.

The man gestured to the west and said something in Pashto.

"He says he saw four men dump the body by the roadside ten days ago," said Daoud. "He and some of the villagers buried it next to a rock outcropping two kilometers from here."

The story was highly unlikely. The villagers knew as well as we did that a soldier's body near the roadside was probably rigged with an explosive device. Still, the man had Forsberg's personal effects.

"Take me to the soldier," I ordered.

The man backed away, waving his hands and speaking rapidly.

"He says he is afraid. The insurgents will kill him if they find out he helped you."

I unsnapped my weapon holster with my right hand.

"Take me to the soldier or I will put you in the front seat of my truck and drive through town where everyone can see you," I replied through Daoud.

I was not bluffing. If Forsberg was nearby, he was coming home with us.

The farmer sighed, then motioned to a decrepit pickup truck. We followed him out of the village, passing illegal poppy fields. When we first invaded Afghanistan, we were ordered to ignore the poppy fields in exchange for the local warlords' assistance in fighting the Taliban. Now we were ordered to make farmers plow over the poppy fields, which were used to make heroin.

"Do you always threaten to get innocent villagers killed?" asked Calvin Estall, a reporter embedded at the Paktika outpost who was sitting behind me in the second truck.

"Only when necessary," I replied tersely. I did not care for Estall and saw no reason to hide my disdain.

The tension in the two trucks was palpable. We all knew we might be driving straight into an ambush. Bussman, sitting next to me in the driver's seat, radioed command with our movements while the others watched for the enemy.

Several bumpy kilometers later the farmer pulled his truck to a stop and pointed to a mound of sand and rocks a few yards away. I motioned for the farmer to walk with me. If he refused, I would know that we were being set up. The old man fell into step beside me. Forsberg was here.

Behind us, I heard Bussman radio command and ask for MA to be sent out. I hesitate to go on with this story. I do not wish to disrespect the dead, or share details that will upset Forsberg's family. I only do so to clarify the stories that have been told about me and what happened that day. Still, I wish I did not feel compelled to do so, as it will only bring pain to those who do not deserve it.

Forsberg had been dead for ten days, and I knew that due to the heat of the Afghanistan weather, we were looking not for a body but for remains, and the mound of rock and dirt bore the telltale signs that decay was taking place underneath. There was the stench of rot, and the swarms of insects, and I knew that what was above ground was nothing compared to what we would find when we began digging.

"Command says the soonest MA can get here is four days," yelled Bussman. Four days. To a civilian, that may not seem like long for a man already dead more than a week. To a soldier's brother or sister in arms, it was four days too long.

"Spread out. Shoot anything that moves," I ordered the men, walking back to the truck to grab a shovel.

I motioned to the farmer.

"Tell him to stand where I can see him until we're done," I told Daoud.

I didn't want the farmer driving away and alerting anyone to our location. If we were caught in a firefight, we were severely outnumbered. Estall grabbed his camera and began shooting pictures of the mound of dirt.

"No photos," I told him. There was no way I was going to let Estall invade Forsberg's privacy. Forsberg deserved better than that, and so did his family.

Estall ignored me.

"I mean it. Put down the camera."

Estall kept snapping. I ripped the camera from his hands and threw it as hard as I could. It landed with a crunch in a field of sand and rock.

"You witch!" he yelled.

"You want the camera back, go get it," I said. The guys snickered from their posts. Landmines were everywhere in Afghanistan. Every step was a gamble. If Estall walked into that field, he was taking his life in his hands.

Grabbing a shovel, I walked to the mound and began gingerly digging around the edge until I found what I was looking for—a swatch of tan camouflage. The smell grew stronger, the swarm of flies thicker, as I moved the dirt away from the body, until I had to wrap a cloth around my face to keep from retching. After twenty minutes I unearthed a patch of withered, pale skin. I stood up and took a step back, then another step and another until I turned away from Forsberg's body and vomited.

"You want to switch places, ma'am?" yelled Bussman from his post.

"I'm fine," I lied.

These men, a couple of them mere boys, were spending Christmas Day, one of the most important dates in their religion, in a war zone. I was not going to have this scene of death be forever linked in their psyches with Christmas. They needed to be able to have normal holidays with their families when they got back.

I picked up my shovel, determined to disinter Forsberg as quickly and respectfully as possible. Oh, how I wished it was not Forsberg! In some ways I had wanted it to be a mistake. I had wanted to believe that Forsberg was not really dead as much as the guys wanted to believe it.

The heat was overpowering, and twice I stopped to catch my breath, worrying that I would pass out from the exertion in the hot sun. I unearthed Forsberg's feet first, working my way up until only his head remained covered. Seeing his face would be the most traumatic for all of us, and while I had faith that the men were keeping their eyes on the horizon, I did not want to take the chance.

Estall was picking his way among the rocks and scrub toward his camera while keeping up a constant stream of obscenities. The man had a colorful vocabulary. No wonder he was such a popular writer.

"Bring me the green blanket from the truck," I called to Daoud after I finished uncovering the body, placing my bandana over Forsberg's face.

Forsberg was taller than I realized and I struggled to lift him onto the blanket Daoud had spread out next to the makeshift grave. I was going to need help. I could not ask Bussman. He had known Forsberg since basic training at Fort Bragg. The soldier who had known Forsberg the least would be the soldier best able to cope with the future trauma brought by this day.

"Clark! How long did you know Forsberg?" I yelled.

"Six months, ma'am!" replied Clark, never taking his eyes off the horizon.

"Hernandez?"

"Same. We all got here at the same time, ma'am."

"He was my buddy. Let me help, ma'am," yelled Bussman.

"Maintain your position," I ordered. Bussman was all of twenty-one years old at the time. There was a very good possibility that Forsberg's body was rigged with an explosive device. I couldn't put Bussman at risk. Plus, someone needed to be around to pick up the pieces of me if things took a turn for the worse. I was going to have to figure out a way to do it myself.

"Let me help you," said Daoud.

"It's against the rules for you to help," I replied. The interpreters were there to translate. They were not expected to engage in the dirty work of war.

He grasped my arm and gave me a pleading look.

"It is against my conscience to not help."

I nodded.

Carefully we slid Forsberg onto the blanket, wrapping him tightly.

"We have him!" I yelled.

The men closed in and gathered at the blanket, their weapons at the ready.

"Are you injured, Lieutenant?" asked Bussman.

"No. Why do you ask?"

"Your hands are bleeding."

Sure enough, my palms were red with cuts and broken blisters. I wiped them on my pants.

"Help me lift him into the backseat," I ordered.

Bussman put his arm out to block me.

"With all due respect, ma'am, we'll do it," he said solemnly.

Hernandez was a mountain of a man. He reached down and cradled Forsberg as gently as a mother would lift a sleeping infant, then carried Forsberg to the trucks and placed him tenderly on the backseat of my vehicle. Estall came panting up as the guys were loading into the vehicles.

"Where is the body?" he demanded.

"Shut up and get in the truck," I replied.

Estall spotted Forsberg, raised his camera to his eye, and reached out to pull back the green blanket covering Forsberg's face. Without thinking, I grabbed Estall by the back of the collar, whipped him around, and slammed him against the metal door of the truck. Estall stared at me. He looked around at the guys, who studiously pretended to not see.

"I have a First Amendment right to take pictures," argued Estall.

"I don't see a copy of the U.S. Constitution around here, do you?" I turned to Bussman. "You got a copy of the Constitution we can check, Bussman?"

Bussman made a show of patting his pockets.

"No ma'am. Left mine back at the tent."

"Well, then," I said to Estall, "until you can show me where the Constitution gives you the right to photograph dead soldiers, you and I will have to agree to disagree."

"I'm taking the picture," said Estall stubbornly.

I'm usually a very calm person, but his actions pushed me too far. I grasped Estall's neck with one hand and pressed him against the vehicle until he made a gurgling sound.

Hernandez materialized beside me. "Ma'am?"

"If you so much as think about taking a photo of him," I said to Estall through gritted teeth, "I will beat you with the shovel and leave you for dead in his grave."

"Ma'am, he's turning purple," said Hernandez, prying my hand off of Estall's throat, leaving a bloody print behind.

Later, Estall would file a criminal charge against me with my superiors, and an investigation would be launched as to whether I should be court-martialed for aggravated assault. Unfortunately for Estall, none of the guys remembered seeing anything out of the ordinary that day, and the case was dropped.

Hernandez shoved a sputtering Estall into the other vehicle, then climbed in after him and we hightailed it back to the compound, where word had spread that Forsberg was coming back. The rest of his patrol from that day was waiting for him when we arrived at a trailer that had an air-conditioning unit and served as a makeshift morgue, and they somberly carried Forsberg into the cool of the trailer. For the next four hours, we all stood watch together over him, his buddies alternating between stories of his hijinks and tears over his loss, until a transport helicopter arrived to bring him to MA in Kabul. Forsberg would be buried in Iowa within the week.

After we watched the helicopter ascend, I went to the medic to get my hands treated before infection set in. I winced as he unwrapped the bandanas that Daoud had tied roughly around my hands on the way back to the compound hours earlier.

"You should have come in as soon as you got back," said the medic.

"There wasn't time."

"The men would have understood." He handed me a pain pill and a cup of water, which I took gratefully.

"It would not have been right."

When I got back to my trailer, woozy from the pain medication, I called Mom and Dad on my encrypted cell phone. When they got on the line, though, I could do nothing but cry.

"Oh, *beta*, what happened?" asked Dad.

"I had a very bad day," I finally choked out.

"You didn't get a tattoo, did you Suraiya?" Mom asked with alarm.

I laughed in spite of my tears.

"No, Mom. I did not get a tattoo."

"Suraiya," soothed Dad, "can you tell us what happened?"

"I just need to hear your voices."

My father would never learn what happened that day, and if I had been given my way, my mother would not have learned of it either. Mothers do not recover from learning the horrors suffered by their children.

"We love you, Suraiya. God loves you and will watch over you until you come home," Dad told me.

"Do you believe in God now, Dad?"

"More and more I believe, little one," said Dad.

"I'm going to hug you now," Mom told me. "Hold the phone close to you, so you can feel my hug."

I did as I was told, clutching the phone close to me and pretending I was safely back home.

That night Bussman joined me as I sat on the step of the trailer. He carried two bottles of beer, one of which he handed to me. We clinked bottles and he drank. The cool of the bottle felt good against my burning hands. I had refused a second pain pill, preferring the pain to mental fog caused by the medication. I envied Bussman his ability to drown the events of the day.

"Today sucked. And yet it was a good day," he said.

I was glad for the dark so he could not see me wipe my eyes on my shirt sleeve. We watched the stars for a while.

"I never met an American Muslim before I met you, Lieutenant. Anybody ever says a word against you, they'll be answering to us," said Bussman quietly, a vow that he and the guys would keep a few years later.

I could find no words to reply. Bussman was only saying what others were thinking. I was a woman and a lawyer and a Muslim. No one expected me to get my hands dirty. No one expected me to spare the men from emotional pain. I would always be expected to prove my worthiness to be their equal. That day the soldiers deemed me worthy.

If only it was that easy to prove my worthiness to the rest of the country. Using my military career as political fodder always made me uncomfortable. It is my experience that those who glorify war are those who have never been on a battlefield. War is not the clean, slow motion experience shown in movies. It is dirty and bloody and chaotic.

Five weeks later I was sent back to Parwan. By that time the judicial tide had begun to turn. Fearless young Afghan lawyers were facing down the old corrupt guard and winning. If there is a moment of my life that I feel is most worthwhile, it is the part I played in helping the Afghan people find justice.

America would have survived, in some way, shape, or form, without me in the White House. I am not so sure that Afghanistan would have survived without the American armed forces helping to rebuild the judicial system. This is not to take credit away from the brave Afghan people. It was the courage I witnessed while there that sustained me in times of trial here.

When I close my eyes, I still smell the grime and the burning of oil and flesh always present in the Afghan countryside. When the smell becomes too much, when the memories push through my subconscious and refuse to return to their compartment in my mind, I run. I find the nearest treadmill or track or street and I run and run and run until my body gives out, and then I pause to collect my breath and run again. I run to escape the mound of dirt near the poppy field.

My husband Greg, too, knows what it is to be haunted by the things a person sees and does in the name of our country. There is a small room in the president's private quarters that other presidents used as a music room. We converted this room into a private chapel for Greg.

Every morning, Greg went into this chapel to pray, a habit he acquired from his grandmother who attended mass every morning. Some days I would accompany him and listen as he recited the prayers he learned as a child.

On other days, on the days when his eyes took on the haunted look of memories that refused to retreat, Greg went into the chapel by himself and closed the door. On the best of these days I would hear the fervent murmur of his prayers as he asked for forgiveness. On the worst, I would hear the quiet sobs of a man unable to escape the smell.

If you want to know why Greg and I chose to not have children, this is why. Because I could never run far enough, and Greg could never pray hard enough, to escape the memories of war.

Chapter Seven

In 2015, I left the Marine Corps and joined the legal practice of my law school friends Grace Dell and Aaron Wallick in downtown Minneapolis. At that time, the Republicans had Vickie Flores in mind for the Third Congressional District, and she was a formidable opponent against the Democrats. Vickie was a professor of accounting at a small liberal arts college in St. Paul. The mother of five grown children, three of whom were adopted from Latin America, she and her husband of thirty years made for a picture-perfect American success story. They were Christian and wealthy and white with a splash of color. In other words, they were the model demographics of most of the people living in the Third District.

Everyone thought Vickie was a shoo-in for the Republican nomination, including me. Then Allah or God or the universe or whatever you want to call him or her stepped in with other plans. My father knew Vickie casually from education conferences the two had attended. He was planning to attend one of her fundraisers, a dinner at the local golf club.

One look at him when he walked through the front door after work, all clammy and red-eyed, and I knew he would not be attending that fundraiser. We did not yet suspect the cancer that would take him from us.

"You go," he said, thrusting the ticket at me. "Maybe you will meet a nice young man."

"Don't worry, Dad," I assured him. "I'll make sure she knows that she has your support."

The only thing I remember about the dinner is Vickie's speech. It was terrible. She talked about the importance of education and little else. Sure, I agree that education is of high importance. I proved in my administration that innovating education is the key to lowering poverty and crime, thereby decreasing the amount spent on entitlements and public safety. Everyone believes in bettering education.

I couldn't believe what I was not hearing. There was no talk about how to end the conflicts in the Middle East in a way to ensure democracy and stability. No mention of the huge deficit and the need to balance the budget. Not a word about energy independence and global warming. Those were the issues I cared about.

My dad was lying on the couch in the den with a damp cloth over his eyes when I arrived home. The lights were off. The television glowed, showing a silent soccer match on the other side of the world between teams from countries that today no longer exist, thanks to civil war and the economic collapse of their governments. In some parts of the world, the borders change quickly.

I curled up in the brown-plaid recliner next to the sofa. Both had seen better days, but my parents refused to part with them. The furniture, while no longer in fashion, was still functional. There was no need to spend hard-earned dollars on something new that would only go out of style.

"What is wrong, *beta*?" my father asked softly from beneath the cloth.

"She said nothing, Dad."

"Define 'nothing.'"

"Her message consisted entirely of platitudes. The substance was not there."

"I see." Dad removed the cloth from his face and pulled

himself upright. “It is a disappointment when we find that those we placed on a pedestal do not deserve to be there.”

“She has a clear field to the nomination, Dad.”

“Yes.”

“She has money, and she has connections.”

Dad took a breath before speaking, carefully measuring his words.

“Message trumps everything, *beta*. But the journey you are considering also takes courage and stamina and a strong spine.”

“In other words, I should put a lot of thought into it before I decide that I can do a better job in Congress than she can.”

He patted the sofa, and I moved next to him. He took my hand and I laid my head on his shoulder as I did when I was a little girl.

“That tugging you feel in your heart is your fate calling you. Do not be afraid to follow it. It will take you where God wants you to go.”

“Will Vickie be angry with you if I challenge her?”

I felt him shrug. “I know Congress will be better off with you in it than with her, and I am not afraid to tell her so.”

Mother and brother Alim were thrilled when we told them. Alim Youssef is not my actual sibling, as Daris is my sibling, but rather we are related as followers of God. The first time I met Alim Youssef I was a child, not yet a preteen, and he was a student of my father’s at the University. Alim, hovering around six feet and stocky, bore little resemblance to the members of my family, and it never failed to amuse Alim to introduce me, at barely five feet, as his sister.

Alim was born in Leicester, home to the most significant population of Indian immigrants in England. My father and Alim’s father never met, but shared a great-grandfather in Africa, which I guess makes Alim and me some sort of distant cousins. My great-grandfather had two wives, and at least twelve children, so our family tree has many branches.

My father sponsored Alim to come to America to study economics and international relations when Alim finished high school in England. Even then, Alim was ambitious and clearly brighter than the students around him.

Alim took great pleasure in teasing me about not being Indian enough or Muslim enough. He would ask me what I thought of the latest movie out of Bollywood, and when I admitted that I had not seen it, he would call me an ABCD, American-Born Confused Desi, an insult lobbed at South Asians for being too American. It was good training for politics.

Alim began his career as an intelligence analyst at the Department of Defense, then moved to the State Department. There he worked his way up from the assistant to the policy advisor on African affairs to a foreign trade policy analyst to the Secretary of State's counsel. Washington is full of people who never appear on the public radar, the people doing the heavy lifting. Alim was one of those people.

As soon as I told Alim about running for Congress, he picked up the phone and called every Indian-American he had ever met.

"My sister is running for Congress. We must support her," he would say, and they would respond by contributing money, and then phoning their friends to tell them about my campaign, and to seek support for me.

The Indian population in America arrived in force in the 1960s and 1970s, and in 2016 we were not a prevalent force in American politics. Bobby Jindal was governor of Louisiana, and Nikki Haley was governor of South Carolina, and they were about the only political clout we had. The entire Indian-American demographic was less than one percent of the American population. If any group was outnumbered, it was us.

While the election of Jindal and Haley was proof that an Indian-American could succeed at the polls, both of them were converts to Christianity. Let's just say that their Christianity was more of a boon than a hindrance to their campaigns.

I may have been new to politics, but I was not naive. I knew that being a Muslim was going to be an issue. While there were two Muslims in Congress already, both of them were African-American men with Anglo names. They were, therefore, less "foreign" than I.

Vickie was livid, using her website to portray me as a poseur.

"If you can't take a bit of name-calling, you'll never make

it through the fight with the Democrats," Dad warned me when I complained about Vickie's attack.

No one in the party took me seriously until we sent in our fundraising report to the caucus. In the initial weeks of the primary campaign, I raised $167,000. Vickie raised $210,000. Suddenly the local Republicans were taking me more seriously. They saw me as a threat. A dark-skinned, Allah-worshipping threat.

The party was not going to hand me the nomination. I was going to have to fight for it. I started campaigning in earnest. No one, not even in my own party, had any idea who I was.

If it wasn't for wearable technology, I doubt I would have been elected. That was the year that droves of people started wearing smartwatches. Ostensibly, these computers would track the wearer's heart rate, steps taken, food digested, and location, and either upload it to the wearer's preferred social media site or compile the information for the wearer's later viewing. I used it to find out where people were congregating. I monitored every social media site available, and would show up wherever there was a crowd, no matter how small.

I would go to coffee shops and introduce myself to three people and talk to them for two hours about the big issues, and hope that they would go home and spread the word. I went to the local high school band concerts and shook hands with the parents. They had no idea who I was, but if there were two or more people gathered on Foursquare, I was there.

I funneled work to Grace and Aaron and lived off my savings so that I could spend all day, every day, campaigning. All this just to try to get enough delegates at the spring nominating convention to vote for me so I would get my party's endorsement. We hadn't even started thinking about the fall campaign.

"If this is what I have to do for the primary, how will I ever survive the congressional campaign?" I asked Alim.

"Keep the faith, sister," Alim assured me.

On a beautiful spring day in May, state Republicans gathered at the Wayzata High School for the nominating convention. There were 156 delegates at the convention; many of them were new delegates attending for the first time. Those new delegates were voting for me.

The old-guard delegates would vote for Vickie. I knew their voting preference because not one of them would return my calls when I was trying to drum up delegate support. The established delegates would not talk to me, so I rounded up my own. It was the party establishment against the rank and file, and no one expected the rank and file to win, not even the rank and file.

The nominating convention works like this: delegates mingle with the candidates and the candidate's campaign staffers, who hand out dozens of T-shirts and buttons, the candidates each give a three-minute speech, and the delegates vote on which candidate they want to receive the party nomination for the fall race. To receive the nomination, the candidate must receive sixty percent of the delegate votes. In 2016, that meant Vickie or I needed ninety-four votes to win the nomination. The party hierarchy expected the nomination to be decided in one vote.

Vickie had experience and name recognition. I had come out of nowhere, but Vickie would never outwork me. No one would ever outwork a Jafari.

The gasps from the delegates were audible when the results of the first vote were announced: seventy-nine for me, seventy-seven for Vickie. Even my devoted delegates were shocked. Delighted, but shocked, although not nearly as stunned as Vickie's devotees. It was not enough to get the nomination, but it was enough to show we were a force, a tactic I would be forced to replay in Iowa eight years later.

Suddenly, Republicans who wouldn't return my phone calls were pulling me aside at the convention, telling me that I needed to drop out for the good of the party. It wasn't my turn, they told me. We needed to present a unified front to beat the Democrats in November.

"What do you think?" I asked Dad, Mom, Daris, and Alim when we had sequestered ourselves in a classroom. "Are they right?"

"Why did you run if you are so easily dissuaded from continuing?" Mom wanted to know.

"I want to do what's best for the party," I said. "I could walk away now and they would owe me. When it's my turn, I'll have favors to call in."

"Do not let these people decide your future for you," advised Alim.

"Dad?" My father paced the room. Political science had been his life for decades. He understood the implications of pushing forward or stepping down.

"People have been telling us for decades that we must wait our turn. We must decide when it is our turn. If not now, Suraiya, then when?"

Tides turn quickly in politics. One minute a shoo-in candidate has a nomination wrapped up. Then an upstart with a two-vote victory comes along and the shoo-in has to swim harder and faster just to maintain momentum. Later that same day, I gained three votes in the second round: eighty-two Jafari, seventy-four Flores. Twelve votes shy of the ninety-four needed for the endorsement.

If neither of us received the required votes at the convention, a primary would be held in September. We would both spend the next four months campaigning for the privilege of representing the Republican Party on the ballot in November. The Democrats would spend those same four months touting the candidate they had chosen for their nomination. The Republicans did not want the nomination to go to the primary.

"Think of the good of the party," Vickie told me over lunch.

"I am," I said. "I'm ahead. I've been ahead since we started."

"You can't beat the Democrats."

"I'm beating you, aren't I?"

It took eight votes and twelve hours before Vickie dropped out of the primary race and I was granted the Republican nomination as their candidate for the Third District, along with John Carlson's grudging endorsement. I spent the next hour shaking delegates' hands and thanking my team, until the sky was dark and the auditorium emptied.

Exhausted, I sought out the relative quiet of the ladies' room, splashing water on my face to wash away the stress of the day. I had won the first battle. All I wanted to do was go home and crawl into bed.

Alim walked with me down the silent hallway, both of us a bit uncertain about where this new path would take us. Mom and

Dad were waiting for me in the car. As I walked out the door of the school that night, I was greeted by a cool, starry night and a lone staffer from the Minnesota Democratic Party, handing out press releases. The title of the press release: *CD3 Republicans endorse right-wing extremist Suraiya Jafari*.

There would be no sleep that night. The war with the Democrats had started while I was in the ladies' room.

Chapter Eight

There are no secrets in politics. Families, on the other hand, harbor all kinds of secrets. You would think it would be the other way around. When family secrets collide with politics, it is best to play offense rather than defense. My dad knew this from his years as a political science professor, but that did not make it any easier for him to decide to play offense when it came to his own family.

The day after I won the Republican nomination for the House, Dad called a family meeting. This time Alim was not included, which should have tipped me off that not only were we dealing with a family secret, but it was a doozy. Daris's girlfriend Neeta was also excluded. Mom, Dad, Daris, and I gathered around the kitchen table.

"We know about your marriage, Daris," said Dad.

Daris gave a start. This seemed weird to me. Of course they knew about his marriage. We all knew about it. Daris and Neeta had been dating for nearly a year. An engagement and marriage was inevitable.

Dad continued. "We know about the ad on the internet. We know about the arrangement you made with Neeta. We know all of it, and if your sister is elected, the rest of the world will know about it too. Secrets never stay in the shadows. The sun always finds them."

"Dad, what are you talking about?" I asked. No one answered. Mom and Dad stared sadly at Daris.

"Daris, what is going on? Is there something you're not telling us about Neeta?"

Daris did not answer me.

"Was she married before?" I asked. "Does she have a tattoo?"

Daris addressed Dad. "How did you know?"

"Alim told me. He sent me an email when he learned about your relationship with Neeta, telling me how happy he was that you had outgrown the bad influence of your friends. He said he had been praying it was a phase, and that God had answered his prayers."

"A phase." That's a euphemism Indian parents use when their children are gay. In our culture, homosexuality is considered a lifestyle choice, a phase that parents turn a blind eye to in the hopes that he or she will grow out of it.

Homosexuality is considered by our faith to be a moral disorder and a sin, and homosexuals are considered no better than thieves and murderers. A Muslim child who is openly gay brings shame to his family and may be disowned, or worse. Some countries execute homosexuals.

If Daris lived as an openly gay man, my parents' dishonor within our extended family and community would be significant. My brother is an honorable man. He did not want his parents blamed for giving him inferior guidance and education, so he did what many Muslim gays did then: he entered into a marriage of convenience with a Muslim lesbian who needed a husband. Hundreds of my people did this in the early part of the century, and still do today, even though homosexuals now have the right to marry in the U.S. and many other countries. Ancient biases are not easily dispelled.

Entire websites were devoted to matching gays and lesbians who needed such an arrangement, and after Alim's email, it did not take long for Dad to track down Daris's personal ad: *I am looking for an Indian Muslim lesbian for marriage. I am gay but would like to get married due to pressure from my family and society. I am open to having children.*

That day, though, sitting at the kitchen table, I did not yet know of the ad, or of Daris's arrangement with Neeta. I was so happy that he had found a nice Muslim girl to marry. They seemed so well-matched. I know it sounds silly now, but sitting at the kitchen table, I hoped Neeta would be able to change Daris's mind, that after they were married he would, indeed, discover his attraction to men was a phase. That Neeta's preference for women was absolute never occurred to me.

"I am so sorry I disappointed you," said Daris to Mom and Dad.

"You and Neeta must marry as soon as possible," Dad told him. "Then you will move and begin your lives somewhere else, far away from here."

Daris nodded, and rose to leave the table.

Mom finally spoke. "My son is not going anywhere."

"Cala, think of the family," said Dad.

Mom turned to Daris. "Will you and Neeta be having children?"

Daris nodded. Mom turned to Dad.

"I will not be separated from my grandchildren."

"The Democrats and the press will be watching our every move," explained Dad. "If they find out about Daris, the world will know our shame."

"What if I don't run for the House?" I offered. "I'll drop out of the race, and no one will find out anything about it."

Granted, there is no requirement that a congresswoman or president's brother be straight, but such a requirement did exist within our family.

"You will not drop out of the race," said Dad vehemently, rising from his chair. "You are going to run for the House and you are going to be elected if it kills me. We must all make sacrifices for the future of the family, Suraiya. Your brother knows this."

Now Mother rose, leaving me the only one still sitting in the midst of the standoff.

"You will not send my son away."

Daris and I looked at each other, then at Mom, then Dad. My parents did not fight. Ever. There was no precedence for this showdown. It was fascinating and terrifying at the same time. Daris sat down, and the two of us waited silently while Mom and Dad decided our fate.

"It is only a House seat," said Dad, finally. "As long as Daris lives a life of virtue going forward, no one will ever know. We will never speak of this again."

Daris and Neeta were married a few weeks later in the civil affairs office in Minneapolis. Despite trying various means, they did not have children.

"Have you tried the old-fashioned way?" I asked Daris when he told me despairingly that the latest round of in vitro fertilization had failed.

"Don't be crass, Suraiya," Daris replied.

He looked so repelled at the thought of being intimate with Neeta that I let the subject drop. By that time, I was a congresswoman and Daris and I were attempting to repair our relationship. He had stopped speaking to me after I voted against a bill that would allow same-sex marriage in all fifty states. We would get together to make my mom happy, but it would be a long time before Daris would trust me again.

Chapter Nine

My opponent in my first campaign for the House of Representatives was a Democrat by the name of Eldon Ronholm. Ronholm was well-known in Minnesota as a four-term state legislator. When the campaign began, he had more money, a donor base to tap for funds, and better name recognition. He also had a burning desire to go to Washington, and he wasn't going to let me stand in his way.

The national committees of the two parties were taking notice of our election as well, sending in scores of campaign personnel and diverting funds away from races considered less critical. Minnesota's Third District was suddenly a hotspot on the political map.

"If you're going to beat Eldon, you're going to have to raise twice as much money and fight twice as hard," John Carlson warned me. This was no small task. Ronholm had two million dollars in his coffers before the campaign even started, none of which he had been forced to use in an endorsement fight. John emailed me his donor list, and suggested that I contact the names on the list to ask for money.

Ronholm would outspend me, and I knew it. One thing my parents taught me was that when the rules are stacked against you,

you need to change the rules to level the playing field. Ronholm's weakness was that he was older and less tech savvy than I. He was still sending snail mail postcards outlining his political positions. I decided to use that factor to my advantage.

I set up a crowdfunding account at rally.org, and notified all of my friends, and all the people on John's donor list, of my campaign platform. I posted the Rally account on all of my social media sites and asked people to go to Rally and donate twenty dollars to my campaign. Only twenty dollars. Then I spent the next three weeks personally calling every single person on the lists and asking them for money. Raising money is a terribly time-consuming task for politicians. I spent the next ten years making those phone calls.

My hope was that I would get enough small donations to get the ball rolling. By the end of the three-week phone campaign, I had raised $150,000. Many people gave more than twenty dollars, some gave less, but it was enough to hire a campaign manager, Olivia Anderson, and a policy advisor, Henry Shaw.

Henry—thin, dark-haired, and easily intimidated—had attended the Humphrey School of Public Affairs at the University of Minnesota, where he received a Master's of Public Policy at the age of twenty-two. It was at the Humphrey School that he studied under my father, and it was Dad who recommended Henry to advise me on public policy matters.

"He's scared of his own shadow," Dad told me, "but he's one of the brightest young people of his generation."

Olivia was one of Dad's political science students as well. She was also only twenty-two at the time, and did not yet have the polish seen now when she steps before the cameras as the White House Communications Director, but she was eager to try out new campaigning strategies and I was a willing guinea pig.

It was Olivia who came up with the *Suraiya-TV* idea. People were tired of feeling as though government was run by backdoor deals. They wanted someone who was willing to be visible all the time. It was Olivia who uploaded videos of every debate, every constituent meeting, every meet-and-greet we did in the months leading up to the election onto the *Suraiya-TV* website.

Every time I turned around, there was Olivia, recording. It

became unnerving, to tell you the truth, and we eventually had to set down some ground rules: No recording in the bedroom or bathroom. I guess that is only one rule. My point is that Olivia's strategy was the basis for the all-access strategy that caused such an uproar when I became president.

We were an inexperienced crew, and brash in our expectations for what we could do to take down the old guard and forge a new day in politics, and that meant using new political tools, especially the Echo Chamber.

The Echo Chamber was a barely established website in 2016, having been started by a couple of political science majors at the University of Ohio just prior to the 2014 election. Galen Haas and Todd Moline were Cleveland high schoolers when the 2012 presidential campaigns descended on their state. The Romney and Obama camps deluged the state with every form of campaign technique imaginable, making life unbearable for the residents there.

Where other students saw an annoying barrage of rhetoric interrupting their media, Haas and Moline saw the vast amounts of dollars being collected by political pundits on television and radio. Dollars that Haas and Moline decided to collect for themselves, while making every United States citizen a part-time pundit unto themselves.

Thereafter was born Echo Chamber Red, for Republicans, and Echo Chamber Blue, for Democrats. Users could log on to either site, or both, and set up their own political opinion pages, espousing whatever political ideal they saw fit. Other users could visit those pages and, theoretically, engage in reasoned debate.

Of course, the political opinions were often of the "that other party stinks and now the sky is falling" variety, and the debate was usually along the lines of "no, you stink." Not the most intelligent political conversation, but no less inane than much of the debate that happens on the House floor.

Haas and Moline had hoped to make a bit of money by selling ads on the sites to political parties. They made money all right. They also turned some of those part-time pundits into stars, thereby destroying the television and radio pundit industry.

Loud men and comely women who had made millions

of dollars spouting political theories and dissecting every word uttered by any politician who opened his or her mouth now found themselves out-of-date and out of work. These men and women had used their platforms to sell everything from books to coffee mugs to baseball caps.

Some of the old pundits tried to make the switch to the Echo Chamber, but the new outlet was quickly taken over by the next generation and the old guard was forced to retire to their mansions.

The pundits, those self-described political experts, handled this exile from the airwaves in a range of ways. One female pundit was so desperate for the spotlight that she "leaked" a video of herself being intimate with a senator's aide, only to become further despondent when she realized no one wanted to watch it. Another pundit, an older gentleman who had once commanded thousands of dollars for a single speech, became so depressed that no one would listen to him anymore that he committed suicide.

The Echo Chamber pundits, however, were numerous and vocal, and the major parties were soon looking for ways to mine the information on the Echo Chamber for their benefit. Most of the opinions were useless. People spouted off indiscriminately from behind the safety of their computers, although the parties did see fit to sponsor some of the more popular online pundits.

But the real value behind the Echo Chamber was in the demographic information collected by Haas and Moline and sold to the parties for vast sums of money. Every person who logged in to the Echo Chamber as a user had to enter their email address, zip code, and party affiliation. The software tracked each user as he or she clicked through the website. This information was then compiled into vast spreadsheets of data.

From this, we could see how many residents from, say, the northwest corner of the district identified as Republican or Democrat, and which pundits they followed. Then we could see which issues that pundit focused on, and we could tailor the campaign around those issues.

It would not be overstating the issue to say that the Echo Chamber changed the political game for those who understood and utilized it early. My campaign staffers in 2016, most of them provided by the Republican National Congressional Caucus, poured over the Echo Chamber data we purchased from Haas and Moline.

Early on, it became clear that Ronholm faced an uphill battle in the election against me. Not because I was a formidable candidate, but because there was another Democrat, Leo Davis, running against us as a third-party Independent candidate. Davis was slicing just enough support away from Ronholm to give me an advantage.

While Ronholm kept attacking my age and race and religion, I stuck to one message: A vote for Ronholm was a vote for higher taxes. If there was one thing the Third District feared more than a five-foot-tall alleged terrorist, it was higher taxes.

That message, coupled with the votes Davis spirited away from Ronholm, meant I won the election by five points. Not a landslide, certainly, but large enough to avoid a recount. It was exactly as we expected after watching the Echo Chamber for weeks on end. Ronholm was devastated. He thought the Echo Chamber was a fad and had been mentally packing his furniture for D.C.

The danger of the Echo Chamber, though, was that politicians and voters could get so caught up in the minutiae available twenty-four hours a day, every day, on the site, that they would lose sight of the big picture. The fact is that no matter how great a politician is, hundreds of thousands of people will not like that politician, and will take to the airwaves to express this discontent.

This was perhaps the most difficult lesson I had to learn as a politician. No matter what I did, no matter how successful the policies I put in motion, half of the people would lionize me and half of the people would demonize me, often over issues that had no bearing on serving in Congress.

Ronholm, while hardly a renegade strategist, had a few tricks up his sleeve. Olivia walked into campaign headquarters one day, openly seething, a postcard clutched in her right hand.

"You are not going to believe this," she snarled, waving the postcard. "I don't even want to show it to you, because it is so offensive, but you need to know, so here."

She lobbed the postcard in my direction. It was sponsored by Ronholm's campaign and pictured a photo of me, surreptitiously taken while I had been jogging a few weeks earlier. My mouth was open in a pant and my complexion was sweaty. A mean trick, yes, but dirty politics enough to justify Olivia's outrage? No.

What had gotten Olivia up in arms, and what made my knees begin to quiver, was the fact that the photo had been retouched to give me noticeably darker skin, and carried the tagline *Suraiya Jafari. She's not one of us*.

Ronholm would say later that he only meant to convey I believed in cutting entitlement programs and limiting abortions and granting tax cuts, but I did not believe him then and I do not believe him now.

"Take a deep breath," I told Olivia, leading her to my chair. As much as I wanted to melt into what my mother used to call a hissy fit, this was a moment that called for leadership, not histrionics.

"Does he think white people are so racist that they won't vote for you if they think you're black?" she fumed.

"He's not trying to make me look black. He's trying to make me look Arab," I informed her. Arab was a euphemism then for Islamic terrorist. "It's his way of playing the Muslim card without saying the words."

"It's not right," she raged. "That racist, pompous, jackass!"

Olivia, with the looks of a Scandinavian angel, was young and not used to the ways of politics. She also had never been face-to-face with this type of racism before. She was a novice in bigotry.

"Olivia, pull yourself together and figure out how we can use this to our advantage."

She gulped down a few breaths. "How can you not want to rip him limb from limb?" she asked.

"What makes you think I don't?" I retorted. "It could be worse. He could have used photos of me from junior high. Now *that* would have been embarrassing."

Olivia laughed. "Any suggestions on how we handle this?"

I thought for a moment. "Call my dad. He'll know what to do."

Ronholm's tactics were no surprise to Dad. He had been waiting for the religion card to be played. In true Rabee Jafari style, he waited to give his opinion until we asked for it. He talked Olivia through some options and let her run with the solution.

Olivia scanned the postcard and uploaded it to Rally and let all of our supporters know about the photo editing. She asked me to approve the text before she sent out: *Ronholm is right. Suraiya is a veteran. That alone sets her apart from the rest of us.*

"Change it to Mr. Ronholm," I instructed.

"Why are you showing him courtesy when he's attacking you?"

"Because we are not going to stoop to Mr. Ronholm's level," I said.

Our Rally newsletter hit our supporters' inboxes thirty minutes before Ronholm's television ads appeared that evening. This time it was video of me jogging, all sweaty and panting and, yes, my skin digitally changed to appear darker. The response was significant.

People of all races were outraged by the ad. Donations began to pour into my campaign from all over the country. Not small donations, either. One elderly white woman in South Carolina sent a check for five hundred dollars with a note that read, "I thought we settled this race thing in 2008," referring, I presume, to the election of President Barack Obama.

Military personnel I knew only in passing from my days in Afghanistan sent money, sometimes wiring it from the Middle East. One enlisted Marine made a credit card donation on Rally, with the note, "He messes with one of us, he messes with all of us. Semper Fi!"

The mixed blessing that almost derailed us, though, were the donations that poured in from wealthy South Asians, some in the United States and some from India.

"You must ask yourselves," bellowed Ronholm in one debate in an attempt to regain ground, "why so many foreigners want to see her elected!"

"I'm going to be one of 435 representatives," I reminded voters. "Does he think I can single-handedly turn over the keys to the kingdom?"

That line makes me laugh now. To be a good sport, I invited Eldon to the White House reception after my first swearing-in.

"Who knew?" I said, shaking his hand when he and his wife went through the receiving line.

"It could be me standing where you are right now," Ronholm replied with a tight smile. Apparently he thought that my ascension was pure luck. It was not luck that got me to the White House, at least not entirely. It also took hard work, some non-ladylike shenanigans, and divine intervention—not necessarily in that order.

Ronholm's cronies in the state house tried to save him in the congressional race.

They attacked my military record: "She was only a lawyer. It's not like she saw combat," said Orville Thompson from Edina. As though I wore combat fatigues and a bulletproof helmet in Afghanistan as a fashion statement.

They attacked my marital status: "She has no husband. She has no children," said Donna Krauss from Duluth, insinuating that I had something to hide about my sexual preference, which of course is quite ironic considering what was happening with Daris.

I went on record as being opposed to legalizing gay marriage, but I served with several lesbian colleagues in the military and I learned pretty quickly that when it comes to facing the enemy, whether in a foxhole or in a courtroom, the only thing that matters about a person is whether she knows how to shoot straight.

They attacked my living arrangements: "She lives with her parents! She doesn't even own a home," accused Karen Swan, the chair of the Minnesota Democratic Party.

"I've lived in this district since I was born," I countered. "My family has been involved in this community for thirty years. Mr. Ronholm only moved here a year ago, when he decided to run for the House."

Yes, I lived with my parents. It's an Indian thing. My parents lived with my grandparents until they married, and I planned on doing the same thing. Before the Great Recession, which drove generations of families under the same roof, this was unheard of in America.

Little did I know—did any of us know—that after winning the election for a Congressional seat, the Jafaris would end up living in public housing called the White House.

Chapter Ten

I managed to disappoint and anger thousands of people before I even unpacked on Capitol Hill. Members of Congress are sworn in en masse in a ceremony led by the Speaker of the House, with each representative raising their right hand and saying: *I do solemnly swear (or affirm) that I will support and defend the Constitution of the United States against all enemies, foreign and domestic; that I will bear true faith and allegiance to the same; that I take this obligation freely, without any mental reservation or purpose of evasion; and that I will well and faithfully discharge the duties of the office on which I am about to enter: So help me God.*

This ceremony does not include any religious texts. Many representatives choose to do a second, private swearing-in so that photos can be taken, and these private ceremonies usually include a religious text such as the Bible or the Torah. Keith Ellison, the first Muslim in the House, caused an uproar when he swore on an English translation of the Qur'an that had been owned by Thomas Jefferson. Hawaii Representative Tulsi Gabbard, a Hindu, used the Bhagavad Gita, and while Christian conservatives were not happy about it, they were not in fear of Gabbard because of it.

Then I came along, a non-observant Muslim, and from the

second the election results came in, speculation swirled as to whether I would use a Qur'an in a private ceremony.

"I won't do a private ceremony, and then it won't be an issue," I told my parents as we watched two pundits from opposite sides of the aisle, neither of whom I had ever met, debate my decision on television.

Dad shook his head.

"You'll miss out on a great photo op for your website."

"Okay, I'll do a private swearing-in, but I won't use any religious text at all," I said.

Now Mother wasn't happy.

"You're a Muslim. You'll use the Qur'an."

"Mom, we don't go to the mosque. We don't pray. We don't fast during Ramadan. Swearing on the Qur'an would make me a hypocrite."

She was not convinced.

"Christians swear on the Bible and turn around and lie, cheat, and steal. Is that not hypocritical?"

"Of course it is! But that doesn't mean I should do it," I said.

"Forget about the public for a minute," advised Dad. "What would you do if publicity was not an issue?"

I thought about this.

"I would swear on the Constitution, because church and state are supposed to be separate, and I am there representing the state."

That is what I did, and boy, were people mad!

A Muslim advocacy group out of New York ran an opinion piece in all the major newspapers, decrying my lack of observance of my faith in one sentence while deriding my decision to forgo the use of the Qur'an in the ceremony in the next.

A Christian group picketed my swearing-in, claiming the country was founded on Christian principles, and that by swearing on the Constitution I was violating those principles.

"Get used to it," Dad told me. "You will face stormier waters than this."

Olivia and Henry and I set about our work in the House. A few of John Carlson's staffers stayed on, and Frank Kirsch, a leading

Republican in the House, sent over a couple of administrative assistants from Senate offices to help out as well.

Our strategy was to let other representatives run around shouting through bullhorns while we kept a lower profile in the press and worked to get legislation passed. Over the years we managed to get bills passed to increase penalties against internet service providers that failed to report child pornography, and to change the tax treatment of charitable contributions from a deduction to a credit for contributions made to charities that battled hunger in America, thereby relieving some of the cost burden to the government food assistance programs.

We also introduced legislation to amend Medicare to include safety and staffing standards for registered nurses, and pushed through copyright legislation to combat digital piracy. We worked hard to negotiate with other representatives, and while no one complained about our work, we often received complaints about my race or religion or gender from people who did not even live in our district.

In November 2020, I was elected to my third term in Congress, and as with all representatives, my team immediately began fundraising plans for our next campaign in 2022. Raising money is an ongoing challenge for elected officials. It would be great if Congress could spend all of its time focused on running the country, but the reality is that fundraising takes precedence over everything else.

On a rainy Saturday in the fall of 2021, a wealthy couple from Minnetonka, Minnesota were hosting a fundraiser for me in their spacious home on Gray's Bay. They coordinated the event with my office, sending us a digital copy of the invitation and the itinerary for the evening gathering. Olivia and Henry went to the home in the early afternoon to help the couple set up while I made an appearance at a local high school football game.

Henry called me at four o'clock in a panic.

"We have a problem. There are two of everything showing up. Two florists demanding to be paid. Two caterers. Two pianists. The couple is freaking out. Everybody is yelling. I don't know what to do," he said.

"How did this happen?" I asked.

"The hosts swear they only booked one of each, but the vendors are all here with invoices, and the hosts don't want to pay for the extra services."

I closed my eyes and tried to drown out the cheering crowd.

"Apologize to the hosts for the mix-up and pay all the vendors out of my private account. Then send the second set of vendors to the homeless shelter at St. Mark's church downtown."

"Suraiya, we're talking thousands of dollars," Henry informed me.

"I know. Tomorrow we need to figure out how this happened."

The day went from bad to worse. Our hosts had sent out fifty invitations to a select list of their friends and acquaintances, expecting that thirty or forty people would actually attend. Instead, more than a hundred uninvited guests showed up, blocking the street with their cars and devouring the food and drinks and messing up the house, then leaving without writing a check to the campaign.

Less than ninety minutes into the event, the hosts called the police to clear the house. Olivia handed me a piece of paper while we watched the last of the interlopers drive away.

"It's a phony invitation to tonight's party," she said. "Someone sabotaged us."

We spent hours cleaning up the lawn and house for our shaken hosts, and it was nearly dawn before I called Alim in New York, where he was working for the State Department.

"It is too early for the Democrats to come after you," he said. "This was one of your own."

I was livid with embarrassment.

"Why? Who would do this to me?"

"Say nothing, Suraiya," he advised me. "Don't talk about it to the press. Don't bring it up in your office when you get back to D.C. The culprit will be waiting for a reaction, and when he doesn't get one, he will reveal himself."

Sure enough, Henry was eating a sandwich at his desk on Monday afternoon when Stanley Radford, one of the administrative assistants sent over by Frank Kirsch, sidled into Henry's office and asked casually, "Anything interesting happen at the fundraiser?"

Henry leaned over and buzzed me on the intercom. "Found him, boss."

Stan was at first belligerent, then contrite, as he explained that he had been passing along confidential information from our office to Frank and other Republicans in the House and Senate for years. The fundraising prank had been the brainchild of Senator Jackson Martin of Texas.

"Didn't he know the fundraising stunt would blow your cover?" I asked.

Stan shook his head.

"Senator Martin assured me that you wouldn't be able to figure it out."

I was preparing to file an ethics complaint against Frank and Jackson when Olivia talked me out of it.

"There's no way you come out of this looking good," she said. "They'll find a way to blame you."

She was right. I fired Stanley Radford, only to find out a few weeks later that Senator Martin had offered him a promotion in his Senate office.

We added our own security cameras to the inner offices, and one of us monitored the workplace on our smartphones or smartwatches at all hours of the day and night. While hard work earned me the respect of many of my colleagues in Congress, some would never be swayed to see beyond the color of my skin.

Chapter Eleven

My father, Rabee Jafari, passed away from cancer in September of 2019, at the age of fifty-seven, during my second term in Congress. The bone cancer had initially responded to the chemotherapy prescribed by his doctors, and we were hopeful that he would enter remission.

That summer, though, the cancer had returned in earnest, turning my father into a near invalid and my mother into his caretaker. I wanted to spend whatever moments with my father that he had left, and I wanted to help my mother. My parents would not hear of it.

"You must go back to the campaign," my father would admonish me when I would visit him.

"I want to be with you," I would protest, choking back tears.

"There is nothing you can do here. I have lived to see my daughter in Congress and my son married to a nice girl. That is more than many men get in this world. Now, go."

I turned to Mother.

"I'll stay with Dad. You go lie down and rest," I begged her.

"Your father is correct, Suraiya. You must go back to the campaign."

So I went back, shaking hands along parade routes and smiling for photos at fundraisers and feeling as though my insides were empty. It was Daris who helped Mom take care of Dad in those last days. It was Daris who was by Dad's side when he passed. Yet, I suspect they never fully reconciled Dad's disappointment in Daris and Daris's resentment towards Dad.

Even though Dad had been sick for some time, it was still a shock to me when he died. He was my father, my rock. He was the foundation of our family. How were we to survive without him?

It was Alim who informed me of Dad's death, as we were leaving a meet-and-greet at a concert in a local park.

"What is this all for?" I asked Alim, gesturing to the crowd we had just spent two hours glad-handing in order to convince them to vote for me. "It all seems so pointless."

"Your father wants this for you. You must honor him with your actions."

We drove straight to my house, where Alim and Daris helped place Dad's body into the funeral director's van to be taken to a washing room at the mosque in Burnsville, a suburb south of Minneapolis. Islam, like Judaism, requires that bodies be buried within hours.

Daris and Alim bathed Dad's body in private, then shrouded his body in a plain, white cloth, wrapping him three times. After being placed in a rosewood casket, Dad was taken to the prayer hall, where Mother, Daris, Alim, Neeta, and I gathered around him while the Imam said prayers in Arabic. I felt the disconnect with my religion most deeply then, unable to understand the words being said for my father.

My father was taken to the Garden of Eden Islamic Cemetery, one of only two Muslim cemeteries in Minnesota. Muslim cemeteries were rare in America then. Most American Muslims were buried in Christian cemeteries, until Muslims created their own burial grounds. Building a cemetery, however, is costly and difficult—almost as costly as maintaining an existing cemetery. When the Burnsville council members found out the local Islamic association was looking for land for a cemetery, they approached the association about taking over a derelict Christian cemetery. Muslims and Christians who would not share space above ground now share space below it.

Today, environmentally friendly green burials, where the deceased are placed into the earth without caskets, are in vogue. Such burials are the norm for Muslims and Jews. My father's body was placed in a custom vault with no bottom, so that his body laid upon the earth.

He was placed on his right side, facing northeast, the path to Mecca. A simple brass plaque would be laid later, listing his name and the dates he walked the earth.

They say that time heals all pain, but they are wrong. The pain changes, morphing into something manageable. It does not heal.

Chapter Twelve

Alim moved to Washington at the same time as I did. He had been assigned to the United Nations in New York. I wanted him to work in my office as a policy advisor, but he was offered a chance to work in the State Department as an aide to the Undersecretary of State, and I urged him to take it.

"I promised your parents that I would look after you," he said when we were talking through the pros and cons of the State Department job.

"The best thing you can do for me is help me build a broad network of important people. The State Department is the best place to do that," I said.

I spent my first years in Washington immersed in my work, and while it was invigorating and all-consuming, there were times when loneliness would creep in, and I would make efforts to create more of a personal life.

My husband, Gregory Mills, and I went to the same high school in Minnesota but didn't know each other as teenagers. Actually, that is not quite true. Greg, blond and blue-eyed, was one of the most popular boys in school—a jock, as they say—and I spent a considerable amount of time surreptitiously studying him from across the classroom. He swears he tried to talk to me one time in calculus and I ignored him, but I have no recollection of that attempt. If he did, I would have assumed he was talking to the person next to me.

After graduation, Greg went west to the Air Force Academy in Colorado Springs, Colorado, and served as an officer in Afghanistan, and while he was stationed at Parwan for a time as well, our paths did not cross then.

When the troops came home, Greg was assigned to the Pentagon as a civilian expert in cyber security. Still feeling like an outsider in Washington, I searched online for other Minnesota natives living in the area, and found a group Greg had started for Wayzata alumni in the D.C. area. I joined the group and emailed Greg to introduce myself, and he invited me to a dinner the alumni were having that night at Cesar's restaurant in Georgetown.

The last thing on my mind that night was marriage. I was a relatively new congresswoman working twelve hours a day and flying back to Minnesota on the weekends to meet with constituents. I was looking only for a social circle in D.C.

I don't know that it was love at first sight when I met Greg again, but it was definitely heightened interest, with heightened being the key word. At six feet tall, Greg towers over my five foot frame. The top of my head barely reaches his shoulder. When he saw me, he smiled and stuck out his hand.

"I'm Greg Mills," he said, gently shaking my hand.

And I, who would become world renowned for my eloquence, turned into a blathering little girl.

"You're taller than your picture," I blurted. *Way to go, Suraiya.*

"My mom says I've been more portrait sized than thumbnail since I was two."

I laughed. He was a smart, handsome man quoting his mother. How could I not fall in love with him? Later I would figure out all the reasons why falling in love was a bad idea—he was white, and Catholic, and his mother wanted grandchildren—but that night the only thing that mattered was getting to know him better.

Greg introduced me to the other alumni at the dinner, Kimberly Anderson, Scott Stearns, and Max Wolcott. Kimberly was an attorney, working as a policy advisor in Michigan Senator Delbert Fletcher's office. Scott was an attorney, working as a tax analyst for the Internal Revenue Service. Max was an attorney, working in the budget division of the Department of Health and Human Services.

You may have noticed that attorneys run the capital, which is as it should be. I mean, we're talking about the constitutional and legislative workings of our country. We're not baking loaves of bread here.

Kim, Scott, and Max would become my friends over time. Well, as much as people in Washington become friends. Politics is more attune to creating allies than friends, and they were smart enough to stand by me during the dustup at the Republican convention in 2024. The potential damage to their careers was significant, but they stood strong and I did not forget. I made sure their loyalty was rewarded when I made my Cabinet appointments in 2024.

In 2020, Greg and I were both thirty-four, and we thought the world was ours for the taking. We went to dinner the next night, just the two of us, and have been inseparable ever since. Or, as inseparable as two people with highly stressful careers and top security clearances can be.

What is the "it" that binds two people together? Call it chemistry. Call it fate. Call it love. Whatever "it" is, it was there with Greg, a most unsuitable suitor, and for the first time in my life, I worked less and had a bit of fun. If the weather was nice, we would drive to West Virginia to hike at Harper's Ferry National Park. If the weather wasn't nice, we would go bowling.

Our most favorite thing to do, though, was to go to the shooting range and compete to see which one of us could get the most points on scored targets. The truth is that I am not the greatest shot unless I practice often, and after leaving the Marines I was a bit rusty. On my birthday, Greg presented me with a bouquet of flowers, tickets to *Sister Act!* at the Kennedy Center, and a 9mm pistol. What can I say? The man gets me.

Sometimes our only "date" during the week would be the plane rides to and from Minneapolis. Greg's parents, Ed and Marlys, had seven children, six of which were girls, and were thrilled that their only son was suddenly visiting them more often. They didn't know yet that the only reason he was flying back and forth to Minnesota so much was so that he and I could spend more time together.

Several months after we started seeing each other, Greg asked me to move in with him. He had a townhouse in Chevy Chase, Maryland, just a ten-minute metro ride from the National Mall. I was sharing an apartment in Arlington, Virginia with two other newer members of the House, Susan Shepherd from Wyoming and Jackie Keystone from Nebraska.

There's a misperception that congresspeople are all rich and make a ton of money, but that's not true. My salary was $120,000 a year—a good income, to be sure, but a fraction of what I could have been making as an attorney in a big firm. I was able to stay with Mom when I went back to Minnesota, which helped out financially, because I didn't have to maintain two homes, but still, I had to be conscious of my expenses. Most congresspeople share residences in Washington to save money.

So when Greg asked me to move in I was tempted but I said no. Even though I was a grown woman, I knew my mother would have a fit if I lived with a man that was not my husband. Besides, moving in with Greg would mean giving up my independence, and I wasn't about to do that without a commitment.

"I don't believe in living together before marriage," I told Greg.

"Then let's get married," he said.

"Gee, with such a romantic proposal, how can I say no?"

"Noted. I will come up with a better proposal, and we can get married this summer."

"I'll be campaigning this summer. I'm up for reelection."

"You can take an afternoon off for a wedding. Besides, it will be good press." Greg was beginning to understand the art of the political campaign.

We opened up a bottle of sparkling water, as I do not drink alcohol, and toasted our impending proposal, but later that night I began to have second thoughts.

What did "wife" mean to Greg? Would he expect me to do his laundry and make his dinner once we were married? I didn't even do my own laundry. I threw all my dirty clothes in a suitcase and had Mom do it when I went back to Minnesota.

Did he want kids? He had never mentioned children. Did I want kids? Children had never been on my to-do list. If we had kids would he expect me to be the primary parent? How would I raise a child when I needed my mom to take care of me?

I wanted to ask other women if they felt the same worries about marriage, but it was too personal. I preferred to agonize over questions such as this night after night by myself.

That weekend Greg invited me to meet his parents for the first time. We were flying back to Minnesota on Friday night for the weekend. I was addressing a Rotary breakfast at 7:00 a.m. at the convention center, attending a League of Women Voters luncheon at noon, meeting with a nurses' union at 2:00 p.m., doing a meet-and-greet at a children's theater matinee at 3:30 p.m., and stopping by a local caucus meeting at 7:00 p.m.

Sunday morning I was scheduled to attend a worship service at Spirit of Hope Methodist Church, followed by serving lunch at the Loaves and Fishes Homeless Shelter and a Three Rivers Chorale Concert at St. Mary's Basilica at 1:30, after which I would bolt for the airport for a flight back to Washington.

In between those appointments I needed to appease my mom by spending quality time with her, and now Greg wanted me to meet his parents. I pulled up my calendar on my iPhone.

"I should be done with the caucus about eight-thirty. I could drive over to your parents' place then. Or, I could meet early Sunday morning. Say six-thirty?"

"That's too late on Saturday and too early on Sunday. What else do you have?"

"I don't. Those are my only options. We can do it another weekend. Let me check and see when I can fit you in," I said, scrolling through the upcoming weekends.

"Fit me in?" Greg said testily. "I'm your fiancé, not a town hall meeting."

"Technically, you're neither. You have not proposed, and I have not said yes."

"You don't want to get married?"

"I don't know. We have a lot to talk about before we make that kind of commitment."

"I love you. You love me. What else is there to know?"

"Do you want children?"

"Maybe. Do you?"

"Maybe. Someday."

"Someday? You need to decide soon, Suraiya, or it will be too late."

"How can I raise a child? I'm never home."

"We could find a nanny. Or you could cut back on your travel. And I would babysit when you needed to work."

"Babysit? You would babysit your own child?"

"I'm the father," he said, rubbing my arm placatingly. "It wouldn't be any trouble."

"You don't babysit your own children, Greg! You raise your children. You parent your children."

"Okay, okay. Sheesh, I can't talk to you when you're all emotional like this."

That remark made me want to throw him out the plane's window without a parachute.

"Greg, if you want to be with me you will need to understand that I have other goals."

"Such as?"

"Such as being Speaker of the House."

"You can't be Speaker of the House. The Democrats have the majority. The best you can do is House Minority Leader."

"Wilkins is expecting another landslide, and the voters aren't going to put a Republican president in the White House and keep a Democratic majority in Congress. The Republicans are sure to take the majority in the next election and then I can run for Speaker."

"That's a long shot, and you know it. You're one of the youngest members there. The Republicans have never elected a female Speaker, especially not a..." He stopped, looking embarrassed.

"A what?"

"You know what I mean, Suraiya."

"You mean someone as short as me? You mean someone with a smart aleck boyfriend?"

"Suraiya, don't be like this."

"Tell me what you mean, Greg."

"The party will never put a Muslim in charge of the House."

His words stung, and I fought back the only way I knew how.

"You know who never has to worry about a Muslim in the house? You. I don't want to get married, and I especially do not want to marry you."

Not a great way to break up considering that we were crammed into adjoining airplane seats. Worst. Plane ride. Ever.

Despite my anger at Greg I suspected he was right. There was still so much fear, so much suspicion, even fifteen years after terrorists attacked us. People painted all Muslims with the same brush, regardless of whether they were extremists or moderates or, like me, culturally Muslim but not practicing. Americans had no issue with Hindu extremists who killed thousands of Muslims in India in 2002 or Christian extremists who killed thousands of Muslims in Bosnia in the 1990s, but every Muslim in America and abroad was approached with caution.

Not even my own party had faith in me. When first I approached Frank Kirsch, the ranking Republican in the party caucus, about someday running for Speaker, he laughed his annoying high-pitched laugh.

That made me all the more determined to run and win.

Olivia and I huddled in my office late one night before the 2020 election, strategizing.

"We need to figure out a way to make it politically attractive for the Republicans in the House to want to vote for me, without me asking them to vote for me."

"Then we need to make you the choice of the people. If the people clamor for you, and the Republicans go with yet another old, white guy, there will be all kinds of murmurings of racism, and the Democrats will accuse the Republicans of being out of touch," she replied. Olivia was wise beyond her years.

"The average age of a House Republican is fifty-four," I pointed out. "If we can start a groundswell of support among the younger voters through social media, by the time it gets to the Republicans' radar, it will be too big to ignore."

I laid out my plan.

"Time is of the essence," Olivia reminded me, jotting some notes on my outline. "We'll have twenty-four hours at most after the election before the House votes."

The morning after Wilkins was reelected, I took extra care with my hair, makeup, and clothes, opting for navy over my customary brown. According to Olivia, navy was commanding, while brown appeared too dowdy on camera.

"Leave through the front door so you can give the reporters an impromptu quote, which I'll write and text to you," she had advised.

"I think you need to look up the definition of impromptu," I said.

"To the press, it needs to look as though you are as surprised as they are."

A swarm of reporters were waiting for me at the front door of my building as Olivia predicted. Unfortunately, Greg had been correct about the Democrats staying in charge of Congress. A landslide for a Republican president and an overwhelming majority for a Democratic Congress. Winston Churchill once said that the best argument against democracy is a ten-minute conversation with the average voter. After 2020, that makes complete sense to me.

"Congresswoman Jafari, is it true that you're being considered as the next Minority Leader?" the woman from the *Times* shouted.

"I don't believe so," I replied innocently. "Where on earth did you hear that?"

"It's all over the Echo Chamber that Republicans want a younger, more diverse image, and they think you're the person for the job," said a man from the Post.

I don't know who Olivia got to post those speculations on the Echo Chamber, but apparently they had laid it on a bit thick.

"No one in the Republican caucus has approached me about being House Minority Leader. There are many older Republicans who have been in Washington much longer than I have who, I am sure, are in line for the position," I said, repeating Olivia's statement word for word. In one fell swoop we had painted my opponents as fusty politicos in a good ol' boys' club.

Olivia was waiting for me in my office when I arrived at

seven, listening to the major news channels while surfing the Echo Chamber.

"Am I in trouble yet?" I asked her.

She handed me a pink message slip. "Frank Kirsch called fifteen minutes ago. He wants to see you in his office immediately."

"Want to watch the fallout?"

"Wouldn't miss it," she said, standing up and shrugging on her blazer over the same skirt and blouse she had worn yesterday.

News crews were waiting in the hallway outside my office, following my every move and shouting questions as we made our way to Kirsch's lair.

"Do you want to be House Minority Leader?" shouted one.

"I will fully support whomever my fellow Republicans elect. I only want what is best for my party and my country."

"Is it wrong to find this fun?" Olivia whispered.

I didn't reply. Those microphones could pick up a cricket breathing, and I wasn't going to say anything to jeopardize my newfound negotiating position. Kirsch opened the door to his outer office for us himself, which is how I knew there would be heck to pay for our little stunt. The two of us stood there shaking hands and smiling for the cameras, until Kirsch's communications officer shooed them out and shut the door.

Frank's smile disappeared as he turned and stomped toward the inner office. Olivia and I followed obediently behind.

"Out," he ordered Olivia, pointing to the outer office. She looked to me. Olivia understood hierarchy but her first loyalty was to me, and she wasn't going to kowtow to Frank no matter what.

"It's okay," I reassured her. "This won't take long."

When we were alone, Frank stood glaring at me from behind his desk, arms crossed over his ample belly, a ring of gray hair circling his red scalp. Then his shoulders began shaking. He was laughing.

"Well played, young lady," he told me. This was quite unexpected.

"Sir?"

"The President's Chief of Staff called me at three a.m., wanting to know why the Echo Chamber was lighting up with criticism of the President for not putting you in charge of the House."

"The President doesn't have anything to do with that decision," I said.

"The President has everything to do with everything! You think the Leader is elected on his merits? He's elected because the President agrees to work with him. Officially, on behalf of the Republican caucus, I am required to chastise you for being an upstart and trying to bend the caucus to your will."

"Unofficially?"

"I now realize that it is better to have you with me than against me. You're a bit of a shark. You remind me of myself at your age."

I did not consider this much of a compliment, so I kept quiet.

"We are going to elect the House Minority Leader tomorrow afternoon, Suraiya, and it is going to be you. We'll float a few names out there to appease the donors. Congressman Eastman is up for reelection next year, so we'll put him out there to make it seem as though he's a valued member of the House, although, as you know, he's an idiot."

"And an addict," I added without thinking. Eastman never met a prescription pain killer he didn't ingest as soon as possible.

"Yes, well, he's still a Republican, and we'd rather have him in the House than a Democrat."

Frank took a seat behind his desk.

"Suraiya, I underestimated your ambition, and that won't happen again. I understand that you aspire to greater things. If you play your cards right, you might be a senator, or even Speaker of the House, someday. But you've got to wait your turn. There are men on the Hill who've spent decades building a political career, and they deserve your respect and your deference. They're not going to let you jump to the head of line again."

"Understood," I said. I was not naive enough to mistake Frank's cordiality for friendship. Frank knew how to play both sides in the political game.

Less than three years later, I was sworn in as president. That time I didn't jump. I was pushed.

Chapter Thirteen

Vice President Theodore Adelson's star rose quickly. He went from Baltimore City Council to United States Vice President under Dennis Wilkins in only six years, a rise unmatched by anyone, except, perhaps, for mine. Theodore went from serving in city government straight to the state capital, serving one term as the Governor of Maryland.

While President Wilkins was a former college football player and had the athletic good looks of his Nordic ancestors, Theodore had the pale complexion of his Irish forebears, with sandy hair cropped closely to his ears. He was scrawny and short and terribly uncoordinated. He always hung onto the railing when descending stairs for fear of falling in front of the press. Theodore was not charismatic enough to go from a governorship to the presidency, but as vice president, he held enough power in the Republican party to be on deck for the next election.

Both Dennis and Theodore were good men. Mostly. Theodore thought he was the smartest person in the room and most of the time he was right, which made him a great second-in-command for Dennis. It's that kind of arrogance, though, that gets people into trouble and Theodore was no different. People like Theodore always think they are superior, that they are more blessed somehow, than the rest of the population, and he was shocked to discover that not only was he not able to fool law enforcement, but that law enforcement would go after him.

Power buys a lot of influence in America, but when the Democrats saw Adelson's blood in the political water, they began to circle. Adelson was the hands-down favorite for the Republican nomination for president in 2024. If Adelson was taken out of the running the Republicans would lose their star candidate, and there was no clear-cut frontrunner to take his place. The field would be wide open. This was good news for other Republicans who were impatient to get their turn at the big chair, but bad news for the party. There was a lot of ground to cover to create national name recognition for someone else if Adelson went down.

The Democrats, though, had begun campaigning for 2024 the second Wilkins won reelection. Their presumed candidate, Bill Lochner, was already stumping for the White House.

In November 2022, rumors began to swirl that Theodore was being investigated by the United States Attorney's office in Baltimore for extortion, tax fraud, bribery, and conspiracy. No one took these rumors seriously at first—I know I didn't—but on December 17th, Theodore was formally charged with accepting bribes of more than $100,000 while he was the Governor of Maryland.

It was a shocking allegation and the initial reaction was that the charges were part of some politically motivated scheme by the Democrats. The U.S. Attorney in Baltimore, though, turned out to be a registered Republican and a contributor to Wilkins's campaign. It's disheartening when you can't blame your problems on the other party.

Dennis read the criminal complaint and had no choice but to admit that the evidence of Theodore's guilt was overwhelming. Dennis was not about to make life easy for the Democrats, though. A lengthy investigation into the charges, followed by a trial, would provide the Democrats with plenty of fodder to use against every Republican candidate running for state or federal office in 2023, and Dennis was too savvy a politician to let that happen.

The U.S. Attorney offered Theodore a deal: plead no contest

to a single charge of tax evasion and resign as vice president, and no further charges would be filed. Dennis ordered Theodore to take the deal.

"Think of the party, Theodore," Dennis told him.

"I'll be disbarred," Theodore reminded the President. "I won't be able to practice law. I'll be banned from politics. How will I support my family?"

"We'll find a private sector job for you," Dennis assured him, and that is exactly what happened. Theodore moved out of the vice president's office straight into an office at an international trade firm, making twice the salary he made as vice president. Theodore always did land on his feet.

The President, then, had a dilemma. Who would replace Theodore?

Politics is the art and science of government. This art and science involves the balancing of multiple interests to seek an end that benefits the greatest number of people. The balance means that no one gets their own way, and voters are always convinced that someone else won and they lost.

You see, bipartisan governance does not mean standing on your side of the aisle with your arms crossed, refusing to compromise. Bipartisan governance means that you give some, and you get some, and everyone ends up unhappy.

President Wilkins had a web of politics to consider when deciding who would replace Theodore. Dennis had been clawing his way to the top in government for decades. He had made promises to many people and made a lot of backroom deals to get to the White House, and people were lining up to collect on their favors. Those were just the Republicans.

The Democrats were an issue for Wilkins as well. They controlled the Congress, and therefore the confirmation proceedings. The Democrats were not going to confirm any Republican for vice president that might present a real challenge for them in the next Presidential election, and they made that clear to Wilkins's people before Theodore resigned.

It was Daniel Hale, a Democratic senator from Hawaii, who passed along that little nugget to Wilkins's Chief of Staff, Samuel Brooks. Sam was in his early forties then, his hair already gone from light brown to gray from the stress of political life, and had been working in Washington D.C. for two decades. The Democrats wanted the next vice president to be the Republican least likely to get elected in 2024. They wanted me.

This was fine with Wilkins, Kirsch, and the rest of Republican leadership. They figured they could play the progressive saviors to people of color by parading me in front of the cameras, yet they also considered me safe. They never considered me a contender for the office of president. I was too young, too female, too brown, and too new to Washington. Any one of those aspects might not be enough to prevent me from being president, but put them all together with a dash of religion, and you have the whole never-going-to-get-elected package.

Just to be safe, though, Frank sat me down and made me promise that I would not seek the Republican nomination for president in 2024. As he told me, "Do your time, do what you're told, and then leave."

"Can I go back to the House?" I asked.

Frank looked at me as though my head had just spun around.

"Why would you want to do that? You will make a fortune on the speaking circuit alone. Plus, there's bound to be a book deal."

"But I won't get to be part of the legislative process anymore. I actually like being a legislator."

"You're going to make a fortune when this is over," Frank sniffed. "You should be grateful."

I was grateful. And annoyed. And excited. And scared. Political power is measured by proximity to the president, and as vice president, I would be closer to the president than anyone else in the world. All I had to do was play their game.

Chapter Fourteen

I'm not sure which news upset Mom more—that I broke up with Greg or that I was going to be vice president. Either one of those things should have been broken to her in person, but there was no time. The official call from President Wilkins came in to my office at three o'clock in the afternoon on a Tuesday. All he said was "Be here in thirty minutes. We want this on the early news."

That was it. No "Would you like to be vice president?" No "When should we announce this?" Just an order to appear, which I obeyed.

I sent Mom a text: *Watch the news. Something big.* I didn't want to say more, in part because I was worried about security, and part because I wasn't entirely convinced I was going to be named vice president. A female, Indian, Muslim a heartbeat away from the presidency? Was it possible?

I arrived at the White House a little out of breath, whether from the rush over or the excitement, I wasn't sure. Sharon Barber, the President's Deputy Chief of Staff, ushered me into the hallway outside the Oval Office.

"The President is announcing your nomination to his staff right now. He will call for you in a moment." She looked me up and down. “You are quite the poster child for affirmative action, aren’t you?”

“I beg your pardon?”

“Some of these men and women have been climbing the political ladder for decades. But you? You’ve been here six years.”

“I am the House Minority Leader,” I reminded her. “Officially I am the third highest-ranking Republican in Washington.”

“Yes,” she sneered, “and I’m sure that was based entirely on merit as well.”

Annoyed, I crossed my arms and peered at her.

“Where is this animosity coming from?”

“My uncle died on 9/11. I have your people to thank for that.”

I rolled my eyes.

“You have terrorists to thank for that. I was born here. I’m an American, same as you.”

“My family has been here for four generations. You are not the same as me.”

After seeing the worst that humanity can do to itself in Afghanistan, staring down Sharon was not a problem.

“You’re right. I outrank you. Perhaps you should remember that.”

The door opened then, and a Secret Service agent ushered me into the room. President Wilkins stood in front of his desk, surrounded by Cabinet members. Secretary Brent Mendelson from the Defense Department and Secretary Claire Herrick of the Department of Homeland Security were huddled together against a wall, whispering. For a moment I wondered if this was all a big ruse to catch me off guard. There was always a fear among Muslims that we would be whisked onto the next plane to Guantanamo Bay.

“Here she is,” President Wilkins said magnanimously. “Our new Vice President.”

Secretary of State Vivian Braunstein started clapping politely, and was soon joined by the Attorney General Edin Sigelman. I knew both Vivian and Edin from the Republican Women’s Caucus. Every month or so we would have a girls’ night at Vivian’s house. Security around Vivian was tight, and the safest place for her was in her own house.

It was one of the few places and times we could let our hair down and not be so serious. Claire used to be part of the group, but stopped coming when Vivian invited me. Claire told Vivian to be careful around me and to let her know right away if I started asking too many questions about defense systems.

Claire needn't have worried. I was only there to talk about shoes and books. I didn't even partake of the wine. Hey, the men got together and talked golf and fishing. Sometimes a woman needs to be around other women.

Anyway, Vivian and Edin started the clapping and everyone else joined in, except for Claire and Brent. They were still whispering. The applause was civil if not enthusiastic. President Wilkins shook my hand, then motioned for me to shake hands with the Cabinet members. In my nervousness, I also shook hands with all of the Secret Service agents, who good-naturedly congratulated me, although I caught Claire rolling her eyes.

A few minutes later, President Wilkins and I drove to the Capitol building in the armored presidential limousine, nicknamed The Beast by the Secret Service. Wilkins would announce my nomination to a joint session of Congress while the news cameras recorded the moment, and we would shake hands with the Congressional leaders and smile and wave for the cameras.

Then the FBI would do a background check and talk to every person I've known since birth to make sure there were no skeletons in my closet, and the House and Senate would vote on whether to confirm me as vice president or not.

This process would normally take eight weeks, but I expected my confirmation would go much more quickly. I'm a pragmatist. I assumed the FBI had been doing a background check on me since the moment I announced my first candidacy for the House, maybe even before, and I doubted they had ever let up.

President Wilkins stood before the lectern and addressed the Senate and the House. When he announced "the new Vice President," I emerged from the side door and joined him at the lectern.

This time, the applause was louder and seemed more genuine. Under the 22nd Amendment to the Constitution, presidents are limited to two terms. Therefore, Wilkins could not seek a third term.

In these circumstances, the vice president would be the frontrunner for the Republican party's candidate on the next presidential ticket. I, of course, had agreed that I would not seek the candidacy. Every Republican in that room was envisioning themselves in the White House.

The Democrats were ecstatic too. They knew Theodore was the brains of the operation, and now that he was out of the picture, they envisioned that Wilkins would take the country downhill. They knew Dennis did not respect me as an equal, and however smart I may be, and however able I might be as a leader, they knew that I was in office as a token.

Sharon was right. It was affirmative action, and I planned to take full advantage of it. I did not know at that time what that would mean or how I would do it, but I knew I could not squander the opportunity for myself, for women, for Asian-Americans, or for Muslims.

As I followed President Wilkins down the steps into the crowd, my phone beeped. It was a text from Mom. She had watched the news and sent me the following message: *Oh Suraiya. Who will marry you now?*

Chapter Fifteen

The vice president's residence is at Number One Observatory Circle, a large Queen Anne-style mansion on the grounds of the United States Naval Observatory next to the White House. While beautiful, the house, at just over 9,000 feet, is much too large for one person. Theodore and Mrs. Adelson were in no hurry to leave the residence, and I was in no hurry to move in.

I had never lived by myself. The thought of spending every day surrounded by staff and the public and then going home alone to that big, empty mansion saddened me.

"Mom, will you come to Washington to live with me?" I asked.

"Why?"

"You're the closest thing I have to a wife," I said.

"What do I do with my house?"

"Keep it," I told her. "We'll need it again in two years."

It did not occur to me that I would never move into Number One, and Mother would never return to her house in Minnesota.

The vice president is given an office in the West Wing and also maintains a set of offices in the Eisenhower Executive Office Building (EEOC) situated next to the West Wing on the White House grounds. I was more excited about moving into the vice president's office in the EEOC than I was about moving into Number One.

The EEOC office is the vice president's Ceremonial Office, used mostly for press conferences. The floor is made of mahogany, white maple, and cherry, and it has two fireplaces surrounded by black marble from Belgium.

But the centerpiece of this office is the desk. The vice president's desk belongs to the White House, and was first used by President Theodore Roosevelt in 1902. I feel a special connection to Theodore Roosevelt. He held the record as the youngest president to ever serve, taking over for William McKinley after McKinley was assassinated in 1901. Roosevelt was forty-two at the time. Later, in 1961, John F. Kennedy, at age forty-three, became the youngest elected president in history. Until I came along, that is.

The desk was used by other presidents, including Taft, Wilson, Harding, Coolidge, Hoover, and Eisenhower, before being placed in storage in 1929. President Truman brought it out of storage and back to the White House in 1945.

It was Lyndon Johnson who brought the desk to the Ceremonial Office when he was vice president, and there it has stayed for more than fifty years. I hope it stays there still. Inside the top drawer is the signature of every president and vice president who used the desk since Truman, including mine.

I spent hours practicing my signature before I signed that drawer. There was this fear that I would misspell my own name, and future generations of schoolchildren would learn about the affirmative action vice president who screwed up her own signature.

Greg and I had not spoken or seen each other since that awful plane ride months earlier. After the breakup I buried myself in my work, my only social life the community events that I attended each weekend in Minnesota, often with my mom in tow. She was my rock, and as much as she badgered me about dating again, I knew she only wanted me to be happy.

When my secretary announced that a Mr. Gregory Mills was on the telephone, I was not sure to which Mr. Mills she was referring. I had met hundreds of people since being announced as vice president, and I was frantically trying to wrap up things in my office in the House before I moved into the vice president's office.

"Did Mr. Mills say what his call pertains to?" I asked.

"He's says it's personal," the secretary informed me.

Personal. Gregory Mills. Greg. I tried to keep my composure as I picked up the phone.

"Hello?"

Silence.

"Greg?"

"Sorry. Hearing your voice again...it threw me for a second."

Silence. *Say something, Suraiya*, my mind screamed.

Greg cleared his throat. "Listen, you probably haven't heard, but I was promoted, and I'll be at the defense briefings, and I wanted to make sure you knew, so, you know, it won't be awkward being in the same room together. At the briefings. On defense. When we're in the same room. Together."

I don't know what came over me. It certainly wasn't an Indian thing to do.

"Maybe we should get together for lunch and talk so that it won't be awkward. At the briefings. On defense. In the same room," I suggested.

Silence.

"Okay."

Lunch turned into dinner, and dinner turned into us getting back together. This time I was more clear about how I felt and what I wanted, and I didn't waste time.

"Nothing's changed and everything has changed," I told him a few days later as we were driving to Harper's Ferry to go hiking, accompanied by my new Secret Service detail. "I know I love you, and I'm pretty sure that I do not want kids, at least not until my tenure as vice president is over. You should also know that I am a package deal. My mother will be living with me, and I cannot foresee a time when she does not live with me."

Greg, sitting in the passenger seat fiddling with the map on his smartwatch, did not seem fazed by this sudden burst of candor.

"I'm fine with not having kids, Suraiya. Let's not mention that to my mother, though. She'll freak out."

"Mine too, but as long as we're not married she won't bug us about it much."

"Then we have a problem, because I don't want to be the vice president's boyfriend. If we are going to be together, then I want a commitment, Suraiya."

What could I do? The official version of our proposal is that Greg asked to speak to my mother privately, and asked her permission to marry her daughter, which my mother deigned to give only after putting him through the wringer about how he would support her daughter. The story goes on to say that my mother called me into the room, whereby Greg dropped to one knee and proposed.

The truth is that I pulled the car to the side of the road on the way to Harper's Ferry, took Greg's hands in mine, and asked him to marry me. It was such an unIndian thing to do. My mother never knew the real story, nor did anyone else until now.

"Are you sure you want to come clean about this?" asks Greg, reading over my shoulder as I type this.

As a matter of fact, I am unsure about admitting this now. Mother is not above coming back from the dead to haunt us.

We decided to keep our engagement to ourselves, our parents, and the President's staff until after the swearing-in. We wanted no big wedding, and announcing our forthcoming marriage would make privacy impossible. Mother and Daris arrived on Tuesday for the swearing-in, as did Greg's parents and three of his sisters, and we all stayed at the Blair House, usually reserved for guests visiting the White House on a state visit.

"Security is going to be an issue," Elizabeth Liu, the Secret Service Director, told Wilkins and me when we met to discuss the swearing-in ceremony. "The closer we can keep everyone to the White House, the better."

What Liu did not say, but what was clearly implied, was that because a Muslim was about to take her place in the West Wing, every crackpot in the country—in the world—was going to be coming out of the woodwork. The safety of those around us trumped our desire for privacy, so I felt I needed to tell Wilkins and Liu of our plans to ask Chief Justice Roberts to marry us immediately after the swearing-in.

The gleam in President Wilkins's eyes was as transparent as it was gleeful.

"Suraiya Mills is much more marketable than Suraiya Jafari. And if you convert to Catholicism, even better!"

"I'm not converting, and I'm not changing my name," I said. Muslim women do not take their husbands' surnames. Until that moment I hadn't given a single thought to whether or not I would be changing my name, but once Dennis thought it was a given, I was against it. Mother was aghast when I told her.

"Suraiya, in America when a man gives you his name, it shows his commitment to you," she scolded me. She was adamant about the name change, until Greg told us his mother was insisting that I take the name Mills.

"Jafari isn't good enough for her?" Mother said, insulted.

"Do you have a preference about this name thing?" I asked Greg when we had a rare moment alone.

He shook his head. "People know you as Suraiya Jafari. You would lose a lot of ground with a name change."

So I kept my name. Greg's mother had a fit, insisting that having the same last name was necessary for family unity, and she did not let up until Greg threatened to change his last name to Jafari. If there was ever any doubt in my mind whether Greg was the man for me, that moment sealed the deal.

Wilkins was not happy about the name, and had to satisfy himself with the political gains from the ceremony itself.

"A wedding is just what this country needs," he exclaimed.

"Not a wedding," I said. "A small, private ceremony."

"Think of the great press we'll get," Wilkins cajoled. "That's worth two million in free publicity alone. Plus another two million in campaign contributions."

"I fail to see how my marriage is going to raise campaign funds," I said.

Wilkins looked at me as though I were a slow child. "Major contributors get to attend the wedding of the century. We can sell sponsorships!"

It was all I could do to refrain from screaming.

"No huge wedding. No sponsorships. A small, private ceremony," I insisted. I could see that Wilkins wasn't listening to me, so I made a huge bluff. "If I can't have a small ceremony, then Greg and I won't get married and we'll live together at Number One."

Wilkins clutched at his heart. "You can't live in sin in the vice president's residence!" he scolded me. "The evangelicals will splinter off again like they did with all that Tea Party nonsense fifteen years ago."

Eventually we settled on a private ceremony in the solarium of the White House, followed by a small reception in the state dining room hosted by the President and the First Lady, Margaret Wilkins. Margaret, of course, made sure every detail was perfect, down to the three-tier red velvet wedding cake with cream cheese frosting.

Mother was conflicted about my wedding dress. In America, brides wear white to symbolize purity, and while Mother wanted very much to celebrate my purity, Indian brides do not wear white, as white is the color of mourning in our culture. American brides also prefer strapless, low-cut gowns—attire entirely too immodest for a Muslim bride. Indian brides wear colorful saris. There was no way I could get married in the White House in a sari. My foreignness was already prevalent in my very being. I knew better than to exacerbate it.

Dennis insisted that I allow Margaret's stylist to help me.

"You look like a dowdy old woman," he told me. "Lose the glasses. Glam it up a bit. This is the White House, not a funeral parlor."

I tried contacts, but I couldn't stand sticking my fingers in my eyes, so after a few days I went back to my black frames. I tried wearing the lipstick Margaret gave me—a reddish hue with the ridiculous name of Berried Treasure—but I kept leaving the tube lying around and within days I had lost it.

Margaret suggested that I wear a pink-colored dress, something A-line and simple with a matching coat for the swearing-in and wedding ceremony.

"This is a big moment in your fashion life," she told me. "The label you choose for your big day will define you."

I thought about what she said, and I decided she was right. If I was going to wear a label, I was going to choose one that expressed who I am as a person. Margaret was not happy when I told her of my choice.

On Monday, April 11, 2023 I was sworn in as Vice President of the United States of America, choosing to take my oath with my shaking hand placed on a copy of the Constitution while our family and friends surrounded us. I was so nervous! I knew the world was watching, and every mistake I made would be scrutinized and analyzed.

Minutes after the swearing-in, I married Gregory Elias Mills in a brief civil ceremony, and unlike the swearing-in ceremony, the marriage ceremony did not make me nervous at all. The Chief Justice told us to face each other and hold hands, and as I looked into Greg's eyes, I saw a man as strong and wise as my father, a man I would trust with my future and my life, and I broke into happy tears. Men like Greg are few in number, and I felt fortunate that we would get to grow old together.

I wore my Marine dress uniform. That is the label that will define me always.

Chapter Sixteen

I could not continue to room with Susan and Jackie in the apartment as a married woman, and the Secret Service had determined that staying in Greg's apartment was unfeasible. It was too difficult to protect: too many windows and doors. It was also too disruptive to the other tenants. The press was camped out in the parking lot and across the street. They scampered inside the front door when tenants went in or out and ducked inside the garage when the parking doors were open for cars. Plus, my mother was now going to be living with us as well.

It was easier for the Secret Service, and safer for us, the agents, and the tenants in Greg's building if we stayed in a location that was already under Secret Service protection. Plus, I had no desire to rush the Adelson family out of their home. They were going through enough already. Theodore's wife and children were facing the loss of their home, their livelihood, and their social status. That is a lot to deal with on short notice.

Even if we had a lot of furniture and other possessions, which we did not, Greg and I had no need to unpack anything but our clothes. The Blair House was fully furnished and staffed. The Blair House sits across Pennsylvania Avenue from the White House.

Known as the President's Guest House, it is used by foreign heads of state when they attend state visits at the White House.

Built in 1824, this row of four interconnected townhouses has borne witness to extraordinary events and exceptional personalities. At just over sixty thousand square feet, it is larger than the White House, and it was to be my home until the Adelsons vacated the vice president's residence.

Being accompanied by Secret Service agents everywhere we went was an adjustment for all of us. Our first night in Blair House, Greg and I decided to take Mom out to dinner at Peking Gourmet Inn in Falls Church, Virginia, a restaurant already accustomed to accommodating the Secret Service. The Peking was a favorite of Presidents Bush one and two, and the Secret Service had installed bulletproof glass in the front windows years ago. We wanted to live as we would if we were ordinary citizens, but yet we didn't want to endanger the Secret Service agents who were literally protecting us with their lives, and this seemed like a good compromise.

The agents ushered us out to the vice president's limousine, which whisked us the fifteen minutes to the restaurant on Leesburg Pike. By the time we arrived at the Peking, the owner was holding the door for us and a table was waiting.

A television over the bar was showing the Senate debate over whether to confirm me as vice president. Jackson Martin, the aging Republican senator from Texas, was warning his colleagues about the dangers of putting me second-in-command.

"This is the first step in the Islamic plan to take over the United States!" bellowed Martin. Martin knew darn well that my confirmation was a done deal. He was making a splash in the news in case he decided to run for president in the next election.

Not that Jackson was happy about my ascension. Frank Kirsch once let it slip that Jackson had taken to calling me the hobbit, a reference to the little people of the Lord of the Rings trilogy. I was surprised that Jackson didn't use a more derogatory racial slur, but he had been in politics a long time, and he knew that such a slur would be a career ender for him if it ever became public. Later I would remind Jackson that the hobbits, while small, were also heroes.

"Well, then," he replied, "I was right for the wrong reason."

Back to the Peking Gourmet and one of my first meals as vice president. It felt strange to be sitting down to eat while the Secret Service agents stood around us, keeping a wary eye on the other patrons, the passersby, and the servers.

"Suraiya, invite them to sit with us," my mom ordered, stealing a glance at the agents.

"I can't, Mom. They're on the job," I whispered.

"Suraiya, you are being a very rude boss," Mom hissed.

I heard a couple of the agents snicker. I was sure they were ordered around plenty by mothers, too.

"Mrs. Jafari," Greg interjected, "the agents are not allowed to sit with us. We'll make sure they get a decent meal later, though."

Mom patted Greg's hand.

"You are a good boss."

"He's not their boss, Mom. Neither am I," I tried to explain.

Greg stopped me. "You want to argue or do you want to eat?"

Before we had even opened our menus, the owner arrived with a roasted duck, plates of pancakes, snippets of green onions, and hoisin sauce. We were eating Peking duck whether we wanted to or not.

"I'm a vegetarian," I tried to explain to the owner, as Mom and Greg dug in. The thought of eating the flesh of an animal sickened me ever since I watched goats being slaughtered for dinner while I was deployed to Afghanistan. I needn't have bothered. A second later a server arrived with a plate of bok choy nestled gently onto shiitake mushrooms. The dishes kept coming, but I could not eat. Every other diner in the restaurant was staring at us.

I leaned toward Zoey Harris, a veteran agent who had once protected the Obama family.

"What would Barack do?" I asked quietly.

"He would greet everyone and pose for pictures," she whispered. I took a deep breath and stood up, turning toward the table nearest us.

"Good evening," I said to the middle-aged couple sitting there watching me. "My name is Suraiya Jafari. I am your new vice president."

I stuck out my hand. The restaurant fell silent. Just when I became convinced that they were going to reject me, the man took my hand in his.

"My name is Steven Westendorf. I hope you'll do a better job than that crook, Adelson," he replied.

"Mr. Westendorf," I replied, looking him dead in the eye, "I will never lie to you. Ever. It won't always be pleasant, and it may not be what you want to hear, but it will always be the truth. Always."

He stood up, still clasping my hand.

"Then, young lady, you are okay by me."

Forty minutes of hand shaking and hugging and posing later, Greg, Mom, and I all climbed into the limousine for the ride back to the Blair House. I hadn't gotten to take even a bite.

"I saved this for you," said Greg, handing me a fortune cookie.

I broke it open and removed the narrow slip of paper. Popping a chunk of cookie into my mouth, I smoothed out the paper and began to read.

"You are a handsome man, marvelous orator, and great leader."

Mother took the fortune from my hand and read it to herself.

"It's got your gender wrong too," she said, without sarcasm.

Greg laughed all the way home.

Chapter Seventeen

The United States has a long and complicated relationship with India. Indeed, India, with its 5,000 years of civilization, has a long and complicated relationship with every country in the world. The fact that India has outlived many of the countries with whom it shares the Eastern hemisphere, as well as the numerous empires that sought to rule it, bears testament to the resilience and strength of its people and culture.

We Americans are the young upstart to India's venerable statesman. Initially, the two countries got along quite well. The first recorded visit of an Indian to America was in 1893. Swami Vivekananda, a Hindu Sage, traveled to Chicago to speak at the World's Parliament of the World's Religions at the World's Fair. Swami Vivekananda began his speech with "Sisters and brothers of America," charming the audience and launching the Swami to stardom as a speaker. He traveled our country introducing yoga and the Hindu religion to the Western world.

The relationship became complicated after World War II, when the United States and the Soviet Union were locked in the Cold War. India became friendly with the communist Soviets, much to the dismay of the Americans, despite India's commitment to remaining a democratic government. Meanwhile, India kept a wary eye on China, which had recently fallen to Communist rule, and which was viewed by India as its greatest threat.

India's wariness was well-founded. The countries did indeed become embroiled in a short border dispute over the China-India border in the Himalayas, culminating in the Sino-Indian War in 1962. The complexities of the relationship between China and India are too immense for this book, particularly as that relationship dates back to ancient times. However, it is important to keep in mind, as one reviews the events that occurred during my term in the White House as vice president and president, that India and China continue to jockey for position as a world power much as they did a hundred years ago.

The relationship between India and the United States improved over the decades as the Cold War dragged on. American leaders saw India as an ally in the battle against communism, and in 1959 President Dwight Eisenhower became the first American president to visit India, thereby creating a new friendship with the Indians.

This friendship grew with the following American administrations. President John F. Kennedy, in 1963, openly assured India that the United States would defend India in the event of a Chinese invasion. The relationship faltered after Kennedy's death, when the U.S. established relations with Pakistan, a land that had once been part of India.

Although this relationship with Pakistan was controversial at the time, and remained so for decades, it later served us moderately well in our search for, and destruction of, terrorists. In the 1970s, though, India considered this relationship an insult.

The friendly relationship was reestablished when President George W. Bush and Indian Prime Minister Manmohan Singh created a new trade program to increase commerce and investment between the two countries. India became quarrelsome when President Barack Obama chose to strengthen ties between the U.S. and China, but ruffled feathers were smoothed a bit when President Obama invited Prime Minister Singh to the White House for a state visit. This status quo was maintained in the intervening years in an effort to appease all of our foreign partners.

Maintaining our relationship with India and China requires a delicate balance: if we are too friendly with India, China is offended. If we are too friendly with China, India is offended. I know of no international relations expert who has a sufficient fix to make all countries happy. I do know that if China and India ever manage to get along for more than five minutes, America is going to make a tempting target. We need to be ever vigilant about our borders.

In 2023, of course, I came into this foreign policy mix. Suddenly, America had an Indian in the upper echelons of government, a fact that did not go unnoticed in India or China. Even President Wilkins, never known for his interest in international affairs, clearly saw the double-edged sword this presented. His first order was to dispatch me on state visits to India, Pakistan, and China.

"In India, be Indian. In Pakistan, be Muslim, and in China, try to be American," Wilkins instructed me.

"I am American," I reminded Wilkins.

He waved away my remark.

"Wear something distinctive so the press can tell you apart from the Indian prime minister," he advised. He was not being sardonic. "Avoid politics as much as possible. This is purely a relationship-building tour. Put on a sari and walk through a temple and shake hands."

"With all due respect, Mr. President," I said through gritted teeth, "there is more to India than elephants and snake charmers."

"Like what?"

"Um..." Shoot, I had never been to India. My view of India was through the media lens that all Americans viewed India, of cows on the street and children begging in the villages.

It was scheduled to be a whirlwind sixteen-day trip with Greg, Mother, my policy advisor Henry, Alim, along with a gaggle of state department advisors and Secret Service agents accompanying me. Once again, I was in the Middle East, surrounded by armed guards, except this time there were five-star hotels in cities instead of a tin trailer in the desert. We never made it to China, of course, fate having other plans.

Our first stop was Pakistan. To the average American, Pakistan is a country of deserts and desolation, a harbor for terrorists and misogyny. But Pakistan is so much more than that. It is a land of gorgeous mountains and crystal lakes and sandy beaches. A land of rich and ancient history and the modern, skyscraper-filled cities of Karachi and Lahore and Islamabad.

The Pakistanis are merchants and farmers and mothers and fathers. They are laborers and landlords, teachers and tenants, miners and manufacturers.

Today, as then, Pakistan is predominantly Muslim, with a smattering of Christians and Hindus. Islam remains the official religion, although the rights of non-Muslims, which used to be quite limited, are being expanded as a younger, more educated and less intolerant generation takes power.

Pakistan is about the size of two Californias. It has its own nuclear weapons, much to the dismay of the U.S., but our consolation is that Pakistan is an ally. I don't think Pakistan and the U.S. will ever be friends, but as long as we are allies, we will avoid worldwide destruction.

It was my job in early 2023 to encourage this continued relationship, in part because Pakistan purchases much of its military equipment from the United States. It is disconcerting to think that the product we ship across the world one day is the very product our military will be facing if relations sour. Pakistan also buys a lot of military power from China. At least we know what we're dealing with if they buy from us. If they buy from China, we're fighting an unknown product, and that's worse.

Mostly, though, I was in Pakistan to buy their continued allegiance. My role was to assure the Pakistani president that billions of dollars of economic aid would continue to flow into Pakistan, provided that Pakistan continued to hunt for and turn over terrorists.

Air Force Two arrived in Islamabad shortly after daybreak, where we were greeted by President Zardari.

Pakistan was enjoying a period of domestic peace at this time. For the first time in decades, the President, the Prime Minister, and the Parliament were cooperating, with no party seeking to overthrow the power of the other, and the Pakistan Parliament session had been completed without interruption by insurgents or domestic terrorists.

President Zardari was the widower of Benazir Bhutto, the first woman elected to lead a Muslim state. She served two terms as Prime Minister, and might have served a third had she not been assassinated by a suicide bomber two weeks before the general election. While women in Pakistan fared better than women in many other Muslim countries at that time, true equality had not yet been achieved. Gender equality has improved greatly since then, but like America, women still struggle to take their full place in society.

President Zardari played host at brunch, at one point leaning over to ask quietly, "Thousands of Americans visit Abu Dhabi every year. What would it take for Americans to visit Pakistan?"

"Peace, Mr. President," I told him. "Americans are afraid to come here. All we hear of Pakistan is terrorism."

"But we are winning our fight on terror. It is very safe here now."

"Perhaps our perception is wrong. In that case, we must change the American perception of Pakistan, and the only way to do that is marketing. Once the world knows what Pakistan has to offer, foreigners will come."

Later he would take my advice, reviving the Hippie Trail, that route popular with hikers worldwide in the 1960s and 1970s. Europeans, Americans, and Japanese would hitchhike from London or Amsterdam through Pakistan and India on a route sometimes referred to as the freak street, due to the general uncleanliness and unique appearances of the hippies. This time, though, there would be no hippies, but rather gap-year backpackers and wealthy baby boomers out for adventure. The Trail had changed too. Gone were the cheap, flea-bag hostels favored by the hippies, replaced by four-star hotels and restaurants. Pakistan became the fashionable place to vacation, a vision unfathomable to Americans born before 2000.

Tourism was not yet a major industry when I visited there, and our visit was only four days, not nearly long enough to hike the Hippie Trail. Greg and I managed to do that a few years ago, with few people knowing our true identity. Throw a baseball cap on my head and I look like every other American tourist.

I accompanied President Zardari on a review of his troops and visited the Faisal Mosque, a stunning, contemporary place of worship located near the Margalla Hills of the Himalayas. The Faisal Mosque, named after the late King Faisal bin Abdul Aziz of Saudi Arabia, holds as many as eighty thousand worshipers within its structure and gardens. It was the first time I had ever been in a mosque, and the traditional Islamic mosaics and calligraphy were stunning.

As I stood in the mosque, I realized again how disconnected I felt from my own religion. America is all about secularized versions of Christmas and Easter, two celebrations that bear little relation to religion. Greg assures me that the Bible contains no talk of Santa Claus or Christmas trees or candy canes or chocolate bunnies that lay jelly beans.

The Jafaris celebrated the secular parts of those holidays as well. We would decorate a Christmas tree and get presents and go on egg hunts, but those were never connected to the stories of Christianity. Yet I realized I knew more about Christianity than about Islam, merely by osmosis from my community, and I longed for a more in-depth understanding of my own faith.

Mom spent the entire visit peppering our hosts with questions—about the history of the city, the country, the mosque, the mountains. The barrage of information was enlightening and annoying, but diverted her attention away from the subject of grandchildren, so I was glad for her distraction. It was a remarkable four days in Pakistan.

Then we went on to India, where I would finally be among my own people.

Chapter Eighteen

Turns out that I am not Indian after all.

I thought I was Indian.

People told me I was Indian.

Then I went to India, and the Indians there told me that I am not Indian.

Or at least, not Indian enough.

We landed in Mumbai, a cosmopolitan city of twenty million people, and were driven straight to St. Xavier's College in the colonial center of the city. Built in the Indo-Gothic style, with high stone walls and arched windows, the campus was founded by Jesuit priests in 1869. I tried to take in the colors and sounds of the city through the shaded bulletproof windows of my limousine. Indians lined the streets of our route waving signs of welcome and Indian and American flags and cheering our motorcade.

Five thousand years of Hindu and Muslim culture in India, and the first place I visit there is a nineteenth-century Roman Catholic college. It was slightly disappointing, but the reality was that the college is a veteran of high-profile diplomatic visits from American dignitaries and accustomed to securing the campus. No one was quite sure which religious or political group posed the greatest security risk for me, only that it was the highest of any American vice president to date.

It was vital to American interests that this visit go well. The majority of India's population, at that time nearly one and a half billion people, were under the age of thirty. These young people were the most coveted consumers and future leaders on the planet because of the sheer size of the group. I expected questions about the U.S. relationship to Pakistan, a sore point with the Indian government and people.

Alim and I had been refining and practicing my response to the most likely question I was to face at the town hall meeting to be held at St. Xavier's College: *Why did America not treat Pakistan as a terrorist state, preferring instead to continue to negotiate with a government openly antagonistic toward democracies such as India?*

It was a reasonable question. On November 26, 2008, terrorists from Pakistan snuck across the border and embarked on a four-day siege, killing hundreds. America condemned the attacks, a woefully inadequate response in the eyes of the Indian population.

My planned answer was carefully measured: I understand your anger and frustration toward the United States and Pakistan. We are forthright with Pakistan about our expectations for them. Making an enemy of Pakistan will not benefit India or America. We want a peaceful, prosperous Pakistan. A stable Pakistan is good for India.

Three hundred students packed the St. Xavier courtyard, known as the first quadrangle, ready to lob questions at the diminutive Indian-American before them. I opened the visit with expressions of gratitude for the warm welcome, noted the generations of freethinkers produced by the college, and touched on America's hopes for a fruitful and warm relationship between our countries, then opened the floor to questions, ready to field questions on Pakistan.

A young man approached the microphone.

"What is your native language?" he asked in lilting English. A sharp intake of breath emerged from both Greg and Mom, seated to my right. A small groan escaped from Alim, standing slightly behind me to my left.

"English," I replied.

"No. I mean, your native Indian language," he persisted.

"I only speak English," I told him.

"Not Hindi?"

"No."

"Not Urdu?"

"No. Do you have any concerns about Pakistan that you would like to address?"

"But your ancestors, they are from Gujarat, are they not?" he continued.

"My great-great-grandparents were born in Gujarat."

"So you must speak Gujarati."

"I do not speak Gujarati."

"Not even a little?"

"Afraid not."

There was stunned silence in the quadrangle now. To this day I do not know if the college administrators were more embarrassed by the student's persistence or by my lack of Indianness. The student turned to my mother.

"Why did you not teach your daughter her native tongue?"

"She is third-generation American," said Mother. "Her native tongue is English."

"Why did you not try?"

"Young man, I was born in the States. I only speak English as well."

The student looked at my mother sadly.

"You call yourself Indian?"

My mother was a very sweet woman when she wanted to be, but when it came to her daughter, and especially to her daughter being insulted, she had no problem turning to iron in an instant, foreign relations be damned.

"I call myself an American. I call my daughter an American. Americans speak English. If you have a problem with that, I suggest you remember your manners and keep it to yourself."

That was the first time I realized that my identity as an Indian was false, and I did not know how to react. All of my life, I had identified as being Indian. Sure, I knew I was an American, but my identity was hyphenated. I was an Indian-American. Or a South Asian-American.

My white friends did not call themselves German-American, or Swedish-American, or French-American. It was an unspoken rule that they needed no such hyphen and that I did, based simply on the color of my skin.

Even Indian-American is not quite sufficient to cover the diversity of my background. My family left India four generations ago. Our more recent history is African, yet no one, not even I or my mother, considers us African-Americans, especially other Africans.

Culturally I am more Indian than African, perhaps, but even that is too simplistic an answer. My heritage encompasses too many angles to be contained in a hyphen. Like America, it is a heritage that defies description, like a diamond with many facets, all of which add to the shine and value of the gem.

"Mom, do you ever wish that I was more Indian?" I asked her when we were alone in our hotel later that night. She sipped her masala chai, prepared by the hotel chef according to her specifications.

"Raising Indian children in America is a challenge," she said after a moment. "In India, parents criticize their children to make them better. Children are expected to obey their parents no matter what. In India, parents show their love through self-sacrifice for the next generation. In America, parents think love is hugging their children. We had to find a balance in raising you. We raised you to speak your mind. Sometimes that made life more difficult for us, but it was what we wanted for you."

"Do you ever wonder who you are?"

"I know who I am. I am Cala Mahdavi Jafari. Mother of the Vice President of the United States," she winked at me.

"You know what I mean," I persisted.

"Let no one define you but you, *beta*," said Mother.

I've been trying to write my own definition of myself ever since.

The next day we proceeded to New Delhi, where we visited Humayun's Tomb and addressed a joint session of the Indian Parliament. We attended a dinner hosted by Indian's President

Shri Pranab Kumar Mukherjee at the Rashtrapati Bhavan, the vast official residence of the president of India. The staff quarters of the Rashtrapati Bhavan, built in the early 1900s by British colonialists, are larger than the whole of the White House. While it was not an official state visit—those are reserved only for the heads of state—the world press was omnipresent.

An American vice president of Indian descent visiting the Indian president made for interesting copy. Mrs. Mukherjee, a sweet woman in her sixties, was dressed in a fuschia sari trimmed in green and gold. I wore a silver evening gown chosen by Margaret's stylist. I still hadn't gotten the hang of dressing for the level of scrutiny to which I was exposed, and I was relieved to have Margaret's input. Greg wore a black suit, white linen shirt, and red tie. It took me two hours to get ready for that dinner. Greg was dressed in seven minutes flat.

Sadly, President Wilkins had been correct in one respect. Headlines in newspapers around the world carried photos of President and Mrs. Mukherjee, myself, and Greg, with Mrs. Mukherjee and I standing next to each other on the red carpet. The photo caption misidentified Mrs. Mukherjee and myself, with my name under her face and her name under mine. The press, it turned out, could not tell two Indian women apart after all.

Chapter Nineteen

The irony of human life is that the mightiest of men may be felled by a single-celled organism smaller than a speck of dust. President Wilkins would rather have died by an assassin's bullet, or a car accident, or a heart attack, or even a painful bout with cancer, than be taken down by a random bacteria moving through his bloodstream. That his body would cling to life as his brain was ravaged by disease was a cruel end to a life of public service.

"Let me die standing face-to-face with my killer than linger in a bed with machines doing my breathing for me," he once told me after we had visited a hospice in Virginia. Now, knowing that he did just that as part of a political deal to benefit me, fills me with guilt. It is his slow crawl toward death for which I feel I must atone.

It is the strange twist of fate that it would be I, not Dennis, who would stand face-to-face with an assassin that jolts me awake in the dead of night. That I would survive an encounter with a madman bent on revolution is more than luck. I do not know the name of the Divine Being, or the earthly dogma this Being prefers, but I know that the Being exists, because I exist to tell you this story.

President Wilkins was in Seattle throwing out the first ball at a Mariners game. As part of the scheduled photo opportunity, the

President walked through the corridors of the stadium, shaking hands with the fans. A local eight-year-old boy, chosen specifically for his wholesome appearance by Chief of Staff Sam Brooks, reached out to shake Dennis's hand, and Dennis, knowing how to work a crowd, kneeled down to the boy's height.

"Do you like hot dogs?" the boy asked.

"I sure do," lied the President. Dennis Wilkins would never deign to eat processed meat in his home, but the cameras were rolling, and Wilkins was not about to offend the processed-meat eaters or manufacturers that might be watching.

"Hot dogs are my favorite," said the boy, continuing to shake the President's hand. The kid had been kept waiting in a side room for an hour for this moment, and he was determined to make the most of it. President Wilkins tried his best to brush the hint aside, to no avail.

"Can we have hot dogs?" the kid asked bluntly.

"Sure," said the President amiably.

One bite of contaminated hot dog. That's all it took to change the course of history. One bite before the President handed the food to an aide, who surreptitiously threw it away. The kid was fine. I've often wondered what my life would have been like if the girl at the food counter had handed the contaminated hot dog to the boy.

But she didn't. She handed it to Dennis.

He flew back to D.C. on Air Force One that night, surrounded by aides and reporters. None of them reported the president appearing ill in any way.

"I have a headache," he told Margaret the next morning. She gave him an aspirin and he dressed for work. Emerging from the elevator connecting their private quarters to the public corridor to join with his Secret Service agents for their walk to the West Wing he collapsed, convulsing with seizures.

Acute bacterial meningitis. I couldn't even spell it when Sam called me on my secure line to tell me the President was in a coma. Mother, Greg, and I were still in New Delhi, visiting the memorial to Gandhi. We climbed onto our helicopter and flew straight to the airport where Air Force Two was fueled and waiting. The rest of the trip was cancelled.

"It's a good thing you've been out of the country for the last several days," said Greg as the plane got underway. "People would suspect you of doing this."

"People have no reason to suspect me of anything," I protested.

"They don't need one. Trust me, the first thing people said when they heard the President collapsed was 'Where was the Vice President?'"

I wanted to tell him that people were not that stupid, but I didn't. I knew he was right. The Echo Chamber was already alight with conspiracy theories.

Let me go on record right now with the truth: There was no conspiracy. Not behind Dennis's illness, anyway. One could argue that the timing of Dennis's death was part of a conspiracy, but I had no knowledge of it at the time. It was a random incident that changed the world, albeit not as much as I thought it would.

Although Dennis gave me much grief, there are things I learned from him in our short time together in the West Wing. I learned how to use people to my advantage. I learned how to massage egos and manipulate psyches. I learned to trust no one. I learned that the president's chair is a lonely place.

Rest in peace, Dennis. It is because you taught me well that I survived the onslaught that was to come.

Chapter Twenty

Camp David is one of my favorite places, and one of the best perks of being president. Camp David is the mountain retreat used by every president since Franklin D. Roosevelt chose the spot in 1942. Located in the wooded hills of the Catoctin Mountain Park in Maryland, a mere sixty miles from the capital, it is officially known as the Naval Support Facility Thurmont. It is, in actuality, a naval installation.

Initially used by the Roosevelts as a family gathering spot to escape the humidity and political pressure of Washington, President Eisenhower changed its nature when he began to hold cabinet meetings there. He also used the retreat to entertain foreign officials, including thc British Primc Minister Harold Macmillan and Soviet Premier Nikita Khrushchev.

Ever since, the lodges and cabins at Camp David have been used for everything from Middle East peace talks (Jimmy Carter in 1978), to weddings (George H.W. Bush's daughter in 1992), to management retreats for administration officials (Bill Clinton in 1993).

In late May of 2023, Greg and I escaped to Camp David for a weekend, accompanied by Dennis's, and for the time being, my,

Chief of Staff Sam Brooks. Sam and I had some things to discuss, and hiking the trails around the camp while we talked gave us a chance for some fresh air.

"We need to discuss your presidency."

Sam kept his hands stuck in his jacket pockets, while I swung my arms back and forth to get my circulation moving in the damp air of the morning.

"That's a bit premature. Dennis could still recover."

"He's not going to get better, Suraiya."

I did not yet know about Sam's secret deal with Margaret Wilkins.

"It is not enough to keep the status quo until the next election. We need to move quickly, to put you in a position for reelection."

That stopped me cold.

"One of the conditions for being named vice president was that I would not seek the nomination in 2024."

Sam met my eyes for the first time since we set out on our walk.

"You made that promise as the nominee for vice president. Now that you are going to be president, things have changed."

I took a deep breath and we began walking through the budding trees again.

"I can't go back on my word."

"If you go into office openly declining to run in 2024, you will spend the next two years as a lame duck president. You will get nothing done. That's not a good legacy."

"There is no way the Republican party is going to give me the nomination."

"You will have to fight for it, but there are ways to make it happen. And once you are elected to your second term, reelection to your third term is all but guaranteed."

That should have been my tip-off that Sam knew something I did not. Under the 25th Amendment to the Constitution, a vice president who becomes president and serves more than two years of the prior president's term cannot seek reelection twice. In other words, if I was sworn in *before* July 1, 2023, I could serve the remaining two years of Dennis's term, plus be elected to one more four-year term.

If I was sworn in *after* July 1, 2023, I could serve the remaining two years of Dennis's term and still be eligible to serve two more four-year terms as president. Dennis was touch-and-go in May. It was possible that he would not survive another ten weeks until July, although I fervently hoped that he would recover.

"You've thought this through, Sam."

"It all rests on your choice of vice president."

"Who do you have in mind?"

"Jackson Martin, from Texas."

I laughed. "Martin! You're mad. He hates me. He's been openly mocking me ever since I took office as vice president."

"Exactly why you should choose him. His change of heart will bring credibility to your presidency."

"He probably wouldn't even agree to do it."

"He'll do it. Being your vice president is his one shot at getting into the Oval Office."

"He would poison my chai to take my spot."

I was certain that Jackson could not spell masala chai, but I was sure he would figure out how to spike it.

"We're going to have to double security around you anyway. Every president in the last one hundred years has had at least three assassination attempts made. With you, I would double that. We might as well add a tea taster to the Secret Service."

I considered his strategy as the sun rose higher in the trees. Spring was turning into summer, and I wondered how hot the season would become.

"He'll have to be confirmed. Would the Democrats go along with Martin?"

"He's sixty-eight years old. He'll be seventy at the next election—too old to serve two terms as president, but his age would be an asset in a vice president. The Democrats won't see him as a threat, even if they did suspect you planned to run, which they don't."

We walked among the spruce and fir trees in silence for awhile, listening to the songs of the White-throated Sparrows. In

Indian culture, being surrounded by birds is a sign of good fortune. I took the songbirds as an omen.

"Convince me," I said. Sam did not hesitate.

"Martin is a rich, white, Christian from Texas. He'll bring in the southern vote, which is important with you being from the upper Midwest. He'll bring in the conservative white vote, which offsets any issues about your race and gender. His presence next to you will provide reassurance to all the racists and evangelicals who are having trouble accepting you in the White House.

"Plus, he's been in Washington for thirty years. He knows everyone, and everyone knows him. He's well-respected in the Senate, and he knows how to get things done. That's important, considering that the Democrats control Congress. Let's face it. Congress isn't going to cooperate with you. They're not going to do anything that will help you look good to voters.

"Most importantly, he is very, very rich, and he has very, very rich friends. Jackson and his wife know who to wine and dine, and how to do it. If you're going to run for reelection, you're going to need money, and a lot of it. They can get it for you."

Sam was right, and that annoyed me.

"So much for a new day in America. We're back to putting a white guy in charge."

"You'll definitely have to let him know that you're the boss. He's a strong personality. He'll run right over you if you let him."

"Okay, so Martin becomes vice president. With Vivian Braunstein as Secretary of State, we have a religious trifecta."

"Pardon?"

"A Muslim president, a Christian vice president, and a Jewish Secretary of State. Equal opportunity at its finest."

Chapter Twenty-One

Much speculation has swirled around whether I knew about Sam's deal with Margaret. I did not. I was not aware of any deal until Sam released his book, *The Bargain*. Most of what I know of Sam's agreement with Margaret comes from Sam's book and Margaret's private papers, released after her death. He never did forgive me for refusing his counsel in 2027.

As I explained earlier, there are restrictions on how many years a president may serve. The most is ten: two four-year terms, plus two years if succeeding a sitting president. If the vice president ascends to the presidency on, say, June 30th, then she may only seek reelection once, because she will have served more than two years of the prior president's term.

Dennis went into the coma in April, and I sincerely hoped for his recovery. I was unaware doctors had informed Margaret in May that Dennis would never regain consciousness. The machines were keeping his heart and lungs alive. The bacteria had destroyed his brain. Margaret, may she rest in peace, was a shrewd and wise woman. It was her ambition, more than Dennis's, that propelled his political career.

Margaret knew if Dennis died she would lose her status as First

Lady, along with all the benefits that such status provided. Margaret had no intention of stepping down. As far as she was concerned, Dennis was going to lay in that hospital bed on life support until the next election, politics be damned.

Sam's ambitions, however, surpassed Margaret's, and he knew that his best shot at another decade as the White House Chief of Staff was to get me into office. He knew that to maximize my years in office, I could not be sworn in as Commander in Chief until at least July 1. It was Sam's idea to do the swearing in on July 4, to play the Land of the Free card to the max.

Sam knew that spending every day at the hospital would be wearing on Margaret. She reveled in her public relations duties. She wanted to be in front of adoring crowds, not stuck in a gray hospital room, surrounded by hospital staff who paid more attention to her husband than to her.

Sam arranged a private meeting with her in Dennis's hospital room in May, after she confided to him that Dennis would not be returning to the White House. Ever. Sam and Margaret faced each other across the sterile white blankets as Dennis lay in his hospital bed, connected to all manner of tube and sensor.

"Margaret, I'm sorry about Dennis. But now we must consider what is best for the country."

Sam knew Margaret did not care one whit about the feelings of the constituents. She did care, though, about her husband's legacy.

"Our enemies see us as weakening. They believe America is ripe for the taking," Sam explained.

"You think we are vulnerable to another terrorist attack?"

Sam shrugged. "Terrorists. China. I wouldn't be surprised if Canada was contemplating an invasion. The point is that the world needs to see a president. An official president."

Margaret shook her head. "Dennis is still the president."

"Congress is making noises about voting to remove him. He would be the first American president to be removed from office that way. Do you really want him to be remembered that way in the history books?"

"Of course not."

"And if we are attacked again, and the country is plunged into war, what kind of reaction do you think Dennis's death will garner?"

"My husband will still receive a state funeral."

"Are you sure? When the country is mourning dozens, if not hundreds of lives lost in battle, do you think they will mourn the death of a man they did not meet, who died of natural causes after a lingering illness?"

"You are a brutal man, Sam."

"You are a smart woman, Margaret. We may be able to help each other out."

"Clearly, your agenda is already made. Tell me what you want."

"Dennis will remain on life support until July 3. On the evening of that day, you will instruct the doctors to remove life support, and he will be allowed to die in peace. The acting president will be sworn in during the early morning hours of July 4. Her first act will be to issue a presidential proclamation announcing the death of President Wilkins, and offer the nation's condolences to your family.

"The new president will order flags at all federal facilities throughout the world to be flown at half-mast for thirty days, and close all federal agencies and offices on the day of the President's funeral in observance of a national day of mourning. President Wilkins will be given a state funeral with full military honors."

"I don't want that woman in my house until after my husband is buried."

I assume "that woman" referred to me. She need not have worried. We were quite happy in Blair House, and I was certainly not going to have the First Lady's knickknacks crated and sent to their home in San Clemente, California before she was ready to go.

San Clemente was the President and Mrs. Wilkins's private estate in California, overlooking the Pacific. It was a gift to the Wilkins from friends in the party after Dennis won his second reelection. Those are the kinds of friends long-term politicians accumulate, and the kinds of friends I lacked. If I wanted to succeed in Washington, I needed those kinds of friends.

So the deal was struck, and Margaret instructed the doctors to remove Dennis's life support on July 3 at eleven o'clock at night.

The President died at 11:18 p.m., surrounded by his wife, his son and daughter-in-law, myself, and the attending physician.

Sam was not in the room. He was in the corridor, waiting with the Chief Justice of the United States Supreme Court. Forty minutes later, in the hospital chapel, I was sworn in as President of the United States of America.

Chapter Twenty-Two

My official inauguration as the forty-sixth president took place at 12:05 p.m. on July 4, 2023, in the East Room of the White House. I was thirty-seven years old, and, following in the footsteps of one of Mom's favorite presidents, Theodore Roosevelt, chose to do my swearing-in without any text at all.

Less than an hour earlier, Margaret Wilkins had stood in the same room, saying farewell to the Cabinet members who had served her husband. She had said her goodbyes to the White House staff earlier that morning. It was not a surprise. They had been busy packing the Wilkins's belongings for transport to California for days.

Margaret, usually stoic, nearly broke down during her goodbye speech. She was leaving behind everything she and Dennis had spent their lives building. After shaking hands with those assembled, I walked with her across the South Lawn to Marine One, the helicopter that would take her to Air Force One and her flight to the West Coast.

This changing-of-the-guard walk is a tradition in Washington. The president-elect walks the former president across the South Lawn on a red carpet laid especially for the event, with the president-elect's wife and the former First Lady following a few steps behind.

Obviously, our walk was going to be different. There was no president for me to walk to the helicopter. There was no president-elect's wife, but rather a husband. The social secretaries had no idea how to handle this.

"Let's forgo the tradition," said one, when Margaret, I, and our teams assembled to discuss the inauguration. "The First Lady will quietly depart the evening before the swearing-in."

"We could have the President walk with the First Lady, followed by the Wilkins's oldest son and, uh, the President's husband," suggested another. They still didn't know how to address Greg.

It all seemed so callous, discussing Margaret's exit in cold detail, right in front of her. I didn't really care one way or the other, but Margaret, well, it seemed like Margaret should get a say in the matter.

"Perhaps the First Lady has a preference," I said.

All eyes turned to Margaret.

"I've earned the farewell walk to the helicopter, and I intend to take it," she said. "My admirers need to be reassured that I am still standing."

Margaret wanted an exit fit for a president, and that's what we gave her. The military band played as she and I emerged from the cool of the White House into the bright July sun. We descended the steps from the portico to the South Lawn, followed by Greg and the Wilkins's eldest son.

Margaret, her back straight as a steel rod, finally seemed to grasp the enormity of the moment when we stepped onto the red carpet.

"I've walked many red carpets, Suraiya," she said. "I never imagined the last walk would be like this."

"No, Mrs. Wilkins. Neither did I."

"You will grow to hate red carpets."

She took my arm in hers, and we walked the rest of the way in silence, hands clasped, two women facing uncertain futures. The fact that I was the president had not seemed real until that moment, walking with Margaret toward the helicopter. With Margaret around, I felt Dennis's presence quite heavily. Once the helicopter was off the ground and Greg and I were walking back to the White House, the enormity of the situation settled on my shoulders, and I reached for Greg's hand.

"Take a deep breath," he reassured me. "You're going to be fine."

The public swearing-in occurred quietly in the East Room, in front of Mom, Greg, his parents, Daris and Neeta, Alim, Olivia, Henry, Frank Kirsch, and the White House photographers. Funny, now, to think how normal the whole scene seemed.

Immediately following the swearing-in, we all walked to the briefing room, where I gave my first address as president. Now it is held up as an example of brevity and brilliance. At the time, it was criticized as too brief and too vague. This is what I said:

"My fellow Americans, we are in the midst of change, but one thing remains steadfast. We remain a government of the people, for the people, and by the people. I was elected to president not by your ballots, but by the republic for which we stand. Barriers have fallen today. There are no more excuses. I accept this difficult job, and ask for your prayers as we do the work outlined for us by the Constitution."

There was no inaugural parade, no inaugural balls, no inaugural parties. The nation was in mourning for President Wilkins, and any outward celebration of my rise would have been in poor taste indeed. We marked the occasion with a simple dinner in the private dining room of the White House with our families and friends, including my Marine recruiter, SSgt. Embers, and the guys from that sad Christmas Day in Afghanistan—Bussman, Clark, and Hernandez. Our clothes and personal items were being transported from the Blair House, where we had dressed that morning, to the First Family's quarters on the second floor.

Mother, naturally, moved with us, taking over a private suite on the third floor, with her own bedroom, bathroom, and sitting room. Greg's parents, Ed and Marlys, having spent the night with us at the Blair House, would be staying in Lincoln's bedroom for a few days. Greg's sisters insisted on remaining at Blair House, claiming that the private quarters in the White House were haunted. By whose ghost, we were not sure.

On July 5, I went alone to the Oval Office and timidly sat down behind the Resolute desk. I ran my hand over the polished wood, thinking of the all the history made at that desk, and blinked back tears. My father would have loved that moment.

I was the President of the United States of America.

Chapter Twenty-Three

I visited Alim and his wife Hasna as often as I could after I first moved to Washington. Their oldest girl, Amaya, was just starting school, and Hasna was expecting their second child, another girl they would name Kira. They introduced me to their friends in the city, and smoothed my way into the local social circles, despite Alim's misgivings about my career choice.

"You should have a husband and children," Alim would admonish me. "Politics is no place for a woman."

"Your boss, the secretary of state, is a woman," I would remind him.

"My boss is the president," he would reply. "I must respect the person he appoints as secretary, but I do not have to agree with the appointment."

"When I am the president, I will make you secretary of state, and then I will be your boss and you will have to do as I say," I would tease him, and he would laugh and laugh. The idea seemed as ludicrous to him as it did to me.

Then I was president, and the time came for me to decide whether to appoint a new secretary of state. I wanted to appoint

Alim, and I suspected that he was waiting for me to call him and offer him the post, but I knew I could not.

If Alim had been a white Muslim named William Smith, a nomination as secretary might have been okay. If he was a Christian named Alim Youssef, that might also have been okay. A foreign-born Muslim with an accent, even a British accent, named Alim Youssef, however, would not be confirmed by the Senate in those years.

The tray with a pot of masala chai was waiting when the door opened and Alim entered the Oval Office. Normally I would invite him to our private quarters in the White House, but this was government business, not personal.

"Madam President." He hugged me to him. "I cannot believe little Suraiya Jafari is the leader of the free world."

"I can hardly believe it myself."

I motioned for him to sit, and poured him a cup of tea as he looked around the office. He lifted his cup to me in salute.

"To you, sister."

"And you, brother."

I tried to sip at my tea, but I felt queasy. I did not want to disappoint Alim or dishonor my deceased father.

"Alim, I need to speak with you about your place in my administration."

"No worries, Suraiya. I am capable of taking orders from you, even though I knew you when you were in braces."

"Alim, I would like you to be the United States ambassador to the United Nations."

His smile faded. "I do not understand."

"You know how to diffuse tense situations. You know how to build bridges across cultures. You know people in high places all over the world."

He placed his cup and saucer on the tray.

"With all due respect, Suraiya, those sound like good qualifications for the secretary of state."

I gave up the ruse of sipping my chai and placed my cup and saucer on the tray next to his. I clasped my hands in my lap to keep them from trembling.

"The ambassadorship places you in position to be secretary of state in the future."

"Do you not believe me capable of being an effective secretary now?"

"I think you would make an excellent secretary. But now is not the time."

"You think I am not 'American' enough."

"I think you are as American as anyone else, but I have to think about how people will react if I try to give the top foreign policy position to you."

"You always said that when you became president..."

"You didn't think I would be president any more than I did."

"Yet here we are, having tea in the president's office. Your office."

"I am so sorry, Alim."

He stood up and paced the room angrily.

"So you are going to submit to those fear mongers who think every Muslim wants to put us on the fast track to sharia law."

"Alim, you are a Muslim with an accent. You know how it would look to people."

"Henry Kissinger was a German-born Jew with an accent when he became secretary of state barely two decades after we were at war with Germany! No one accused him of being too foreign. Yet I, British-born, am too foreign?"

"I need to think politically right now. I need to do whatever I have to do to get reelected."

The ambassador to the United Nations was appointed. There would be no confirmation hearing. Alim would still be close by as one of my most trusted advisors, while breaking ground as the first Muslim United Nations ambassador from the U.S. It was a fair compromise.

A few months after this exchange, Hasna confided to me that Alim had indeed been expecting me to offer him the position of secretary of state, and had been planning to turn it down. The secretary of state travels more than three hundred days of the year, and Alim did not want to be away from Hasna and the girls.

"His greatest joy is reading bedtime stories with them. He refused to give up that time with his daughters," Hasna told me.

"Then why was he so upset with me?" I asked her.

"Because you took away his choice, Suraiya. It hurts when someone decides your fate for you," she explained. That, I understood.

Alim moved to leave, stopping as he reached the door. Refusing to turn to face me, he spoke.

"Promise me something, Suraiya."

"Anything brother."

"Do not be the first female president, or the first Indian president, or the first Muslim president. Be the president. It is the only way we will ever belong."

One day I hope Alim will tell me that I fulfilled that promise.

Chapter Twenty-Four

The air clung to my skin the July evening I summoned Texas Senator Jackson Martin to my office at midnight on the day of my swearing-in. Rumors were flying as to whom I would choose for vice president, and a few senators were hanging around Capitol Hill in the hopes the phone would ring with an offer, despite Jackson Martin being the odds-on favorite for the office.

As one of the highest-ranking, well-known Republicans in Congress, Jackson knew that the summons could only mean one thing: I was going to choose him as my vice president. If I was going to choose someone else, I would either give him a courtesy call to let him know he was out of the running, or not contact him at all. If the situation was reversed, he would not bother to call me.

Henry Shaw, who I brought with me to the White House as an advisor, ushered him into the Oval Office, and my new secretary, GeriAnne Basse, whom I inherited from President Wilkins, followed us in with a tea tray. GeriAnne, a reedy woman in her sixties with a penchant for enameled brooches depicting every shape and form of birdhouses, had been with Dennis for eighteen years, and was fiercely loyal to him. She had not yet warmed up to me, often keeping me waiting outside the Oval Office when I was vice president. GeriAnne placed the tray on the coffee table between the two sofas.

I was seated on one chintz-covered sofa. I did not rise to greet Jackson, but rather motioned for him to sit across from me. This was the first inkling he had that this would not be any ordinary meeting.

"Thank you," I said to Henry and GeriAnne before the tea was poured. "That will be all."

It was unusual for any senator to be left alone with me since moving to the White House after Dennis fell ill. It was especially unusual for a male to be left alone with me. For appearances sake, I always made sure that I was not alone with any man. There was always some White House staffer nearby to take notes, but not tonight. Perhaps if male presidents took the same precaution to safeguard their virtue, they would not get into so much trouble.

I made no move to serve either him or myself. I merely sat there, considering him. Finally he could not stand to wait any longer.

"You wanted to see me, Madam President?" he asked.

I entwined my fingers, and placed my hands in my lap.

"The Democrats tell me that if I choose you to be vice president, they will vote to confirm your appointment in a matter of days."

He nodded. I went on.

"The Republican caucus tells me that I must choose you to reward your loyalty to the party. They want me to send you on a six-month goodwill mission to Latin America and Asia."

That was not how he expected the meeting to proceed. The caucus might lobby for a particular person to be appointed, but it did not order the president to do anything. That was the moment when I watched Jackson begin to squirm.

"They've decided on someone else to run as the Republican candidate in 2024," he said matter-of-factly. "They want me out of the way."

I nodded. "It would seem so. Everyone knows you and I hate each other. They expect that together we will self-destruct, thereby clearing the way for one of their more favored candidates."

Jackson released an angry breath. "All of my years of service have come to this, being banished as less than even an ambassador!" He sank into the couch, deflated.

"There are things in this world that I hate more than you, Jackson," I said with solemnity. "I hate being pushed around. I hate being treated as a second-class citizen. And I hate, *hate*, watching people put their own needs in front of the needs of my country."

Jackson stared at the tea tray, looking as empty as the unfilled cups.

"So the question I have for you, Jackson, is how strong is your hate for me?"

There are defining moments in life, and Jackson knew then that his response to that question would define not only the rest of his life, but the rest of mine and the future of the country. The woman before him, whom he had dismissed as weak and insignificant, was preparing to stage a coup. Did he want to go along for the ride?

"What do you have in mind?" he asked.

"We let Congress appoint you as vice president. As soon as you're sworn in, we announce that we will be seeking the Republican nomination in 2024."

He let out a low whistle.

"Everyone will be angry," he said.

I couldn't help but give a slight smile. "Would you rather shake hands on two continents until being forced into retirement?"

He sat for a moment, thinking. "We will have to find a way to work together."

My smile disappeared. "No, Jackson. It is you who will have to find a way to work with me."

Jackson was being offered power surpassed only by the president herself. Could he take orders from this person he had denigrated, both personally and publicly, in order to gain that power?

Jackson had never poured a cup of tea in his life, much less served tea to someone else. He picked up the teapot and filled both cups. He picked up the saucer under the cup, balancing a silver teaspoon on the side, and offered it to me.

"I take it you have a plan for this insurrection of the establishment," he said as I took the saucer.

"I do." We drank our tea in silence then, Jackson wincing at his first taste of chai. I had no intention of filling him in on my strategy quite yet. At 1:00 a.m., I rose, silently dismissing him.

"One more thing," I said matter-of-factly as he walked toward the door. "If you give me reason to believe that you are not one hundred percent loyal to me and the American public, if I even suspect that you are putting your own interests ahead of us, I will bury your bloody carcass in the Rose Garden."

He considered this.

"I would expect nothing less, President Jafari."

Jackson Martin was now on my side.

Chapter Twenty-Five

If you had asked me at my inauguration, "What one issue will derail your presidency?" never in a million years would I have answered Christmas trees, a pagan symbol that, as far as I can tell, has no relationship to the birth of Jesus whatsoever. Yet, that is what happened.

I knew my first press conference would set the tone for my time in office, and I wanted to be rock solid on the main issues of the time: the economy, health care policy, the threat of terrorism. Every morning I met with the Cabinet to discuss these issues, and every afternoon, Jackson, Sam Brooks, and I met in the Oval Office to go over the briefings in detail. In the evenings, we were joined by my Senior Advisors Henry Shaw and Gordon Palmer, and sometimes the new House Minority Leader, Kevin Gilbert. The guys would pretend to be the Press Corps and fire questions at me about everything from labor unions to education reform to energy policy to transportation guidelines.

They asked about possible appointees to the U.S. Supreme Court, and I would reply, "If such an appointment is necessary, I will take all qualified candidates into consideration regardless of their political affiliations."

They asked me about peace negotiations in the Middle East: "Direct negotiations between Israel and Palestine are needed to arrive at a peaceful solution. The U.S. will assist in these negotiations in any way we can."

They asked me about Social Security reform: "We need a gradual raise of the age at which people may receive full benefits, from 67 to 70. This age raise would increase by two months every year, until 2040. This, combined with stricter definitions on who may receive disability payments, will keep Social Security operable."

So when it was time to give my first press conference on public policy less than two weeks after being sworn into office, I thought I was ready.

"You'll do great, kid," Jackson said, giving me a light punch on the arm. I felt like Jackson was the coach, giving a pep talk to the new quarterback in the locker room.

Alim was supportive too. "Hold your head high. Be authoritative," he instructed.

Even Mom had an opinion. "Wear heels. Otherwise you won't be able to see over the microphone." Thanks, Mom.

Jackson and I followed the new Press Secretary, Anna Plainfield, who had until then been Jackson's public relations officer, into the James S. Brady Press Briefing Room. The press correspondents, who each paid $1,500 for their seat, were sitting expectantly in their chairs.

Anna made a brief introduction thanking the correspondents for coming, and then turned the lectern over to me.

"Thank you, Anna," I began. "These are, in many ways, unprecedented days in the history of the United States. My goal in the coming months is to uphold the power and prestige of our country. The Cabinet appointed by President Wilkins will remain unchanged for the time being. Congress will proceed on schedule. To our enemies, I say this: do not mistake the changes you see as weakness. This time of new beginnings is a sign of America's strength. The American people remain as strong and resilient as ever. I will now take questions."

Nigel Rayment of the podcast Politico Watch went first.

"Madam President, will there be a Christmas tree in the White House this year?"

This was not a question that any of us anticipated, and at first I thought perhaps I had not heard him correctly.

"What do you mean?" I asked.

"As a Muslim, will you allow the White House to be decorated for the Christmas holidays?"

Every year, people bemoan the fact that Christmas decorations hit the store shelves in October, so perhaps I would have considered this question more relevant if it had not been a humid summer day and a hundred and two degrees in Washington, D.C.

"It's July," I said. "There are more important issues right now than Christmas trees."

"Are you saying you won't allow a Christmas tree in the White House?"

I threw my hands in the air, which is not a presidential move that looks good on camera. When I want to torture myself by watching embarrassing footage from those days, I begin with that moment.

"I'm saying that Christmas is the last thing on my mind right now."

"Is your opposition to Christmas based on your belief as a Muslim, or is this purely a political statement?" asked a guy in a gray suit and an awful striped tie.

"I have no particular feelings about Christmas at all," I protested. My stomach churned. How much longer could this continue?

"Will any Christmas decorations be allowed?"

This line of questioning was too inane, moving me to lash out in frustration, a mistake I would take pains to not repeat in later months.

"I don't care about the stupid Christmas decorations. Does anyone have a question that doesn't involve Christmas?" I said hotly.

Hands shot up. I called on a gentleman in the second row.

"Madam President, does this mean the annual Easter egg hunt is canceled as well?"

"Santa hijacked your press conference," Greg said later, sorting through the newspaper headlines.

There it was, splashed across the major papers in black and white: *President says she doesn't care about Christmas* and *President declares Christmas unimportant*.

I rarely swear. Mother always warned me that swearing makes women look trashy. That day, though, lying on the chaise lounge in our private sitting room while Greg read the newspapers to me, a string of profanity left my lips before I realized its escape.

Greg laughed. "Honey, I'm glad to see you let off a bit of steam."

"Don't tell my mother," I said.

He laughed harder, throwing the newspapers to the floor and wrapping himself around me, and we lay quietly together for awhile.

"I have no idea what I'm doing, Greg. People are looking at me to lead a nation, and I don't have a clue."

"No one understands the pressure of being president until they get to the big chair. If they did, no one would want the job," he assured me. I didn't answer.

"You're not expected to do this alone, you know. There are dozens of very smart people at your disposal, just waiting to give you their opinion."

"Maybe I should serve out the two years and forget about reelection."

"Run, don't run, it's up to you. I only ask that you don't make the decision based on fear. It's the one reason for which you will never be able to forgive yourself."

Greg is a very smart man, with very good advice. It was the last talking we did that night—we were newlyweds after all—and in the morning, after thinking about what Greg had said, the task ahead did not seem quite so daunting.

I went to the *Suraiya-TV* website and added the following statement:

The White House belongs to the people, and the people are of many faiths. Of course there will be Christmas trees! My husband is

Catholic, and as a Muslim I would no more ignore the holy days of his faith than the holy days of mine, or the holy days of our friends, or the holy days of any American. We will celebrate Christmas, and Eid al-Fitr, and Yom Kippur, and Diwali, and any other days we see fit. Now, let us not focus on the religious points on which we disagree, but on building a stronger America.

Less than a minute after I posted those remarks, an online news source ran the following headline: *President Calls America Weak.*

Chapter Twenty-Six

Jackson expected his vice presidency to be a well-paid vacation. In 2023, the vice president received an annual salary of $250,000. Far above the national average, but a fraction of Jackson's net worth, estimated at that time at thirty million.

Jackson had been sworn in at the end of July and gave his first speech as vice president immediately after. It was conciliatory, and while it wasn't exactly a ringing endorsement of my presidency, it did not openly call into question my ability to lead.

In his speech, Jackson humbly stated that "I want to be useful to President Jafari, who, in my opinion, has opened the door on a new era. I accepted her nomination because I feel there is a national and worldwide crisis of very serious proportions, but I am now extremely optimistic about the country's future."

He arrived at our first private meeting dressed casually, in a sport shirt and khakis.

"Is it casual Friday?" I asked, as GeriAnne brought in a tea tray.

Jackson poured me a cup. "There's no press here," he shrugged, handing me the cup and saucer.

"It's still an official meeting," I reminded him. "We're going to discuss the next two years of your life."

He took a sip of his tea and winced at the taste. Jackson was not yet a tea convert.

"Where are you sending me? Asia? Africa?"

"You're going to the Senate chamber."

He wasn't listening. "I've never been to Alaska. How about starting with a domestic tour? There are a number of governorships and Senate races up for reelection this year, even a few house seats I could stump for until November."

"Jackson, you're going back to the Senate."

He stared at me.

"I don't understand."

"The vice president is president of the Senate. So you're going back to the Senate."

"I'm well aware that I'm the Senate president now," he snapped. "I've been in politics longer than you've been alive!"

"Exactly," I said calmly. "You know every person in Congressional hall, down to the secretaries and interns. You know how to get things done, and I need you there to help me get things done."

He stared at me sullenly, then his face brightened and he started to laugh.

"You were serious when you said that you're thinking of running for reelection!"

I nodded. "Not thinking. Planning."

He laughed louder. "Suraiya, you've got guts, I'll give you that. But you gave your word that you wouldn't seek the nomination."

"That was when I was being vetted for vice president. I'm the president now. The incumbent president always gets the party nomination."

Jackson ran his hands over his face. "I don't know how to tell you this, but the party will never give you the nomination. Ever."

"They will if the public wants me in office."

"You can't get anything done in two years. Especially not if Congress blocks you every step of the way. And believe me, Suraiya, Congress will block everything you try to do."

"That's where you come in. You know every skeleton in every closet. You know how to make backroom deals. You can get things done."

"Even I have my limits. I can't move heaven and earth to make you look good."

"I don't need you to move heaven and earth. I just need you there to keep things running smoothly," I told him.

We sipped our tea in silence for a moment.

"Do you have a running mate in mind?" he asked.

I glanced at him over my cup. "You, of course."

"What if I don't want it?"

"That's your prerogative, Jackson," I said. "But you want it."

"You sound pretty sure of that."

"You have money. You have prestige. You have power," I said bluntly. "You would not have spent decades in the Senate if you didn't care about this country. Together, we can change America."

"The gridlock in Congress is a mighty opponent," said Jackson. "It will not be easy to overcome."

"I was not elected to this office. I made no campaign promises to lobbyists or corporations or power brokers in exchange for campaign funds. The only debt I owe is to the people who rely on me to lead. I can take risks that no other president in history has dared to take. Win or lose, Jackson, it's going to be a heck of a ride."

"It's bound to be an interesting chapter in my memoir," agreed Jackson, setting down his tea and reaching for a pad of paper and a pen. "Tell me your plan, Madam President."

"Keep Congress in line, especially the Senate. Cajole. Threaten. Get on your knees if you have to, just make sure the legislative wheels keep turning."

Jackson stopped writing and looked at me, his eyebrows raised.

"Let's work on an above-the-belt strategy, shall we? My knees are feeling a bit creaky these days."

"If you insist," I laughed.

"Oh, I insist," he said.

"I do have one idea. It involves Junie," I said.

"Does it involve her getting on her knees?" he asked.

"No."

"Let's hear it."

"Entertaining powerful people is a skill, and Junie is good at it. No, she's great at it," I said. "You and Junie host a series of dinner parties at Number One."

Jackson interrupted me. "We decided to stay in our house in Virginia. It's much nicer than Number One."

"You'll be moving into the vice president's residence," I corrected him. "You need to be a man of the people, and that means making do with a Queen Anne mansion next to the White House."

Jackson sighed. "Fine. But I refuse to use Air Force Two. That thing is a dump. Either I get to use my private plane or I'm going to seriously rethink taking over as vice president."

"You can use your own plane." He was right. Air Force Two was always breaking down and had an unnerving rattle on takeoff. Technically, Air Force Two is not an airplane but rather the call sign assigned to the vice president, just as Air Force One is the call sign that applies to any aircraft on which the U.S. president is present.

Back to the plan for Jackson and Junie. "Half of the guests at the dinner party will be Republicans and the other half will be Democrats. Inform all guests that this is a social gathering. No work talk allowed."

"I fail to see the point of that," said Jackson.

"Think back to when you first came to Congress. You had no problem working with people on both sides of the aisle then."

"We all knew each other better then," he said.

"Exactly. Congresspeople stayed in Washington on the weekends. Their families lived here. Their kids went to school together. They socialized with each other outside of work. Now their families live in their home states and they fly back and forth every week. They don't know each other as friends, only adversaries. We need to change that."

"You think a dinner party is going to change the acrimonious nature of Washington?"

"It's a carrot. Guests who behave well get a second invite to the White House. Guests who misbehave do not."

Jackson stopped writing and laid his paper and pen on the coffee table.

"You're using playground logic to make grown men and women fall in line. You want them vying for your attention and favor."

"I think it might work."

Jackson picked up the pen and paper. "Oh, it will work. These people are unbelievably susceptible to peer pressure. The playground might be different, but the politics are the same."

He was right. I called Junie myself to enlist her help in what Jackson began calling Phase One. I knew she would have invaluable insight into how to carry it out, and once I explained the goal of the dinners, she said "I'll take it from here," and she did.

Here's a little secret about Junie: She kept a list. Actually, it was a spreadsheet. She kept track of which congressperson was married, and whether the spouse lived in Washington or in the politician's home district. She kept track of who had kids, including the children's names and birth dates. She knew every politician's hobbies and interests. She had two secretaries who did nothing but monitor congressional social media pages. If there is a singular reason for Jackson's success in politics, it is Junie. She was a force of nature, and became one of my most-trusted advisors, as well as a surrogate mother after the loss of my own.

Junie began hosting Sunrise Thursdays at Number One, opting for breakfast gatherings rather than dinners.

"People are fresher then. More open," she informed me.

Every Thursday afternoon at 3:00 p.m., a dozen congresspeople (six from the House and six from the Senate) received a personal call from Junie, inviting them to the Vice President's residence the following Thursday for breakfast.

"This is a casual gathering," she would tell them. "No business allowed."

She and Jackson would deftly steer the conversation away from politics, toward more personal topics. This is where Junie's spreadsheet would come in. If a senator was into skydiving, she would also invite a representative who was into skydiving, or aviation, or something related. If a representative was, say, a hockey fan, she would also invite a senator who loved hockey.

The first group of invitees spent an hour connecting over scrambled eggs and hobbies, then were driven to the Congressional office buildings. The other congresspeople or their staff members saw this little group arriving together from Number One and immediately sensed that something was up.

They wanted to know why these particular senators and congresspeople had been invited. They could not believe there were no politics going on in that house, and it drove them crazy to think there were dealings going on that did not include them.

That afternoon, Junie made her second set of calls, inviting another group to breakfast the following Thursday. Capitol Hill nearly went mad, trying to figure out her angle. Who was being invited, and why?

Senators and congresspeople started hovering around their phones on Thursdays at 3:00 p.m., willing them to ring with a personal invitation from Junie. Sunrise Thursday became the social event of Washington, and as the weeks wore on, any senator or congressperson not invited yet became very nervous. In Washington, if you are not in the loop, you have no influence, so everyone wants to be in the loop, and the loop circled directly around Number One Observatory Circle.

Junie became a power broker in her own right. Her spreadsheet expanded to include two new pages: the Yes page and the No page. Politicians who abided by the "no politics" rule, who were well-mannered and acted as charming guests, were placed on the Yes page. Those who attempted to spread their agenda or who did not carry their weight in the conversation or spent the time on their smartphones were placed on the No page.

These pages were forwarded to my staff every Thursday afternoon. Names on the Yes page were included in upcoming White House events. Names on the No page were excluded. Junie included notes next to the names on the Yes page, letting me know how to best utilize that connection.

Several congresspeople were sports fans, so Jackson bought club seats at the FedEx Field for the Redskins (football), Nationals

Park for the Nationals (baseball), and the Verizon Center for the Wizards (men's basketball), Mystics (women's basketball), and Capitals (men's hockey). We would then invite people from the Yes page to join us in the club box at one of these sporting events. After the games, the players were invited to the club box for a meet and greet, which thrilled the politicians to no end. At heart, these grown men were still little boys in heroes' jerseys.

Quite frankly, Greg enjoyed these events more than I did, and he was a willing ally in this part of my presidency.

"This is my favorite part of being First Husband," he said in The Beast after a Wizards game. "The best seats in the house and we don't have to worry about parking."

We had a "no politics" rule at these games, too, but make no mistake, this was work time for me. I was briefed on every detail of every politician who sat next to us. I asked them about their spouses by name. I asked them to tell me how little Johnny or Joanie was doing in school. "Is he enjoying chess club this year?" "I hear she is studying Spanish. How is that going?"

It wasn't only sports. One Sunday evening in March, Junie called me in our private quarters.

"Sadie Williams is pregnant!" she practically shouted. I like babies as much as the next person, but I failed to see the need for her to call me at home to tell me that a senator was going to have one.

"So?" I asked.

Junie sighed. "Williams is a Democrat from Virginia. And this is her first baby."

I still didn't understand Junie's excitement.

"Sadie is forty-two years old. She is having the first grandchild on either side of her family. Her entire family lives within two hours of Washington," said Junie, breaking it down for me. "The families are going to be over-the-moon about this baby."

"Riiight," I replied, trying to follow her line of thinking. "This is great for me because..."

I could feel Junie rolling her eyes on the other end of the phone line. "Sadie is on the Yes list," she said, as though speaking to a small child. "Imagine how excited she and her family and friends would be to have a baby shower at the White House."

I was the leader of the free world, and Junie wanted me to throw a party where guests had to use a roll of toilet paper to guess how big Sadie's stomach would get during pregnancy.

"It doesn't seem very presidential," I hedged. "Wouldn't it be better for my image if I declared war on North Korea or something?"

"It's a girlie thing," agreed Junie reassuringly, "but babies are a great photo op. We could plan it for the Saturday of Easter weekend, when you'll be at the White House anyway for the Easter egg hunt."

"No stupid baby shower games?" I asked.

"Not one," she reassured me. "Have Ruby call me tomorrow to set up the details."

Officially, I hosted Sadie's baby shower in the White House living room, but it was Ruby Bennett, my social secretary, and Junie who planned the event. Sadie, her mother, and her mother-in-law attended in their Easter best, even though it was a Saturday. Sadie's friends were shy when they first arrived, but I asked Sadie to introduce me to them one by one, and we were soon able to find common ground for conversation.

As I write this, Sadie has eyes on occupying the White House herself as Commander-in-Chief, and I dare say that would not be a bad thing, despite the fact that she's a Democrat.

I wish I could tell you that the partisan posturing in Washington permanently eased through these methods, but that would be a lie. The truce was short-lived. Politicians continue even now to bluster on with their sky-is-falling rhetoric.

In private, however, the officeholders soon realized the only way to get seated next to the power in Washington (me) was to play nice. Childish behavior, in Congress or out, meant no invitation to Sunrise Thursday, and no invitation to the White House or state dinners. Congress as a whole became a more closely knit community, and if there is one legacy I leave, I hope that is it.

As soon as it became clear that the Republican party would not willingly give me the nomination for president in 2024, however, all civility ceased. There was blood in the water, and the sharks wasted no time in circling.

Chapter Twenty-Seven

Harry Truman once said, "I remember when I first came to Washington. For the first six months you wonder how the hell you ever got here. For the next six months you wonder how the hell the rest of them ever got here."

That pretty much sums up how I felt at my first Cabinet meeting. The Cabinet was created by George Washington to assist him in running the country. Washington's Cabinet consisted of only four men: Secretary of State Thomas Jefferson, Secretary of the Treasury Bricker Hamilton, Secretary of War Henry Knox, and Attorney General Edmund Randolph.

Today the Cabinet is made up of fourteen secretaries who head the federal executive agencies plus the Vice President (Jackson), as well as the Ambassador to the United Nations (Alim), the White House Chief of Staff (Sam), the Administrator of the Environmental Protection Agency, the Director of the Office of Management and Budget, the U.S. Trade Representative, the Chairman of the Council of Economic Advisors, and the Administrator of the Small Business Administration.

All of those people come with their own aides and agendas, making Cabinet meetings crowded and often antagonistic. The secretaries are chosen by the president and confirmed by the Senate, the way Jackson and I were chosen and confirmed for vice president. The U.N. ambassador and Chief of Staff are chosen by the president, and do not require confirmation. All, though, serve at the pleasure of the president and may be fired or reappointed at will.

That day, it was my will as to whether they continued in their posts, and the Cabinet room was ripe with uncertainty. My heart was pounding as I entered the room. This was my first Cabinet meeting as president, and as nervous as the Cabinet members were as to what was going to take place, I think I was even more nervous about being in charge of people with a lot more knowledge and political savvy than I possessed. By the time I made the short walk from my office to the Cabinet room, I could feel the sweat soaking through my silk blouse. I could only hope I wouldn't sweat right through the blazer too.

"Relax, everyone, you are still employed," I said when we were all seated. Minute puffs of breath escaped the lips of the secretaries. They did not know what to expect from me, but at least they were still employed in the West Wing. That counts for much in this world, regardless of who is in charge.

My chair was in the center of the group to the right of the table, with Secretary of Defense Brent Mendelson on my left and Secretary of State Vivian Braunstein on my right. Jackson was seated across from me, between the Attorney General and the Secretary of the Treasury. Alim was seated at the end of the table to my left. The other secretaries filled in the remaining chairs. Grace and Aaron had closed the law firm in Minneapolis and come to Washington to serve as my policy advisors, along with Henry and Gordon.

There was some jostling as the cameras maneuvered to set up to capture everyone. I kept my hands under the table so people wouldn't see them shaking. Alim gave me a reassuring smile.

"Let us begin," I said.

Vivian cleared her throat. "Madam President, Cabinet meetings do not officially begin until the cameras are removed."

"Today the cameras stay."

A murmur made its way around the table.

Brent spoke up. "President Jafari, sensitive topics are

discussed at these meetings. Topics that are not appropriate for the public at large."

"We will not be discussing security issues at this meeting, Brent," I said. "As for the other topics, it is time we removed the veil of secrecy on our government and let the people see how decisions are made."

Ripples of panic moved through the Cabinet members. This was not how government worked. In their minds, they were smarter and better qualified than ninety-nine percent of the population, which gave them the right to make decisions for the masses, regardless of whether the masses liked those decisions.

In all fairness, they *were* smarter and better qualified than ninety-nine percent of the population. This move was purely political in nature. The only way I was going to earn the public's trust was to show them there were no tricks, no hidden agendas, in my presidency. If I failed at that, then I would be a lame duck president for sure.

I continued. "This is a difficult time for all of us. President Wilkins was much admired, and while he and I share the same number-one priority—the well-being of our country—our approaches vary quite vastly. It is time to embrace innovation in our education, our healthcare, and our trade to relieve the burden on the taxpayer. There are no longer any sacred cows in Washington. Everything, and everyone, is fair game."

I looked at Vivian. "President Wilkins was in the process of appointing a new national security advisor to the National Security Agency when he became ill. You will be taking over that role, along with being secretary of state. That will save the taxpayers nearly $200,000 a year."

The move was not unprecedented. Other presidents had recognized that the duties overlapped and combined the duties under one role.

"With all due respect President Jafari," interrupted Vivian, "that is merely a drop in the bucket when it comes to the federal budget."

"Drops make oceans, Vivian," I replied.

I turned to the Secretary of the Treasury, Reuben Garcia.

"Mr. Secretary, you will be heading a new White House economic team to oversee the financial progress of our country. You will be working with the House and the Senate to come up with a ten-year prosperity plan."

Reuben's jaw dropped. This news was a shock to him, which was quite unfair of me. I had just handed him an onerous task. If he performed this task well, I would get the credit. If he did not, he knew full well that it was he who would wear the blame. The Cabinet members were scrambling to take notes now, except for Jackson, Sam, and Alim. They had created this opening salvo with me. I went on.

"Our goal is to reduce the deficit by a quarter within a year. In the meantime, I expect every department to identify cost-saving measures while maintaining the current level of service. Every agency is required to reduce their operational expenses by a minimum of ten percent. I am also instituting a federal government hiring freeze, effective immediately. We will add no further burden to already overburdened taxpayers. Please have your austerity proposals on my desk in three days."

Reuben spoke up. "Madam President, these measures will need to be approved by Congress."

"Congress has eight weeks to either approve our plan, or to create and agree on a plan of their own. If they refuse to do their job, then they will suffer the same fate as any employee who fails to perform his or her job. I will order the Office of Budget and Management to withhold their paychecks until they bring their performance up to par."

Dead silence.

"I'm not sure you have the constitutional authority to do that," sputtered Reuben.

"The Compensation Amendment prevents Congress from voting itself a pay raise. It does not prevent me from issuing executive orders to the Budget Office," I explained. "The rest of America is required to work for a living, it seems only fair that Congress plays by the same rules."

With that, I rose and, without giving the shell-shocked

secretaries any opportunity for discussion, left the room, my knees shaking.

I doubted that withholding Congress' paychecks would withstand a legal challenge, but it didn't have to. It was the public's imagination I needed to engage. On the other hand, I know my constitutional law. There was a chance that I could carry out my threat and have it upheld.

In 1789, twelve Constitutional amendments were submitted to the state legislatures for ratification. Ten of these amendments were ratified immediately and became the Bill of Rights in 1791. Two amendments were not ratified. The first regarded how members of the House of Representatives would be apportioned to the states. The second, the Compensation Amendment, stated that any pay raise for Congress would only take effect after the next election.

In theory, it prevented Congress from voting itself a pay raise. In reality, many of those in Congress were reelected, so they benefited from a pay raise anyway. Plus, the amendment did not preclude cost-of-living adjustments. Congressional pay was not in danger.

At that early stage in the country's history, ten states needed to ratify the compensation proposal in order to make it a Constitutional amendment. Only six did so, and the proposal was forgotten until 1982, when a student at the University of Texas at Austin came across the amendment while doing research for a paper and realized that it included no time limit for ratification. The Compensation Amendment, it turned out, was still in play.

The student received only a mediocre grade on his paper, but his interest in ratification of the proposal was infectious, and within a decade the compensation proposal received the required number of state ratifications, then thirty-eight, to become the 27th Amendment to the United States Constitution, more than two hundred years after its original proposal.

A group of congressmen launched a legal challenge against the amendment, claiming that its ratification was illegal and no such limits could be placed on congressional pay. After my announcement, another group of congressmen, including some of the same men who originally insisted the Compensation Amendment was illegal, would claim that it prevented me from stopping their paychecks. Unfortunately, it did not come to a face-off in court. I'm still curious how that would have turned out.

The calls for impeachment were immediate and came from my own party. Under Article One of the Constitution, the House of Representatives must first pass articles of impeachment by a majority of votes. These articles must allege some type of crime. Whether a crime constitutes an impeachable offense is defined by the House of Representatives, which seems to me like the fox guarding the chicken house.

The new House Minority Leader, Kevin Gilbert, took the lectern in outrage, accusing me of overstepping my authority.

"She's not supposed to actually make decisions!" he bellowed to the House.

If Gilbert had simply kept quiet no one would have paid much attention. The hits on the Cabinet meeting video were barely into the four digits. Outside of Washington, few people tuned in, and most of those viewers were leaders of other countries. Gilbert's insults, though, caught the attention of every women's group and political pundit in the nation, and they met his outrage with their own.

Gilbert's statements were carried on every newscast that very night, and the video of the Cabinet meeting, available on the White House website, received a million hits over the next twelve hours.

Both sides of the Echo Chamber lit up:

"What did he expect her to do? Sit in the White House and knit?"

"Clearly he is disappointed that she's not willing to be the Republican puppet."

"Gilbert is right. We don't want or need a foreigner making decisions for us."

His hubris cost him more than he could have imagined. Gilbert had planned to launch his candidacy for president that fall, following his presumed reelection to his House seat. Instead, he found himself fighting to just get back to the House. He barely managed to fight off a primary challenge by a Democrat, Miggie Jensen, who painted him as a dinosaur. She ran what is undoubtedly my favorite campaign slogan of all time: *Gilbert. Out of touch with voters and reality.*

Gilbert spent precious campaign time and money defeating Jensen for the seat. In the end, Gilbert managed to win by a narrow margin. Battle weary and broke, he returned to his seat in the House with empty campaign coffers. At the time, I doubted there would be a national campaign for Gilbert that year, or any year after. He was too tainted to raise the funds necessary. That was a lesson I learned too late: never, ever underestimate an opponent.

Chapter Twenty-Eight

The economy was improving slowly, but not quickly enough to satisfy me or the voters.

"If you want to keep your job in 2024, you need to be able to point to a lower deficit," Jackson warned me in our daily briefing. He, Sam, and I always met privately in the Oval Office for thirty minutes each morning. Neither GeriAnne nor any aides were allowed in that meeting. Washington D.C. is terrible at keeping secrets, and we were not about to let the world know about our plans for reelection before we were ready.

Dad taught me the basics of economics at a young age: spend less than you make. Otherwise, there is no way to balance the budget. The problem with the federal deficit, however, is that it was greater than five trillion dollars. There was no way to cut enough from the government's budget or to bring in enough taxes to meet our obligations and pay down the debt.

"It is not enough to make the payments, we need to show a substantial reduction," said Jackson.

"How much?" I asked.

"One-tenth would be good."

I nearly spit out my tea. "You want me to find a way to cut five hundred billion dollars from the deficit in two years?"

Sam jumped in. "One year. We need it done before the election. The sooner the better."

"Oh sure, I'll press my magic button and start deleting zeros," I said sarcastically.

"Try to do it under the radar," Sam said. "The less notice our political opponents have, the better."

There were few groups making significant amounts of money in those years, and the group making the most money was the group that profited from the wars in Afghanistan and Iraq, the war industrialists. It is a common misperception that wars are fought to defend freedom and fight injustice.

That was true for World War II and, arguably, Afghanistan, but most wars are fought to protect American business interests overseas. In 1900, American troops were sent to China to put down the rebellion of local Chinese against the American, Russian, Japanese, and German corporations that were drilling for oil off China's north shore and exporting the oil to their countries.

In 1903, the American navy arrived in South America to protect the interests of American companies that imported bananas, tobacco, and sugar cane. In 1915, American troops were sent to Haiti and the Dominican Republic, ostensibly to restore order after rebels overthrew the governments. In reality, the wealthy American owners of sugar plantations asked for military help in putting down a revolt by their slave workers. American troops spent nearly two decades in the Caribbean, protecting the island governments installed by the U.S.

A hundred years later, American men and women were still being sent to foreign lands to protect American interests, usually involving oil. The cost for this protection was staggering. Defense contractors made billions of dollars producing everything from guns to latrines to providing meals to the soldiers. Oil companies received billions of dollars' worth of armed security paid for by the American people. Worse, this protection filled veterans' hospitals with living corpses, men and women who suffered traumatic physical and emotional injuries that required decades of health care.

I bear no qualms about storming beaches to protect freedom. When it comes to private entities attaining great wealth at the expense of the common person, though, my stomach churns. If I could add one amendment to the U.S. Constitution, it would be that only those people willing to physically go fight a war would be eligible to declare war.

When Jackson, Sam, and I next met to discuss the deficit, I laid out my plan.

"I'm going to bill private corporations for the cost of providing military troops to protect their overseas interest," I informed them. "Anything we collect will be applied directly to the deficit."

Jackson turned pale. He'd made millions from such private corporations.

"Please tell me that you are joking," he choked out.

"Not a joke. I am going to give the taxpayers the same break that is being given to Wall Street and the industrialists. If American corporations want their interests protected by our military, then they have to pay for it."

It is a credit to Jackson that he did not spew platitudes about the good of the corporations being good for the average American. He knew as well as I did that war was largely a matter of lives being exchanged for money for the benefit of a few. The president of Allen Steel, of which Jackson held considerable shares, received a three million dollar bonus in 2014 alone, thanks to Allen Steel's profits that year of fifty billion dollars. War is big bucks for a few lucky ones, but not for the ones who fight it or the taxpayers who foot the bill.

Sam chimed in. "How do you plan to carry this out?"

"The Defense Department is going to prepare invoices for the corporations that benefitted from the American presence in the Middle East, including the defense contractors. Any corporation that chooses not to pay will be put on a debtors list on the White House website as having an outstanding balance."

Jackson groaned. "I thought you were going to do this under the radar."

"Would they pay if I did it quietly?"

"Of course not," said Jackson.

"Then why waste time? We are going to take the profit out of war. That way we'll reduce the deficit and save American lives at the same time. From now on, no American troops will be used for the gain of a private individual."

"This is a fool's errand. You won't see a dime from those companies," Jackson admonished.

"Oh, they'll pay. And they will do so openly and willingly. Otherwise, I am going to spend my next press conference calling on Congress to pass legislation stating that politicians and corporate executives get paid the same wages as the men and women in the trenches."

"That's minimum wage!" Jackson protested.

"Exactly," I replied. "American men and women are dying on foreign soil for less than they could make delivering pizzas, while energy companies are taking private airplanes to island resorts for board meetings. You wanted a solution to the deficit? There it is. Corporate responsibility."

"There goes the reelection," sighed Sam, looking defeated.

"The public will love it," I argued.

"The public doesn't buy elections. Corporations and wealthy donors buy elections," said Sam.

"Then we'll have to rely on democracy to win," I replied.

Jackson and Sam looked at each other, then at me. Jackson drained his teacup and, with shaking hands, set his cup and saucer on the tea tray.

"Oh, Suraiya, you do have a lot to learn," he said sadly.

Chapter Twenty-Nine

"You need to get a dog," Sam told me one day over tea.

I opened a desk drawer to put away the intelligence report on China that I had been reading and pulled out a stuffed Santa. Ever since the Christmas tree press conference, Grace, Aaron, and Greg had taken to hiding this twelve-inch doll around the White House, letting me find it at inopportune moments and creeping me out to no end. They thought it was funny.

"He knows when you're awake," Grace would taunt me, and I would fling the elf at her. It never occurred to me to hide the Santa from them so they could not annoy me with it. What fun would that be? I threw the Santa into the corner. GeriAnne would pick it up later and return it to Grace, who would then hide it somewhere else to await detection.

"I don't want a dog," I replied. Silly me, I thought that would end the conversation.

"You need to either get a dog or have a baby," he persisted.

Not the baby conversation again.

"I'm the president. I'm in charge of 300 million people, and those people own nearly eighty million dogs, so I'd say I have enough on my plate the way it is."

"You look too tough. Too masculine. You need to appear nurturing," insisted Sam.

After all the lectures about appearing too feminine, suddenly I was not feminine enough because I didn't have children. The bottom line was that I was working twelve to twenty hours a day. When would I take care of a dog?

"I think a dog is a great idea," Greg told me over dinner. "It will take some of the baby heat off of us."

"Actually, people will assume that we're breaking ourselves in for parenting," I told him.

Mother chimed in, as I knew she would.

"A dog is a nice compromise between a baby and no baby."

This surprised me. I assumed Mom was adamant about having grandchildren.

"Don't you want a baby to coddle and coo over?" I asked her.

"I do not want my grandchild to be a media event," she explained. "That baby would be the most scrutinized kid in the world, and that is a terrible thing to do to a child."

This was a new side to my mom, at least to me.

She went on. "In a year you won't be president anymore. Then you can have a baby. You'll need something to do."

"I'm running for reelection," I reminded her.

"Yes you are, dear," she said, cupping my chin in her hand as though I had just told her I was running for third-grade class president.

Greg rubbed his hands together. "It's settled. What kind of dog should we get?"

"It is not settled," I protested. "I don't want a dog."

Mother put her hand on my arm and whispered in my ear. "You're working all the time, dear. Men need companionship. Give in on the dog."

I rolled my eyes. Mother turned to Greg.

"Schnoodles are nice," she offered. "Mrs. Debevec down the street had one. It was very well-trained."

"Great! We'll get a well-trained schnoodle," Greg said.

"Do you even know what a schnoodle is?" I asked him.

"A cross between a noodle and a schnoz?" he offered.

"It's a cross between a schnauzer and a poodle," I told him.

Greg frowned.

"That doesn't seem like a very manly dog," he admitted.

"It's more like a stuffed animal that barks," I said.

"You don't want a manly dog," Mother chimed in. "You need a small fluffy dog that you can cuddle."

"A cuddly dog would look more nurturing on television," I told Greg.

"Sorry, Mrs. Jafari," Greg told Mom. "A schnoodle is not going to work out. How about a German Shepherd? That's a manly dog. And they're known for being intelligent and loyal."

Mother was pouting. My mother, who had never owned or cared for a dog in her life, was suddenly very attached to the idea of a schnoodle in the White House, and she was not going to go down without a fight.

"German Shepherds are herding dogs," she told Greg. "They need to run and work. It would be cruel to keep such a dog in the White House. It would be bored."

"Labrador Retriever?" Greg offered.

"Too big," sniffed Mom. "A Pomeranian would be better."

"Too yippy," said Greg. "Golden Retriever?"

"Too...golden," Mom ventured. Even she knew she was pushing her luck with that one.

"Let's get a rescue dog. A mutt," I suggested, but Greg and Mom ignored me. They were having too much fun torturing each other with the negotiations.

"A Siberian Husky," said Greg.

"A Husky would hate the humid summers in Washington," Mom told him.

"It's only for another year, remember?" He teased her, winking at me. "After that, we'll be living back in Minnesota. Huskies love that weather."

Mom considered this. "It's still a big dog. I would agree to a miniature husky."

"This isn't really your decision, Mom," I said.

"Let's get a miniature husky from a rescue group," said Greg.

"Do they have those?" I asked.

"Of course, they do," said Mother, as though she would know. "You just need to go on the Google and find it."

"You don't go 'on the Google,' Mom," I started, then dropped it. If we started down that path, we would be at the dinner table all night. I turned to Greg.

"I still haven't agreed to get a dog," I reminded him.

"Sure you did," he insisted. "You were the one who said you wanted a rescue dog, so that's what we'll do. And we'll give it a manly name, like Duke or King."

"What if it's a girl?" Mom asked.

"Then Coco. Or Cleopatra," Greg offered.

"I don't like those names," said Mom. "I like Princess for a girl."

"Princess is too hoity-toity. Suraiya's advisors would never go for it," Greg told her.

"How about Luna?" I offered.

"Shhh, Suraiya," Mom chastised me. "This doesn't concern you."

I sighed. I knew the conversation would be pretty much the same if we ever had children.

That weekend, we flew with Mom on Air Force One to Kansas City, Kansas. We had invited the senators and congressmen from Kansas to join us for the trip, a honor bestowed to members of Congress rarely, and with an intent for them to return the favor by siding with the Executive Branch on a vote in the future. The Kansas governor and local press were awaiting our arrival at the Kansas City airport.

An animal shelter in Springfield had a red and white miniature husky male awaiting adoption, and the foster family and shelter owners were going to bring him to the airport where we would all meet in an empty hangar.

Mom, Greg, and I were met by the Governor and the local press as we disembarked the plane. We shook hands for the photographers, then piled into The Beast, flown in earlier by the Secret Service on a C-131, for the ride across the tarmac to the hangar where our furry baby awaited.

"I'm more nervous now than on our wedding day," I said to Greg.

"That's because you knew on our wedding day that I already

liked you," he said, squeezing my hand. "Plus, you didn't have to worry about me peeing on the rug."

I laughed so hard I snorted, earning a disproving look from my mother, and a snicker from the governor's wife.

"My rugs should be so lucky," she deadpanned, which sent Greg and me into a fit of nervous giggles, further aggravating Mom.

He was the reddish gold of a fox, with bright blue eyes and pointy black nose, tugging at his green nylon leash. He seemed to think he was the star of the event, and, as much as it chagrins me to say this, he was right. Every news outlet in the country ran the headline "President and First Husband Adopt!" before we had even taken hold of his leash.

Greg and I walked into the hangar, hand in hand, to meet our new baby.

"We don't want to frighten King, so approach slowly," Greg had advised me earlier. He should have spent more time advising Mother.

She pushed past us and marched right up to the dog, crouching down on her haunches so they were eye to eye. She held out her hand to him, palm down, and he sniffed it, his tail wagging furiously. The foster father loosened the leash, and the little dog climbed into my mother's arms. She turned toward the photographers, who were going nuts snapping photos, and said in her most cooing voice, "Cuddle with me, my little noodle. You are just the sweetest canoodler ever. I'm going to call you...Schnoodle."

With that, she stepped forward and looked Greg straight in the eye.

"Meet Schnoodle."

Greg's clasp became so tight I thought my fingers would break. Cala Jafari had won again.

Democrats took to Echo Chamber Blue to rail against the cost of flying Air Force One to Kansas to pick up a dog.

"Children are going hungry, and she's wasting tax dollars on an animal!" they wailed.

"There are so many dogs in shelters in Washington. Why did she have to fly all the way to Kansas?" they complained. That's easy. If Schnoodle had been in Virginia, we would have driven across the

Potomac and picked him up. But he wasn't in Virginia. We went to Kansas because Schnoodle was in Kansas.

Republicans who were eyeing their own run for the presidential nomination took to Echo Chamber Red to bemoan the uptick in the rush to adopt miniature huskies.

"She should have known she would start a fad. What will become of these poor puppies once the trend subsides!" they complained, as though it was my fault that people adopted animals.

Both sides hated the name. *Schnoodle?* they cried. *Schnoodle is not regal enough for the White House dog.* Of course, if we had named him King like Greg wanted, they would have accused me of considering myself above the average citizen.

Greg took the opportunity to try to reclaim some of his control.

"If people really hate the name Schnoodle, can't you issue an executive order changing it?"

"Sure," I said. "As long as you agree to be the one to tell my mother."

"Schnoodle" the dog remained.

The controversy around Schnoodle and how he came to be in our family became so distracting on the Hill that even the White House press corps got involved. At a press conference to explain our proposed changes in the education system, the first question was about Schnoodle.

"Will Schnoodle remain at the White House, or will he be exchanged for a pet that is more presidential?" asked the reporter from the Times. I took a deep breath. This was getting too stupid.

"I understand that our lives are open to constant scrutiny," I began. "My opponents make attacks on me, on my husband, on my mother, and now on my little dog, Schnoodle."

The reporters chortled quietly. I went on.

"Now, I don't mind the attacks on me, and my husband and my mother are strong enough to withstand the attacks on them, but Schnoodle is a sweet, good-natured dog, and he's starting to take these attacks personally."

The reporters were snickering more loudly now. Even they were beginning to realize how silly the controversy was, and they made a living by creating contention where none existed.

"If you would like to discuss education or transportation or immigration or tax policy, then I am willing to listen and respond. If you want to continue picking on Schnoodle, then I am not willing to grant you the time or energy it would take even to ignore you. I am a busy person. If you have nothing better to do, then I suggest you find some purpose for your life."

It was the only time in my presidency that the Echo Chamber fell silent. The silence lasted only twenty seconds, but in internet time, that's the equivalent of years. Schnoodle was finally free to claim his title as White House dog.

Schnoodle got better press than I did. A poll by the American Institute of Public Opinion asked people to name the three most trustworthy people in the United States. Schnoodle was ranked first. The fact that he was not human did not seem to matter at all. Mother was second, and Jackson was third.

"Outclassed by a dog," muttered Jackson when he heard.

"At least you made the top three," I reminded him. "I was ranked fourth."

"How close do you think the rankings were?" Jackson asked.

"I'm guessing you and I were pretty close for third. But there was probably a pretty big gap between us and them," I said, not even attempting to sugarcoat it.

"Maybe I should walk Schnoodle a few times to improve my image," he suggested. He brought that up a few times, but he never could bring himself to appear holding Schnoodle's leash.

Schnoodle's every move was captured by cameras. One enterprising photographer put together a calendar with photos of Schnoodle on every month and sold it through his studio website. Fifty thousand copies sold out in hours. Schnoodle appeared on the cover of tabloid magazines, under headlines reading, *Schnoodle Gets Private Tour of Area 51*, and, *First Dog Sleeps in Second-rate Doghouse.*

For the record, Schnoodle never made the trip to Area 51, and while I doubt he ever saw any aliens, I do not know that for sure. He never said. As for his sleeping accommodations, Mother insisted on having a replica made of her bed for Schnoodle. Every night she would send him to his mini-bed, and every morning when she awoke he was snuggled up next to her.

Mom would take him for walks through the public areas of

the White House when school groups were visiting so the children could see Schnoodle in person, until the tour guides complained that Schnoodle's presence was too disrupting. What child wants to listen to the history of the presidential seal when there is a friendly pup nearby waiting to be adored?

Sam, of course, saw Schnoodle as a gold mine of money and publicity. It was his idea to commission a series of children's books about Schnoodle's adventures in the White House. Never mind that Schnoodle rarely had an adventure bigger than forgetting that the tail he was chasing was attached to his own body.

Schnoodle and the Easter Bunny, a mystery in which Schnoodle must help the Easter Bunny find missing Easter eggs, was released first. This was followed closely by *Schnoodle and the White House Squirrels*, in which Schnoodle stopped chasing the dozens of squirrels that lived around the White House long enough to help them find their missing acorns. (Spoiler Alert: A mean squirrel was stealing them and hoarding them in a sculpture on the South Lawn.)

Millions of books were sold.

"We can't keep that money," I told Sam.

"This could finance half of your campaign costs," he objected.

"We're not the kind of people who use a dog for personal gain," I said.

He persisted, but I held steadfast. All of the profit from the Schnoodle books, and it was several million dollars, was dispersed to charitable organizations that helped animals, either rescue organizations or veterinary care for the pets of the poor.

"At least let me arrange photo ops for the donations," Sam begged.

"Of course," I said.

I'm a smart woman. The free publicity—positive publicity—from those donations was priceless, and I have no doubt that it is one of the reasons I was reelected.

Chapter Thirty

There is one person in the White House who yields more power than any other, and it is not the president. Every president answers to a higher power, and it is not God. Throughout American history, one rule has stood clear: antagonize the First Lady and you are out. Doesn't matter how much the president likes you, or how many people owe you political favors, or how well you do your job. If the First Lady isn't happy, nobody is happy.

My administration did not have an official First Lady. I had a First Husband, who was willing to put up with a lot, and a Cala Jafari, who was not. Mother filled the First Lady role while I was president, and if Cala Jafari was not happy, nobody was happy.

I had my hands full with running the country, and Greg, who had taken a leave of absence from the Pentagon to make public appearances on behalf of the Republican party, had no interest in dealing with interior decorators, so Mom took on the task of redecorating the White House after the Wilkins's belongings were removed. The White House is accredited as a historic museum, and First Families have the option of bringing their own furnishings to the public and private spaces, or choosing furnishings from the

White House collection, overseen by the White House Office of the Curator.

Greg and I had no furniture suitable for the White House, so Mother met with the curator at the time, a fussy gentleman by the name of Bertram Lottleby, to choose items from the White House collection. The meeting did not go well. Lottleby refused to bring Mother to the temperature-controlled warehouse where the art collection and furniture were kept, insisting instead that she choose items from photographs he had assembled of what he considered appropriate pieces "for your situation."

"What situation would that be?" Mother asked.

"Temporary," said Lottleby.

Lottleby further insulted Mother by suggesting that Junie would be better equipped to choose pieces of historical significance for the public rooms.

"I have a degree in history. I'm perfectly capable of making those decisions," Mother told him.

Lottleby gave her a skeptical look.

"This is *American* history, Mrs. Jafari," he told her.

Mother stormed into the Oval Office to tell me about the exchange with "that pile of mint chocolate chip." Not even GeriAnne was brave enough to try to stop her. Lottleby, for his part, complained to the White House Chief Usher that Mother was being difficult. I buzzed GeriAnne and Lottleby was fired from his position within the hour and replaced with his assistant, who was only too willing to work with Mother, lest she be relieved of her duties as well.

Mother could certainly be difficult, but she was also fair. She was willing to give White House staff the benefit of the doubt when it came to their uncertainties in working with an Indian-American family for the first time, a fact discovered by the White House chef, Jason Kenner.

The White House Executive Chef is, technically, appointed by the president, but usually the incoming president just reappoints the chef currently in residence, as long as that chef is able to get along with the First Lady.

The WHEC is more than a chef. The chef plans, manages, and prepares all meals for the First Family on a daily basis, any private entertaining the First Family does, and any official state functions at the White House. The chef manages a staff of four sous-chefs, who assist with the actual food preparation.

Desserts and pastries are the responsibility of the White House Executive Pastry Chef. One of my favorite parts about being the president? My own pastry chef. If more women knew, as president, they could order chocolate mousse every day, politics would be overrun with estrogen.

When I was vice president, I had very little interaction with Jason. Jason interacted almost exclusively with the First Lady, Margaret Wilkins. When I took office, Jason was flummoxed. I am a vegetarian, but Greg and Mother were not, and every night we sat down to dinner to Jason's idea of Indian cooking until Greg couldn't take it anymore.

"Doesn't he know how to cook anything besides curry?" Greg demanded, pushing away his plate.

"I think he's trying to be accommodating to our culture," I soothed.

"We're Minnesotans. Our culture is tator tot hotdish," said Greg stubbornly.

"I'll have a talk with him tomorrow," I promised.

"You know nothing," interrupted Mother. "I will take care of this chef business."

"I'm not trained in Indian cuisine," Jason said sheepishly to Mom the next day when she stormed his kitchen. "The night President Wilkins passed away, I stayed up researching Indian cooking on the Internet."

He was also flummoxed by the fact that no First Lady existed. Jason was used to collaborating with women. Now there was a First Husband.

"I had visions of serving buffalo wings and pork rinds alongside tandoori chicken and naan," he told her.

Greg and I were not exactly foodies. We were used to grabbing takeout on the way home from work. When we were too tired to do even that, we were perfectly content to settle for bowls of cold cereal. Suddenly, Greg and I were sitting across from Jason, answering his questions about our food philosophy. Food philosophy?

"I like avocado ice cream," I said.

Greg nodded. "And apple pie. Can we have apple pie?"

Jason looked at us as though we were insane. Mom shook her head in embarrassment beside me.

"I told you they're hopeless," she told Jason. She turned to us. "You children run along. I'll take care of this."

We were so happy to get out of there, we didn't stop to think about how it looked to the White House staff that we were so easily dismissed by my mother. Although initially wary of what it would mean to have an Indian in the White House, Jason relaxed when Mom put him at ease.

"There's more to Indians than curry. Let whatever is in season in the White House garden guide your menu," she told the chef.

"Will that be okay with the President and the First Husband?"

"They will eat what you put in front of them," she told Jason.

Jason, of course, went on to write that book about his time with Mom, *More Than Curry, Cooking with Mother Jafari*. I didn't realize how much time they had spent together in the kitchen until I read it. Just another indication that I did not give her the credit she deserved for smoothing the road for me.

She would meet with Jason every morning to review the plans and menus for the day, and every Monday mid-morning, typically a slower time in the White House, Mom would join Jason in the kitchen and teach him how to make an Indian dish, including our daily masala chai.

While they cooked they talked, with Jason telling Mom about his life as the only openly gay teenager in his conservative Montana town, and Mom telling Jason about her grandparents' early life in Africa, and their culture shock of moving to Minnesota.

Jason kept several journals of these cooking tutorials and the recipes, later publishing them in honor of Mom. I weep when I flip through the pages of his book. All those photos of him and Mom in the kitchen, the two of them laughing as they share their lives. How did I not know this about my own mother?

Chapter Thirty-One

Mother was bored. She wanted to be supportive of my career, but she soon learned that she could not win. If she left the White House, the critics claimed she was carousing. If she visited me in the Oval Office, there was speculation that she was trying to influence me in political matters. If she stayed in her quarters, the tabloids described her as aloof.

"What am I to do?" she asked while Skyping her friends in Minnesota.

"You need a purpose," they told her.

"I need a job," she announced to Greg and me at dinner.

"What kind of job?" I asked warily.

"I don't know," she replied. "I only know that if I don't find something worthwhile to do, I am going to go crazy, and a crazy mother isn't going to do you much good in the next election."

"She has a point," agreed Greg.

"Mom, I can't give you a government job."

"I didn't say I want you to give me a job. I said that I need a job. I can find one on my own."

"Mom, you can't get a job."

"Why not?"

"Because you would need a security detail. Besides, you're not trained for anything. The only thing you've ever done is be a wife and mother."

Mother slammed her fork onto her plate.

"Oh, is that all?"

"Mom, I didn't mean it like that."

"I raised a president, didn't I? Doesn't that count for something?"

"Of course it does, Mom. What I mean is that you don't have any skills."

My husband groaned.

"You might want to stop talking, Suraiya," nudged Greg.

"No skills!" exclaimed Mother. "I have a history degree."

"There's not much you can do with that, Mom."

"Suraiya!" said Greg, sharply.

"What?"

"You're insulting your mother."

"I am not! I'm trying to give her a reality check."

"You think you know everything, Miss President," yelled Mom. "You watch. I can take care of myself."

Mother threw down her napkin, pushed her chair back from the table, and marched out of the room. As she passed the butler, she whispered, "Tell Jason the potatoes were excellent. The roast beef, though, was a little dry."

Greg gave me an exasperated look.

"What?"

"You could have been a bit more supportive."

I threw up my hands.

"She lives in the White House! She has a maid, a butler, a chef, a driver. How could I be more supportive?"

"Your mother left everything she knows to be here with you. The house she lived in for thirty years, the friends she hung out with her entire life, are now fifteen hundred miles away."

"She has Skype."

"She's lonely. And bored. She needs a reason to get out of bed in the morning."

I sighed. “Fine. What should I have her do?”

Greg got up and kissed the top of my head. “It’s not up to you. You need to ask her what she wants.”

I trudged up the stairs to the third floor, where I found Mother standing at the solarium’s windows, staring out at the National Mall like a bird trapped in a gilded cage. Staring out of a window is a sure sign of a person’s despondence, and it is a fool who ignores this sign in those around her. When she became aware of my presence, Mother moved slowly to one of the yellow chintz sofas. I sat beside her, taking her hand.

“Let’s pretend that I am not the president, and this morning you won the lottery.”

“How much?”

“A million dollars.”

“A million dollars doesn’t go as far as it used to.”

My jaw clenched involuntarily and I made an effort to relax.

“Fine. A hundred million dollars, Mom. That’s how much you won. What would you do?”

“How much would I have to pay in taxes?”

“Forget the taxes, Mom.”

“Forgetting to pay taxes is how you became the president, young lady.”

I closed my eyes and took deep, calming breaths.

“The hundred million dollars is after taxes, okay? You’re rich. Filthy, stinking rich.”

“Please tell me you didn’t forget to pay your taxes, Suraiya.”

“Mom. Focus.”

“Taxes pay for the roads, Suraiya. And schools. What if everyone decided they didn’t need to pay taxes? Where would we be then?”

“Mom, I know where the tax money goes, believe me.”

“So why didn’t you pay your share?”

I dropped her hand and jumped off the sofa.

“Mom! I paid my taxes!”

“No need to yell, Suraiya. I only asked you a simple question.”

I counted to five and tried again.

"I came up here to ask you what you would like to do. What is it that would make you happy?"

Mom stood and went back to the solarium's windows, her face aglow from the setting sun.

"I would like to travel. I want to visit my great-grandparents' graves in Africa. And I want to see penguins. And pet a tiger. And visit the great museums of Italy."

I rose and wrapped my arms around her, resting my head against her shoulder. We had never stood like this before, and it felt strange. It was Mother who had always comforted me. Our roles were shifting.

"Then travel is what you shall do," I promised her.

"Where do penguins live?" I asked Jackson the next morning over tea.

"The zoo."

"I don't think the zoo is going to cut it."

"Is there a new penguin constituency? Because I don't believe penguins pay taxes, and if they don't pay taxes..."

I set my cup on its saucer too forcefully, the chai spilling over the cup.

"I don't want to talk about taxes!"

The vice president held up his hands in surrender.

"I'm sorry. My mom needs something to do. She's moping around the house all day and driving me crazy."

Jackson was confused.

"And you want to give her a penguin?"

"No, she wants to see penguins. Africa and penguins."

"There are penguins in Chile. We could send her down there. In fact, we could send her on a goodwill tour all over Latin America and Africa," Jackson suggested.

"We can't use government funds for that. The Democrats would have a field day, and I don't have the resources to privately fund a tour that big."

"I know people with those kinds of resources. Let me take care of it."

Three telephone calls. That's all it took for Jackson to line up private financing for Mother's goodwill tour. Three calls to old friends in private industry, with factories in Argentina and Colombia and Mexico, and the next thing Mother knew, she was on a private plane to Chile, accompanied by a hair and makeup artist, social secretary, clothing stylist, and security detail.

"First, the penguins," Mother insisted, when I told her of the tour.

"Yes, Mom, you will start with the penguins."

When the plane touched down in Chile, a band was waiting on the tarmac to greet her. The Chilean president and the U.S. ambassador to Chile waited for Mom with their families. The Chilean president's five-year-old granddaughter, a pretty dark-haired girl, bedecked in layers of bright pink chiffon, presented Mother with a small bouquet of orange marigolds. Mother leaned down for the little girl's soft-spoken greeting, "Welcome to Chile, Mother Jafari."

The girl was so sweet, and Mother's responding kiss to the girl's forehead so sincere, the press went wild. Photos of Mother with her lips pressed to the child's brow were splashed across every major newspaper in Latin America the following morn, with the headline "Mother Jafari Visits Chile." The moniker stuck, and within hours the U.S. State Department was deluged with requests from Spain to Brazil to China to South Africa for visits from "Mother Jafari." Cala Jafari, the woman who was treated as a second-class citizen in her homeland became, in an instant, the most recognized and adored woman in the world.

Mother saw her penguins. She started with the rockhopper penguins on Isla Pingüino, near Puerto Deseado. She visited the Magellanic penguins at Puerto Montt, and the Humboldt penguins along the Pacific Coast of Northern Chile, and everywhere she went, fawning crowds greeted her with chants of "Mother Jafari," and local dignitaries feted her with flowers and banquets.

My gracious Mother, initially surprised by the outpouring, soon warmed to her new role as mother figure to all, to her daughter's chagrin.

"I've created a monster," I said to Greg as we watched CNN coverage of mother's trip to Argentina.

"She's found herself," said Greg, as video of Mother Jafari, laughing and clapping along as a group of schoolchildren serenaded her in Buenos Aires splashed across the screen. "She may never come back."

Chapter Thirty-Two

In October of 2023, I was thirty-seven years old and had been president for barely four months. The Iowa primary was fifteen weeks away, on February 1 of 2024. No one other than my family, Jackson, and Sam knew of my intent to seek reelection. Both of them knew better than I did that surprise was our only chance to take Iowa, and Iowa was our only chance at the nomination.

"Politicians do not take Iowa seriously," Sam explained to me earlier in August as Jackson nodded in agreement. "But the press does, and if you can take the lead in Iowa, you will be splashed across every news outlet in the country, and that is how you become the front-runner for the nomination."

I was still unwilling to believe my own party would blatantly refuse to back me.

"Won't the party want to save face by clearing the way for me?" I asked.

Sam and Jackson both laughed.

"There is too much money and too much power involved," Jackson said. "We've got one shot at this, Suraiya. We simply have to take Iowa, and to do that, we need to be on the ground in Iowa as much as possible."

"Without tipping our hand about the reelection," admonished Sam.

So in the late summer and early fall of 2023, Jackson made six trips to Iowa, appearing at fundraisers for local politicos and county fairs and mustering volunteers to stump for the Republican party in the upcoming year, and by the middle of November we were ready to declare our intentions.

I called Frank Kirsch, my replacement as House Minority Leader, Kevin Gilbert, and my senior advisors Henry and Gordon into the Oval Office for a meeting with me, Jackson, and Sam. Jackson was seated to my right on the sofa. Sam stood behind my left shoulder.

GeriAnne brought in the tea tray, and I saw Frank smirk as Jackson poured a cup and passed it to me. GeriAnne served the others, then sat near my desk to take notes.

"Gentlemen, I've brought you here today to make an announcement," I began.

"Congratulations!" said Frank jovially.

"Excuse me?" I asked.

"You're going to tell us you're expecting," Frank replied.

"I'm not expecting," I informed him. This constant baby watch was getting on my nerves. Frank looked disappointed.

"There goes a photo op," he muttered.

I ignored him.

"I've decided to run for reelection," I announced.

Silence. Kevin looked at Frank. Frank blinked furiously. Frank turned to Jackson.

"She's kidding, right? Tell me she's kidding."

Jackson chuckled.

"She's serious, Frank."

"But you promised you wouldn't seek the nomination," Frank said.

"I made that promise when I was going to be vice president. I am the president now. By all rights, the Republican nomination should be mine."

Henry and Gordon, seated in the wing chairs between the sofas, watched our faces as Frank and I stared each other down.

They had expected to be out of jobs when my term was up. Now, suddenly, they realized they might get four more years in the West Wing. I noticed Henry's face turning blue.

"Breathe, Henry," I ordered. Henry did as he was told and took a deep breath. His color returned to normal. Gordon moved to the edge of his seat, silently watching to see how this meeting would play out.

"It isn't fair, Suraiya," complained Kevin. "I've been in Congress longer than you. You don't deserve that nomination."

"I deserve it because I am the president, my popularity rating is above fifty percent, and I am doing a good job."

Frank regained his composure.

"None of that matters," he protested. "The party has been making other plans."

Jackson stepped in.

"Frank, Suraiya is the president. The *Republican* president. Any plans to give the nomination to someone else should have been run by her first. Think of the good of the party."

"I am thinking of the party!" Frank snapped. "Giving you the nomination would be a waste of time. There's no way the American people are going to elect a Muslim to the White House. I'm sorry you made me say it out loud, Suraiya, but there it is."

Henry caught his breath again, and did not let it out. I glanced at him and mouthed, "breathe." He let out a gasp. Frank's outburst was not unexpected. I looked from Frank to Kevin.

"From now on you will address me as Madam President, even in private meetings," I told them. "Frank, I am running for reelection. If the party will not place me on the ballot as its nominee, then I will win the nomination at the convention by a majority of delegate votes. You and Kevin are excused."

Neither Frank nor Kevin moved. Jackson stood.

"You heard the President. Out."

Once Frank and Kevin had left the office, I turned to Henry and Gordon.

"You two will be leading the campaign in Iowa. Go home and pack your bags. You leave tonight."

Henry and Gordon deserve the credit for Iowa. They both

worked twenty hour days in the weeks leading to the primary. Some nights they did not sleep at all, such as when Calvin Estall, the annoying reporter that was embedded with my unit in Afghanistan, wrote a scathing article about my alleged assault on him when I was serving in the Marines. Estall accused me of disregarding the freedom of the press, and predicted an usurpation of the First Amendment if I was reelected. I'm not sure how I would accomplish that, what with every citizen armed with a phone and camera on their wrist, but Estall's charge made an interesting sound bite.

"Can we talk about Forsberg now?" asked Sam. He knew about the young man's death from the FBI profile done on me when I was being vetted for vice president, and I had forbidden him to discuss it. I refused to put Forsberg's family through more pain.

When my hands healed from recovering their son, I wrote to Forsberg's parents, Hedda and Albert, telling them that not only had their son died with honor, he had been buried with care by the Muslim villagers, and recovered with respect by his countrymen. I did not give them the details of the recovery. No parent should have to hear that.

His mother invited me to lunch at their home when I returned to the States, and every May after I returned from Afghanistan, I quietly visited Forsberg's grave with his parents in Cedar Rapids on Memorial Day until I became vice president. My appearance on Memorial Day as the vice president would have drawn a crowd, so I visited the weekend prior to the holiday, and Forsberg's mother and I sat on the couch in their small family room, and she showed me photo albums of her son.

"We will not talk about Forsberg, no matter what Estall does," I commanded, threatening Sam with the loss of his job if he went against my orders. Henry and Gordon were working nonstop, trying to do damage control.

The Forsbergs, however, refused to let Estall or anyone else disparage the name of the woman who had helped to bring their son back to them. Hedda and Albert called the *Des Moines Register* and told the city reporter about my visits to Iowa, and how I had been part of the mission to find their son. Their photo ran above the fold of the Sunday edition. Sam was over the moon.

Soon Bussman, Clark, and Hernandez joined the conversation, accusing Estall of trying to profit from the deaths of American soldiers.

"The President will always have our support," proclaimed Bussman to reporters outside the Jafari for President headquarters in Cedar Rapids.

"Have at it," I told Sam as we watched the press conference unfold.

Stories of my so-called heroism in the Middle East began appearing in the press, manufactured by Sam and placed there by Henry and Gordon. Those stories made me uncomfortable then, and still make me uncomfortable today. I was lucky. I came home. Eric Forsberg did not.

People love a good story of compassion, though, and when it came to me caring for one of their native sons, Iowans were impressed. I won the primary by an overwhelming margin. The press declared me the front-runner for the Republican nomination, and articles began appearing questioning why the party was not treating me as the presumed candidate for the party nomination.

Charges of racism and sexism soon followed. A few weeks after Iowa, Frank requested a private meeting with me and Sam. Jackson was not invited. I thought Frank would see my win in Iowa as a reason for concession. Instead, Frank saw Iowa as a reason to negotiate.

"He's going to throw me under the bus," said Jackson bitterly, after I told him of the secret meeting.

"I won't let that happen," I promised. Sam pulled me aside.

"Don't make promises you won't want to keep," he said.

"Why would I not keep that promise?"

"Let's hear what Frank has to say."

Frank, Sam, and I gathered in the Oval Office once more at the end of March 2024. I remained behind my desk, and Frank and Sam took the chairs facing me. GeriAnne brought in the tea tray and set it on the edge of my desk.

"Thank you, GeriAnne. You may go."

GeriAnne rolled her eyes at me and left. Frank glanced from

the tea set to me. Sam watched Frank. I studied Frank. Finally, Frank broke the silence.

"Is there coffee?"

"It is tea or nothing," I replied.

"You could order GeriAnne to find a coffee for me."

"What do you want, Frank?" I asked.

Frank gave me an ingratiating smile.

"Good news. I've talked to the Republican leadership, and we've decided to give you the nomination."

The tea tray sat between us, untouched.

Frank looked from me to Sam.

"That's good news for you, Sur—um, Madam President," said Frank.

I did not reply. Sam leaned toward the tea tray, pulling back his hand when I cleared my throat in warning.

"Why the change in heart, Frank?" asked Sam.

"We've decided to change with the times," said Frank, waving his arms expansively. "A new day and all that."

It was clear to me by that point that Frank did not understand how the Jafari game was played, and I was impatient for this meeting to end.

"Sam, please pour me some tea," I requested.

Sam did so. He did not offer a cup to Frank. I took a sip and set the cup and saucer on my desk.

"What is the cost of this new day?" I asked Frank.

Frank shifted in his chair, suddenly uncomfortable under my gaze.

"The party feels that this is a good opportunity to showcase other talent in the party. Younger talent. Talent that could run the White House in the future."

"Who might this new talent be?" I asked.

"Kevin Gilbert." There it was. Jackson had been right. Frank was offering me the nomination in exchange for putting Kevin on the ticket as the vice presidential candidate.

Sweat broke out on Frank's forehead. My hands clenched. Disloyalty makes me irritable.

"The ticket is full," I reminded him.

"Let's not be hasty, Madam President," interrupted Sam.

"Listen to your Chief of Staff," advised Frank.

I rose and walked around the desk, stopping by Frank's chair. I smiled at him.

"Thank you for the visit," I said, motioning for him to rise. "Sam will see you out."

Sam sighed.

"You should have poured the tea, Frank," he mumbled to himself.

Frank's face turned an ugly shade of violet.

"You're making a mistake," he growled as he stood. "A huge mistake. We will fight you every step until the convention."

I met his glare and calmly stepped closer until our noses practically touched.

"You don't scare me, Frank." I said. "Everything about me scares you. So bring on the fight. I guarantee you that I'll be the one standing when this is over."

Frank slid past me and left the office, slamming the door behind him.

"That man is going to rain down a storm of trouble on you," said Sam, coming to stand beside me.

"Then you better decide now whether you are in my camp or his. Because I will not tolerate you playing both sides of the fence."

Sam nodded. "I'll stand by you, Madam President."

Stand by me he did, although there is no doubt that he would have jumped the Jafari ship had it appeared by the end of summer that we were not going to have enough delegate votes to win. The next eight months were a blur of campaign appearances. The Frank Kirsch-Kevin Gilbert ticket did their best to oust me in the polls and primaries, but our lead after Iowa was too strong.

Hedda and Albert became media darlings, telling their story to anyone who would listen. Their earnest Midwestern plea for votes on my behalf, along with that of the guys from Afghanistan, did more to garner support than any advertising campaign cooked up by my campaign staffers.

Campaign buttons and bumper stickers reading "I'm voting

for Greg's wife" began appearing all over the country, which I found insulting.

"It's sexist," I complained to Sam.

"When Bill Clinton ran for president, there were buttons and bumpers stickers that read 'I'm voting for Hillary's husband,'" he reminded me.

"That's different," I protested.

Sam was amused. "How?"

"It just is."

Kirsch and I were in a dead heat going into the Republican National Convention in August. Oddsmakers in Las Vegas had Frank getting the presidential nomination by ten points. I often wonder how many people from my own staff were taking those odds.

When the vote came back, the nomination had my name on it by less than a hundred delegates. Jackson and I were waiting in a reception room at the arena when it was announced. Our families and staffers were in a nearby room with Sam. Normally we would all be together, but Jackson and I wanted to be alone when we received what we thought was going to be bad news. My stomach was churning, and sweat was running down my back, despite the coolness of the room.

"The fewer people with us, the less they can write in their memoirs about how we took the news," Jackson advised me, and I agreed. So when we heard the distant cheering coming from Greg and Junie and Mother and Alim, we looked at each other in disbelief. Was it possible?

Fifteen minutes later, I officially accepted the Republican nomination for United States President. Twelve weeks later, on November 3, 2024, the American people elected me president by a narrow margin. I was no longer the accidental president.

Now I had a new problem. I did not know how to dance.

Chapter Thirty-Three

Most of the Jafari for President contingent, including Henry, Grace, and Aaron, watched the election returns on huge screens in the ballroom of the Graves Hotel in downtown Minneapolis. I was too nervous to do that, so Greg and I and our immediate families all gathered in a suite upstairs.

We were crowded onto the king-size bed in front of the television, with Greg on the right, me next to him, Mother in the middle, and Daris and Neeta next to her. Greg's nieces and nephews took turns piling on top of us, telling us knock-knock jokes and spilling juice on our blue jeans. By that time I had learned to keep my dress clothes out of reach until the children were ushered out of the area. Alim sat in a chair nearer the television, while Greg's sisters and parents took turns chasing after the children.

I was so nervous. I wanted to believe that the country believed in me, but I wasn't sure if my work had been enough to make people look past my race and religion. By nine o'clock that night, the numbers were too close to call, with seventy-three electoral votes for me and ninety electoral votes for the Democratic challenger, Bill Lochner, former Governor of Oregon. My skin alternated between clammy and itchy.

"Take deep breaths," Greg whispered to me at one point, and I reached for his hand, holding it close to my heart.

"Suraiya, stop that!" Mother ordered. "There are people around."

"For heaven's sake, Mother, we're just holding hands," I argued.

"Be a lady," she hissed.

"Yeah, Suraiya," Greg teased. "A nice girl doesn't taint her husband's virtue in public."

I rolled my eyes.

"You lost your virtue long before you met me," I reminded him.

"In that case, close your eyes Mother Jafari," said Greg, wrapping his arms around me and kissing me on the cheek. The pile of children on our laps squealed and scattered.

I slapped him away, embarrassed.

"Not in front of my mother!"

"Really, Suraiya, you must learn to accept affection from your husband," scolded Mother, turning to Daris. "And you should show your wife more affection."

Daris and I both gave Mother an exasperated glare.

"Shhh! The latest numbers are coming in," Alim chided us.

We all stared intently at the screen. One hundred fifteen electoral votes for Lochner, ninety-six for me.

"It's still early," said Greg.

"I need air," I told him, getting out of bed and weaving my way among the children to the balcony off the living room. The November night air felt sharp as I inhaled, and I regretted not grabbing a jacket on my way out.

I could hear people below making their way to the hotel ballroom, and see the lights at the nearby Target Field, the home of the Minnesota Twins baseball team, where thousands of people waited to hear either a concession or victory speech from me. The door to the balcony opened behind me, and Greg placed a blanket around my shoulders.

We stood like that, holding each other, enjoying a rare moment of peace.

"No matter what, we have each other," Greg murmured. "Even if you win."

I smiled into his shirt. He continued.

"We have our families who love us and drive us crazy, and our friends who keep us sane."

He lifted my chin and wiped away a tear he found on my cheek. I hadn't realized I was crying.

"Everything you've done has been enough to pave the way for the one that follows," he reassured me.

Was it? I wasn't sure. Would the next Indian or Muslim seeking office face a higher hurdle because of something I did? Or had I proven myself to a level that they would be judged the same as a white Christian counterpart?

The election was too close to call, and Jackson called at midnight from Texas where he was watching live coverage online.

"Get out there and say something," he advised.

So Greg and I led a parade of the Jafari for President campaign staff down Seventh Street to Target Field. News cameras surrounded us. After the first block, Henry reached forward and tapped me on the shoulder to tell me that the wireless ear bud I was wearing was not turned on, and that Jackson was trying to talk to me.

I pressed a button on my smartwatch and turned on the ear bud in time to hear Jackson screech, "Smile for heaven's sake! You look like you're all in a friggin' death march!"

Henry and Olivia took it upon themselves to lift the mood by leading the group in singing *This Land is Our Land*, taking us to the third verse as we entered the stadium and I took to the stage to thank the revelers for their support.

"The final results will not be in until morning at the earliest," I informed the crowd. "As much as I would like to hang out with you here all night, it is very cold and we all have to work tomorrow. Thank you for being here, and for supporting me and my family. Thank you for voting. Whatever happens tomorrow, I am humbled and honored to serve you."

The Lochner camp took this as a concession, and partied until dawn, certain the Democrats would be taking up residence in the West Wing. It was not until noon on Wednesday, November 4, 2024, that I was officially declared the president, with electoral college results of 297 votes for me, 240 votes for Lochner.

"This election gives you validation," Jackson told me later when we returned to D.C.

"That's a relief," I agreed.

"No, that's bad," Jackson said. "You're a bigger threat now than you were when you were here by accident, because now there are vested interests in seeing you succeed or fail."

"A threat to whom?"

"Everyone."

Junie sent me a text less than a minute after the election was declared in my favor. "Can you waltz?"

"No," I sent back.

"We have so much work to do!" she replied.

The 20th Amendment to the United States Constitution requires that a newly elected president be inaugurated on January 20 of the year following the election. Until the 20th Amendment was ratified in 1933, presidents were sworn in on March 4, leaving the country subject to four months of lame duck government. The 20th Amendment did not apply to my first round as president, because I took over from Dennis. This time, though, there would be a full inauguration with a parade and fancy dress balls.

I didn't care so much about my dancing ability—or lack thereof—until my detractors lit up the Echo Chamber with jokes about the inaugural balls featuring Bollywood-style dance numbers and wondering if I would be prancing around in a veil, barefoot. Suddenly, learning to waltz was a priority.

Before the election, my days began at 5:30 a.m. with a run, followed by reading a current-events recap sent by Henry or Gordon. That was followed by a shower and dressing in whatever Junie's stylist had prepared for me for that day, then breakfast with Greg and Mother. The rest of the day was filled with meetings and public appearances.

After the election, my days—and those of my staff—began at 5:30 with a dance lesson by Benji Patino, a friend of Junie's, whose job was to make us look light on our feet at the inaugural balls.

“You’re kidding, right?” Greg said when I told him about the dance lessons.

“Do you know how to waltz?” I asked.

“No.”

“Then I’m not kidding.”

Greg dug in his heels. “I’m not spending the next eight weeks learning to waltz.”

“Fine. You call your mother and explain to her why her son is going to look like an oaf on worldwide television.”

So there we were before dawn in the White House ballroom, when Junie arrived with Benji Patino in tow and a grumpy Jackson lagging behind.

“You could have lied and told her you already know how to dance,” Jackson grumbled to me.

“You know my policy about always telling the truth,” I reminded him. “Plus, she scares me a little.”

“Me too,” he admitted.

Day after day, Patino attempted in vain to teach us the basic waltz, clapping his hands furiously as he yelled.

“Weight on your right foot!” “Left box turn! I said LEFT!” “One-quarter turn! Not that way!”

We would stop and Benji would reposition us, and when I say “us,” I mean me.

“President Suraiya, you must let the man lead,” Benji would say in exasperation.

“Benji, that goes against every fiber of my being.”

“Don’t argue with the teacher!” Mother would yell from the sidelines.

“Suraiya, you need to be subservient,” Greg would murmur, snickering and making me giggle.

“Gregory! You must take this seriously!” Mother would yell.

“Sorry Mother Jafari.”

I was never so relieved as I was the day of the actual inauguration, knowing the torturous dance lessons would end.

“We should have appreciated those days more,” says Greg now. “We got to spend every morning together, holding each other.

As soon as the inauguration was over, you were back to work as usual."

Jackson and I were sworn in on the steps of the U.S. Capitol, then joined the Presidential Inauguration Parade, a procession of military regiments, marching bands and floats, as it wove its way along Pennsylvania Avenue toward the North Lawn of the White House.

Junie's stylist had chosen a peacock-blue silk dress for me, with matching three-inch heels.

"How long is the parade route," I asked Junie.

"One and a half miles."

I threw the shoes at the stylist.

"Try again."

We finally settled on a pair of navy pumps with one-inch heels. My feet were pictured on every worst-dressed list in every fashion magazine in the world after the parade, but I didn't care. My feet hurt bad enough even in those shoes. My combat boots were more comfortable. Mother liked the peacock-blue dress so much that she adopted the color as her own, wearing it on her public appearances abroad because she said it nicely offset the saffron-colored marigolds her thousands of fans brought to greet her.

Greg and I walked the entire inaugural parade route, with Jackson and Junie alternating between walking with us and warming up in The Beast as it drove slowly in front of us. Mother and Schnoodle walked a little ways with us, but the crowds became unruly in their quest to get to Schnoodle, so he and Mother rode most of the way in the car.

We waved to the crowds and greeted as many people as we could. We were the center of attention, but I knew the parade was not about us. It was a celebration of democracy, of being a free people. It was about the future we were creating for ourselves and those to come after us.

We reached the parade stand where the inaugural address was to take place. Greg and Junie went ahead into the shelter with Mother and Schnoodle to warm up. Jackson and I walked slowly to say hello to the spectators in the nearby stands. Those seats were reserved for major donors. We would need them again in four years.

After shaking what seemed like the thousandth hand, Jackson took my elbow and we approached the steps to the shelter. Jackson leaned over and spoke in my ear.

"Turn around. Take it all in. Few people get to stand where you stand today."

"We'll be back in four years."

"Nothing in life is guaranteed, Suraiya."

I did as he said, turning and looking—really looking—into the eyes of the people around me, and a chill crawled from my scalp to my neck and through my shoulders. Jackson had not told me to enjoy this moment because he did not think we would be reelected in 2028. Jackson had told me to enjoy this moment because he knew the odds of my being alive in four years were against me.

One out of every ten American presidents is assassinated while in office, despite the best efforts of the Secret Service agents in the Presidential Protection Detail (PPD), and those presidents were mostly white and Christian. Agents in the PPD are so close to the president that agents refer to the area around the president as the Kill Zone. The Kill Zone now referred to the space around me.

Soon after the inauguration, the formation of the American Liberty League was carried in all the major news outlets. The League announced that it was forming to "maintain the Constitution," but did not specify any particular threat to the country. It did not matter. I knew that the threat they feared was me. Everything Jackson had predicted was coming true. The roster of names involved in the League was impressive. These men were not to be trifled with, and if I had not taken Jackson's warning to heart before, I was taking it seriously now.

The League's National Executive Committee was headed by Grayson Murphy, head of a Manhattan brokerage firm. Murphy's net worth was somewhere north of a hundred million dollars, and he was notoriously hard-bitten in his business dealings.

The League had maneuvered its incorporation papers to hide the fact that it was financed by some of the wealthiest, most ruthless, men in the country. The formation of the League was hardly headline news, but nevertheless it was top news in every mainstream organization, a fact that indicated to me that publishing giants were backing the League as well.

Sure enough, four weeks after the League announced its formation, news articles criticizing me and my administration began appearing in newspapers, podcasts, newscasts, and online outlets. It did not matter if the news organization was conservative or liberal. Each one carried the same theme: My presidency was un-American.

The League called for a centrist government, but what the League called a "centrist government" was thinly disguised fascism of the kind invoked by Mussolini and Hitler. Later we would learn that the League's plan was to install a president, preferably Jackson or Frank Kirsch, to carry out the wishes of the wealthiest Americans. They couched their plan in patriotic terms, as in "we are saving the nation from socialism," but it was a dictatorship all the same, and the game, as always, was at the expense of the weak and gain of the rich.

Even a group of wealthy men need a ringleader, and the clandestine ringleader of the League was none other than Frank Kirsch. If only I had suspected Kirsch of treachery, we might have avoided the bloodshed that was to come.

Chapter Thirty-Four

When President Barack Obama was reelected in 2012, twelve states collected signatures on petitions stating that they wanted to secede from the United States. There is no legal method for secession, a fact the confederacy found out the hard way when they lost the civil war in 1865, but that did not deter the President's detractors, so I was not surprised when, upon my reelection, the talk of secession began, secession being the grown-up equivalent of "you won't let me have my way so I am taking my ball and bat and going home."

I am, of course, first and foremost Rabee Jafari's daughter, so when reporters asked me about the secession petitions circulating on the web, I replied simply, "Show me the economics. If they can support themselves as a separate country, we'll talk about a plan for them to go."

"Suraiya," asked Aaron the next morning, "did you tell the New Republic that they could secede?"

"Who is the New Republic?"

"The states that want to leave the union. That's what they're calling themselves. The newspapers are reporting that you said the

New Republic could go out on their own if they present you with a financial plan."

"I guess I did."

"Doesn't this make you a bit nervous?"

"Not a bit." Oh, how naive I was!

I was relying on the Pareto principle, named after an Italian economist, which states that eighty percent of the effects come from twenty percent of the causes. In other words, I expected that the New Republic, formed by Mississippi, Alabama, Arkansas, Louisiana, Georgia, and the Carolinas—would run the numbers and realize that they contributed only twenty percent of the country's tax dollars, while consuming eighty percent of the resources.

The New Republic ran the numbers alright, and they found exactly what I predicted. If they seceded from the union, the New Republic would be a third-world country. Their health care would disappear. Welfare and food stamps would be non-existent. State income taxes would rise to seventy-five percent.

The state governors of the New Republic were forced to appear before the press and sheepishly admit they could not exist on their own, and that all talk of secession would cease. Except it did not cease. The other states—the ones who contributed eighty percent of the taxes to support the states in the New Republic—decided this imbalance was unfair and unconstitutional, and decided the New Republic should secede as soon as possible.

Among all the talk of secession, the average voter became alarmed. People from the New Republic states became convinced they needed to get to the North as soon as possible in order to stay in the United States. Residents of Mississippi and Alabama swarmed across state borders, flooding their northern neighbors in Tennessee and Missouri.

Those states, ill-equipped to deal with the influx, sent state defense forces, also known as SDF, to stop any more people from crossing state lines. Fewer than half of the states in the union have SDF, and unfortunately the ones that did were located largely along the boundary lines of the New Republic.

Rich Southerners, frantic at the thought of losing their wealth to entitlement programs if the poor were not allowed to leave, pressured the New Republic governors to send their own SDF to prevent the transients from getting back.

Tent cities sprang up along state borders. Unable to move forward and forbidden at gunpoint to go back, American citizens became refugees in their own country. The SDF, made up of civilians who had no military training, were often disorganized and trigger happy. Fearing that the conflict would escalate, I signed an executive order that all SDF were to stand down, and ordered the National Guard units in the border states to set up patrols to keep the peace.

The SDF had no intention of following orders from me, and the newscasts were filled with homegrown soldiers vowing to fight to the death, although when asked what they were fighting for, the soldiers would stare blankly at the camera for a second, then raise their guns in the air and yell, "Freedom!"

"Great," said Sam. "They have no friggin' clue what's going on, they just want to play *Braveheart*."

I was concerned that the SDF would open fire on the National Guard when it arrived, but once the SDF got a good look at real soldiers, highly trained and heavily armed, they dispersed quickly.

Those tent camps were filled with the most vulnerable of the population—children and the indigent—and they needed protection, from each other and sometimes from themselves. The Red Cross mobilized to help the refugees. Citizens were allowed to cross borders at will, but most eventually went home when they realized there would be no secession.

You can bet that video of tent cities of American refugees played on every news outlet in every country across the world. Our enemies declared the American empire dead, and China threatened to call in our debt note, a move that would have rendered America bankrupt and would have downed our entire banking system.

Alim spent more time reassuring the United Nations that the U.S. was still a viable country than he did negotiating treaties on trade. Vivian took over part of the U.S. embassy in Beijing to explain to Chinese party officials that America is a vast country, and the secession crisis was overly hyped.

Once the New Republic disbanded and state relations returned to normal, I turned my attention to another matter I thought would secure my place in the Republican hierarchy and avoid another presidential primary challenge: ending abortion.

Today, Republicans oppose state-funded birth control and abortion in its political platform, but it was not always so. Planned Parenthood, which grew out of a family planning advocacy by feminist Margaret Sanger, was supported by everyone from Martin Luther King Jr., who was given the Margaret Sanger Human Rights Award, to Republican President Dwight D. Eisenhower. Future Republican President Ronald Reagan lifted restrictions on abortions when he was Governor of California, then later, when he sought the Oval Office, he blamed his actions on political inexperience.

In 1968, Republican President Richard Nixon asked Congress to increase federal funding for family planning, a plan supported by a Texas congressman and future Republican president named George H.W. Bush. As the elder Bush argued in the House of Representatives, "We need to make family planning a household word. We need to take the sensationalism out of the topic so it can no longer be used by militants who have no knowledge of the voluntary nature of the program, but rather are using it as a political stepping stone."

What a difference an election makes. In 1971, incumbent President Richard Nixon's political advisors informed him that he would need the Catholic vote in order to retain the White House. This presented a difficulty for Nixon. The Catholic Pope had recently issued the *Humanae Vitae*, condemning both abortion and birth control.

Nixon had to court the Democratic Catholic vote—as one of his strategists wrote in a memo "Favoritism toward things Catholic is good politics"—and Nixon did so by reversing his decision to allow doctors in military hospitals to perform abortions on indigent women. Abortion and birth control were suddenly a political platform.

It is unfortunate that such deeply personal circumstances as unwanted pregnancies are used for political gain, and while I condemn it, the fact is that I used it to my advantage as well. I believe that life begins at conception, and the interruption of life after conception is the murder of an unborn child. Disagree with me if you like, that is what I believe.

I also recognize futility when I see it, and futility was staring Republicans, indeed all Americans, in the face when I became President. Pro-life forces had been trying to overturn *Roe v. Wade* for forty years, to no avail. Conservative presidents had appointed conservative judges to the U.S. Supreme Court with the intention of making abortion illegal once again, but *Roe* survived all such challenges. Meanwhile, millions of babies did not survive.

The only way I could see to keep babies from being aborted was to prevent babies from being conceived, and the only viable way to do that, other than banning people from having intercourse for purposes other than procreation, was to make birth control inexpensive and easily accessible.

It should be noted here that while many of my fellow Republicans promoted abstinence as a solution to unplanned pregnancies, few if any of them were willing to take that particular path themselves. It was my premarital abstinence, a private matter that was made public by my roommates, that was the subject of much derision among my congressional colleagues. Hypocrisy knows no bounds.

I knew that my views on abortion would be scrutinized. This is true for all politicians. I also knew that no one on either side of the debate would like the plan I introduced. As Dad used to say, "If both sides are complaining, you know you are doing something right."

This was the impetus behind the Women's Health Initiative I directed the Secretary of Health to create in 2025.

The goal of the Women's Health Initiative (WHI) was to eliminate abortion by making birth control pills available without a prescription, and to provide extensive sex education to whomever wanted it. I was willing to concede to abortion in cases of rape, incest, and the life of the mother, but barely. I don't think it is the unborn child's fault that its conception occurred as an act of violence, but I am also not monster enough to put a woman through carrying her rapist's child.

I didn't bother trying to get sex ed into the schools. That battle would have been time-consuming and expensive and unnecessary.

All we had to do was make it available on the Internet for free. Teenagers could look it up on their own time, and they did, in droves.

Conservatives had managed to get mandatory coverage of contraception written out of the Affordable Care Act. The ACA, also known as Obamacare, required insurance companies to provide coverage for birth control. I had no intention of requiring insurance companies to pay for contraceptives. I had no intention of getting the government to pay for it either. Instead, I provided a benefit that did not cost them tax dollars.

In 2025, birth control pills were a billion dollar industry. That's a lot of cash to chase. It seems obvious now, but back then, in order to get birth control pills, women had to make a doctor's appointment, get an examination, get a prescription, take the prescription to a pharmacy, fill the prescription, then return to the doctor every twelve months for another examination to get the prescription renewed. For a woman working full-time or unable to pay for a doctor's visit, getting a birth control prescription was an obstacle to family planning.

Jackson let his contacts in the healthcare industry know that if a manufacturer of birth control pills filed an application with the Food and Drug Administration to sell their product without a prescription, the White House would order the FDA to grant permission. There were only six manufacturers of such pills then, and three of them filed applications within weeks. Once their products were on the store shelves between the tampons and the condoms, sales skyrocketed and competition for customers drove down prices.

The pro-life advocates had a field day. It seems incongruous that people who oppose abortion also oppose the prevention of unplanned pregnancies, so let me give you a little background. Pro-life advocates believe that birth control is an incentive for single people to engage in sexual intercourse without thought for the consequences. I don't disagree. The question as I saw it, however, was not whether I thought single people should be engaging in intercourse. The question was how to prevent unplanned conception, and therefore, abortion, and the answer was birth control.

This did not sit well with my in-laws, Ed and Marlys, who are staunch Catholics, especially after Greg was notified by the archdiocese that if he did not convince me to change my mind, he would be excommunicated. For the record, Greg never asked me to reconsider my stance on birth control. Marlys did not speak to me for several months, until Greg gently told her that holding a grudge on the issue would mean forfeiting her invitation to the family Christmas gathering at the White House.

The WHI did not please the pro-choice advocates, either, particularly Senator Sedona Hart. Hart was a die-hard feminist who named her children Omega Dawn (her daughter) and Midnite Chardonnay (her son), and never quite got the memo that the hippie revolution had ended decades earlier. Hart came of age in the 1960s, when the Pill forever changed contraception and sexual habits worldwide, and almost all abortions were illegal.

Hart and her followers wanted fewer restrictions on abortion, not an elimination of the need for abortion. Another incongruity, in my opinion. They saw the WHI as the first step in taking away the reproductive rights of women. Feminists argued that WHI was racially motivated, equating "poor" to "minority." I think that equation says more about them than it does about me.

Both sides argued that the WHI would not prevent all unplanned pregnancies, and of course they were right. Nothing is one hundred percent guaranteed. We had to weigh the number of birth control failures against the number of pregnancies, and possible abortions that would be prevented. If we could prevent even one abortion, I was willing to give it a try.

The other part of the WHI was to encourage women to not have abortions by paying their medical bills for carrying the babies to term. The government would pay for prenatal care and the maternity ward for any woman who was considering abortion because of lack of financial resources. My party went nuts. They wanted to cut welfare benefits, not add to them. According to them, they should not have to pick up the tab for some woman's inability to say no.

Jackson did his best to threaten and cajole the Senate to pass the WHI as a whole, to no avail. He struck a deal that upheld the FDA's decision to make birth control pills available over-the-counter but cut the coverage of maternity costs for indigent women.

In the first year of WHI, the number of abortions dropped by half. That is, 750,000 fewer women sought to kill their unborn babies than the year before. The pro-life and pro-choice advocates both claimed the WHI a colossal failure for not eliminating all abortions. It was the first time the two groups had ever agreed on anything. Sometimes I think the abortion debate is less about saving babies and more about one group getting too much action, and one group getting too little action, although I'm not sure which group is which.

Today we take free contraception for granted, assuming that it was always so and always will be so. Not true. I fought that battle, and while it was a battle I won—the number of abortions performed in the United States has dropped by eighty-seven percent—I did not win the war. There are still nearly 200,000 abortions performed every year. It is my most significant achievement and defeat, all in one.

Chapter Thirty-Five

The month after the inauguration, Mother visited her friends in Minneapolis, then left for a two-month goodwill tour of the Middle East and Europe, arranged once again by Jackson's corporate friends. I assumed their cooperation meant they had forgiven me for those invoices that raised enough money to cut a chunk out of the deficit.

The tour began in Spain, where Mother was entertained at the Palacio de la Zarzuela by King Felipe and Queen Letizia. The King and Queen were struggling to guide their daughters safely through the teenage years. Mother fixed a pot of her masala chai, and over tea proceeded to give the royal couple the benefit of her years of mothering experience. Mother told the King and Queen to assign the princesses to duties in service of the poor, which they did. Nothing changes a spoiled teenager's perspective like spoon-feeding an abandoned toddler in an orphanage for the disabled. The princesses now run a non-profit global initiative to battle child hunger, which they named The Cala Project, after mother.

Mother made stops in London, Paris, and Munich as well, visiting hospitals and schools and spreading her particular brand of diplomacy, before heading to the Middle East. It was one o'clock on a sunny day when the first earthquake struck in southern Israel, near Eilat. Every newscaster in the country warned Israelis to prepare for aftershocks, and urged calm and cooperation.

Mother was visiting schools in the coastal Dan area, in central Israel, when the second quake, measuring 7.1 on the Richter scale, ripped through the region thirty minutes later. The Dan area, housing almost half of the country's population, was ill-equipped to withstand that amount of rattling from the earth's crust.

Not one of the three hundred schools in the Dan was built to meet the earthquake-resistance standards, enacted in 1980. As the earth shook, the buildings fell. Some children were trapped and later rescued, but most were killed.

Rescuers frantically searched the rubble for days, not stopping to weep when they recovered the body of yet another child. Praying as they dug, they hoped they would find one child, please God, even one child, still alive.

As Israel and Palestine reeled from the disaster—7,000 dead at last count, and thousands more injured—Greg and I accepted the Israeli President's invitation to stay at his private compound while the search for Mother and the rest of the children continued.

"I can't just stand by," I told Greg as we paced our suite in the compound.

Much to the Secret Service's dismay, we went to the nearest hospital and offered our services, holding the hands of patients and comforting them as best we could. Hour after hour, body after mangled body, they came in, some barely breathing. The doctors patched them up as best they could. I let mothers weep on my shoulder as they mourned their children and I wondered when it would be my turn to grieve. My beautiful mother was surely lost.

I was holding the crudely bandaged hand of a young woman in the waiting room when the headline on the television set in the corner caught my eye.

"Mother Jafari found," cried the words. Then video of the somber rescue workers, gathered around a figure in peacock blue. The camera zoomed in for a closer look as the workers removed their hard hats and pressed them against their hearts. *Why weren't they helping her up? Shouldn't they be checking her pulse? It's possible!* I wanted to shout.

Then I saw the scene as the rescuers saw it: my mother's lifeless body wrapped around the bodies of two small children in a vain attempt to shield them from the falling rubble.

Had they been killed instantly, I wondered? Had they lain under that debris, alive and scared, before death took them? I remembered all the times my mother had sung to me at bedtime, when I had been scared of the dark. Had my mother, a Muslim woman, sung to these Jewish children in their final moments to relieve their fear?

I felt my knees buckle, and the young woman rushed to my side and took me in her arms, and held me as together we wept.

The world mourned for Mother Jafari. Flags flew at half-mast from Detroit to Istanbul to Beijing. Prayer services were held in her honor in mosques and synagogues and churches.

The Spanish King, who had been so charmed by Mother's nurturing spirit, broke down during his public condolences in front of Parliament. The Turkish Ambassador proclaimed at the news of her death that he felt as awful as he had when his own beloved mother had died.

Sympathy cards arrived at the White House by the truckloads. American families planted saffron-colored marigolds in her honor.

Mother was given a nondenominational memorial service at the Washington National Cathedral on a chilly March morning in 2025. I had wanted a small graveside ceremony in Minnesota, but Congressional leaders wanted a state funeral.

"The world is in mourning. Other countries are sending delegations to the service," Kirsch insisted. "Your mother is more popular than you."

The memorial service, privately funded by the corporations that had sent her around the world, and televised on every network, was a compromise. She had been interred next to my father at Garden of Eden Islamic Cemetery within days of her death in Israel.

"Mother would be appalled if we spent thousands of dollars to memorialize her when millions of children went hungry last night," I told Greg.

"She would be honored by the attention, though," he reminded me.

He was right. Mother delighted in her time in the spotlight.

Following the memorial service, the visiting dignitaries were escorted to the White House, where they attended a reception hosted by Jackson and Junie. The new Israeli Prime Minister Eli Barash and the recently elected Palestinian President Yonas Haniyeh were both demanding a meeting with me before departing to their countries.

"Why?" I asked Alim.

"They want foreign aid to rebuild."

"They will only send bombs again."

"Your mother has given you this moment, sister," said Alim gently. "Do not waste it."

I did not want to talk to them. I did not want to see anyone. I was an orphan and I no longer cared about their fighting. Israel and Palestine had never known peace, despite decades of negotiations by my predecessors in the White House. I was in no mood for their bickering.

Alim and Vivian showed Barash and Haniyeh to the inner court of Olmsted Woods, known as the Contemplative Circle, next to the National Cathedral, where I waited on a piece of cut stone, meditating. Neither was happy to see the other. They glared at one another and waited for me to speak.

I took a calming breath, opened my eyes, and addressed them both.

"Nothing I do or say will change your fighting. Go home. Bury your dead. Dig extra graves for the boys and girls who will die when the rockets fly again. Do not expect a dime from us. We will not help you kill each other any longer."

"President Jafari, promises were made to Israel," Eli complained.

"Not by me," I interrupted. I turned to Yonas.

"Don't look so pleased with yourself, President Haniyeh. Israel will live on to fight with you, whether we give them money or not. I am only ensuring that the war escalates as you try to annihilate each other. And when your people are half dead from battle, who will invade Palestine then?"

Haniyeh's eyes widened despite his efforts to prevent any display of emotion.

"I do not understand, President Jafari."

"Do you really think that your neighbors will stand by and let you limp along? One of them will decide to claim your lands for their own, and you will be too weak to stop them. Who will it be I wonder? Egypt? Turkey? There may be a new president in America by then. Perhaps he will decide that a colony of Westerners is just what the Middle East needs for stability. Perhaps he will make me ambassador. Don't worry. I will be sure to visit you in your prison cells. If you live, that is."

"Westerners! In Palestine!" cringed Yonas.

"Palestine and Israel," I corrected, turning to Eli. "The two lands unified at last under an American-controlled government. The West Bank carved up and sold to American housing developers. Condos filled with Baptist evangelicals and Mormon missionaries determined to spread the word to your people. Now leave my country and do not come back with your hands out until you are at peace."

Barash and Haniyeh turned and walked away. Alim told me later that as they were walking to their limousines, Barash turned to Haniyeh, horrified.

"Baptists. In our lands."

Haniyeh shook his head in panic. "Oy vey."

The loss of monetary aid—and a mutual dislike for me—drove both sides to the bargaining table for the first time in decades. A tense peace emerged, until I was no longer in office and my American successors reinstated the financial backing for each country. Once the financial incentive for cooperation was gone, negotiations broke off. Will Israel and Palestine ever manage to find a solution? I doubt it. Too many leaders in that region built their careers on violence for peace to prevail.

Chapter Thirty-Six

It's always the quiet ones you have to watch, according to Greg. He was talking about girls, warning his nephews about the dangers of wayward women. On the day after Christmas in 2026, on a bitterly cold afternoon, I learned that it applies to countries as well.

Our private living quarters were filled with Greg's sisters and their families, including at that point more than a dozen children under the age of eighteen, all high on sugar from the Christmas celebration the day before. Every year we attended Christmas Eve services at the National Cathedral, even though I was always criticized for doing so by Muslims and Christians alike. Nevertheless, the service was important to Greg, and therefore, to me. Plus, it gave me a chance to light a candle in honor of Forsberg, something I still do every year on Christmas Day.

The next morning Greg and I hosted a huge Christmas brunch for our families. This brunch, to put it mildly, sometimes got a bit raucous. To get a break from the family hoopla, I went to the Oval Office to get some work done. I never required my staff to be in the office the day after Christmas, but a few insisted that if I was at work, they would be there too. Jackson was in Texas, celebrating the holidays with his family.

Our defense and security departments kept a constant surveillance on the Middle East and North Korea and China and, yes, even India. No one thought to keep an eye on Canada.

"Suraiya, there is a situation along the border with Ontario," said Henry, after GeriAnne showed him into my office, her scowl a bit less severe. After three years, she was warming up to me.

"What kind of situation?"

"The Canadians have started construction on a pipeline to transport water from Lake Superior to their western provinces."

I set down the latest update on a proposed transportation bill and checked to see if he was smiling.

"Please tell me you're joking."

"The planned pipeline runs all the way to Alberta. They've kept it well under wraps until now."

Lake Superior is one of the five freshwater lakes, known as the Great Lakes, along the northern middle border of the United States. Only one, Lake Michigan, lies wholly within America's borders. The Canadian-American border runs through the others. The Great Lakes make up twenty percent of the world's supply of fresh surface water, and mostly escape political attention.

There was a dust-up when oil companies wanted to pipe water from Lake Superior to North Dakota to be used in hydraulic fracturing operations for oil drilling, but the Minnesota government placed an exorbitant price tag on doing so, and the oil companies found alternative means to extract oil from the ground. All the while, our neighbors to the north were planning their own water hijacking.

Henry continued.

"It gets worse. They've installed ground troops along the pipeline route."

"They're prepared to militarily defend themselves?" I couldn't believe this. It was one thing to commit a political faux pas, to ask for forgiveness rather than permission. It was another to prepare for military action.

Within the hour, Sam, Vivian and I were in the Situation Room with the senior members of the Joint Chiefs of Staff, viewing satellite images of the Ontario border. A silver line snaked across the screen.

"How did we not know about this?" I demanded.

Vivian cleared her throat. "No one was watching Canada. We didn't know anything about this until an environmental watchdog group in the Boundary Waters got wind of it and launched a protest. That's when the Canadian army showed up."

"Any aggression on Canada's part?" I asked.

"Not so far," said Vivian.

"Do you want me to get the Canadian prime minister on the phone?" asked Alim.

"Not yet," I said. "Do you think Russia is behind this?" Russia was the largest importer of Canadian oil.

"Maybe. If we send troops to the border, Canada may call in Russia as backup, then China. We're talking about World War III here," said Sam.

"I'm aware of that," I snapped. "I also know that we can't sit by and let them steal our water."

Everyone in the room knew my view of war. No one who has seen the horrors of war, who has smelled death, considers lightly the prospect of sending sons and daughters to the trenches. Sometimes, though, we must take a stand. This was one of those times.

"Tell everyone to get back to Washington immediately. We'll hold a press conference in one hour. We're going to let the people know what's going on and what we plan to do about it."

"What are we planning to do about it, Suraiya?" asked Vivian.

"Prepare for war," I replied.

"You've read the file on the prime minister?" I asked Sam when the others had left.

He nodded.

"Your impression?"

"He's smart. Cautious."

"Would you say he's more interested in domestic affairs than in world domination?"

"Yes," said Sam.

The press was aware of the pipeline and the military buildup on the Canadian side of the border by the time I walked to the lectern in the press room

"My fellow Americans, this afternoon we learned that Canada

is claiming rights to the entire body of water known as Lake Superior, including that which lies within America's borders. This invasion constitutes an act of war against the United States. Until today, Canada has been one of America's fiercest allies and greatest friends. Make no mistake. Canada's ambitions do not stop at the shores of Lake Superior. If we fail to answer this action, the next stop will be an invasion of Lake Huron, Lake Erie, and Lake Ontario. We will not allow this to happen. I have instructed the Defense Secretary to prepare to defend our borders. There will be many difficult days ahead. I ask for your prayers and your strength for the families of the soldiers. We need each other now more than ever."

"Are you out of your mind?" Jackson shouted at me over the video line when I got back to my office. He had watched the press conference on Air Force Two. "You've just declared war! On Canada! That's like kicking a puppy!"

"That 'puppy' laid claim to our water supply. We need fresh water as much as they do."

"Americans care a lot more about a gallon of oil than they do a gallon of water," Jackson reminded me.

"We're going to run out of water before we run out of oil. My job is to protect the citizens for generations to come."

Jackson rested his head in his hands.

"What did the prime minister say when you called to reason with him?"

"I didn't call."

Jackson stared at me through the screen. "You committed troops to battle and you didn't even call?"

"The prime minister will be calling me any minute now."

"How can you be so sure?"

"Because the only thing a white man in power can't stand is when a woman like me acts uppity. He'll expect me to back down."

In Ottawa, tucked into the southeast corner of Ontario, Canada, Prime Minister Rodney Hunter and his Cabinet watched the press conference with growing alarm, a scene portrayed in a subsequent movie version of the event, *Two Days Under Water*.

"She's crazy," said one Cabinet member.

"She's bluffing," said another.

“Get me the President,” said Hunter.

Hunter and I faced each other across the miles, he on his secure computer line and I on mine in the Situation Room, located in the basement of the West Wing.

“Remove your troops, Mr. Prime Minister. Stop the pipeline, and we will help you find a solution to your problems. Continue your present course of action, and we will take all necessary means to protect ourselves.”

Hunter attempted to stare me down.

“We have Russia on our side,” he informed me. “Any action on your part will be met with combined resistance by our allies.”

“Russia is a fickle friend,” I reminded him. Russia has been both an American ally and enemy over the years. Sometimes both at once.

“And whom do you think India will support?” I asked.

The irises in Hunter’s eyes flickered. When I played poker with the Marines in Afghanistan, that is what we called a “tell.” India has more than a hundred million people in the prime military draft ages of 18 to 25. No nation wants to face a military force of that size.

“India has no stake in this matter,” Hunter choked out.

I laughed.

“I am a daughter of India. Do you really think the land of my forebears will stand by while we face this act of aggression?” In truth, I had no idea what India would do. India had no stake in the conflict at all. White people, though, assume a racial loyalty that may, or may not, exist. It was a bluff, and one I was confident in taking.

Hunter attempted to call that bluff. “Russia is on our side, and China will side with Russia as a fellow Communist country.”

“You would be mistaken to send your country to war on that assumption, Mr. Prime Minister,” I warned.

Prime Minister Hunter, with a slight tremor, reached forward and severed the connection.

I turned to Sam.

“Get me Beijing.”

Sam began entering a series of confidential pass codes into

the computer, asking for a secure line to Premier Zhin, head of the Communist Party of China.

"It's the middle of the night there," said Henry.

"They're awake. You can bet they saw the press conference too," I told him.

"China won't promise to back you against Russia," warned Alim.

"I don't need them to back us. I only need them to sit out the dance," I replied.

When Premier Zhin came on the line, every person in the room fell silent. We all knew the outcome of this call would dictate whether lives would be lost, and how many.

"Mr. Premier, please allow me to speak openly."

I could see the Premier's eyes dart to the translation ticker running across the bottom of his screen. Premier Zhin nodded.

"I am the first Muslim, Indian, and woman to hold the office of American president. My place in history is assured. Yours is not. The only question we need to discuss is how you want to be remembered. Do you want to go down in history as the man who grew China into a superpower? Or do you want to be remembered as the man who sent millions of only sons to their deaths?"

I noticed the skin around his jawline begin to pale.

"Are you asking China to be your ally in a war against Canada?" he asked tightly.

I shook my head reassuringly.

"Not at all, sir. I only ask that you let it be known that China will not take part in this dispute in any way. Even if asked to do so by your comrades in Russia."

Zhin steepled his fingers together, thinking. His eyes moved beyond the computer screen, checking the reactions of the unseen communist party officials seated off camera. I found myself holding my breath. Now I understood how Henry felt all the time.

Finally he nodded.

"You have my word, President Jafari. We will not interfere, on one condition."

My stomach churned. Would he demand lower tariffs on imports? More humanitarian aid? Higher interest rates on our debt?

Zhin continued. "You must invite a Chinese delegation to the United States for an official state visit."

I let out my breath, not even trying to hide my relief.

"It would be my honor, Mr. Premier." India was going to be furious when they found out.

When the connection was severed, Vivian let out a whoop and the others began to cheer. With China out of play, the odds of warfare were even, and only a fool would take those odds.

There's an old adage: Behind every successful man there is a woman. Rodney and Clarissa Hunter's forty-year marriage, according to scrambled-together reports from American intelligence gathering, was marred by alcohol abuse and fights that often turned physical. Clarissa had a taste for expensive jewelry and grand homes. The only way for Rodney to satisfy those tastes was to get into bed with the oil companies, and the oil companies wanted water. The water was pushed underground in the oil fields to create pressure that pushed oil to the surface. In one year, more water was used in oil drilling in Alberta, Canada than by all the residents of the three largest cities in Alberta combined.

The oil companies had already drained the reservoir near Lethbridge in Alberta, as well as the surrounding rivers and underground aquifers. Farms and towns in the area were deserted. There was no drinking water, no water for crops, no water for cattle. The oil companies had taken it all, and not paid a dime for it.

"You're risking hundreds, maybe thousands of American lives," said Alim after hearing China's official position.

"Yes."

"If we could negotiate..."

"The time for negotiation is over, brother. They will understand only a show of force."

"If Hunter is intent on keeping the pipeline, then the only thing he'll understand is a show of force so totally unhinged that it makes shock and awe look like a children's fireworks display," said Sam.

I spent that night in the map room, pacing along the floorboards once paced by Franklin D. Roosevelt and Winston Churchill, hoping some of their wisdom would emanate to me. In this room they had strategized the movements of World War II, sometimes knowingly sacrificing the lives of their own people to save civilians later.

I did not want any American bloodshed, and I knew Hunter was counting on this unwillingness as a bargaining chip. As long as I was afraid to send my people into battle, Hunter would keep building the pipeline. Shortly after midnight, Vivian joined me in the map room and handed me a sheaf of papers stamped "Confidential."

"We're not supposed to know about this," she told me. "In 1985, an American employee at the Defense Department was convicted of passing American secrets to the Israelis. In truth, we were using him to collect information on Israel. The employee died in jail last year, and Israel never discovered the truth. We used the information we planted to gather information on an Israeli attack on Saudi Arabia."

I thumbed through the sheaf of papers, stopping at the grainy photos of a Saudi airfield runway. I looked at Vivian.

"Are those what I think they are?" I asked, pointing to dark gray images lying on the tarmac.

She nodded.

"I know it's a bit unusual, but it might be enough to persuade Hunter to back down, and it would risk minimal American lives," she said.

"If we do this, Israel will know we were spying on them," I pointed out. "It's the only way we could know about this stunt against the Saudis."

Vivian shrugged.

"We spy on them. They spy on us. It's how the world works. Even among friends."

Alim, Sam, Vivian, Jackson, and my policy advisors crowded into the small map room in the hour before dawn. There was disbelief as I laid out my plan. Alim was the last to file out of the room.

"Have you sold your mother's house in Minnesota yet?" he asked.

"No. Why?"

"Because if this goes wrong, you're going to be impeached

and I'm going to be out of a job, and we're all going to need a place to live."

I pulled him to the side.

"Do you think it's unhinged enough to get my point across?"

"Sister," said Alim, "it's so unhinged, I'm starting to wonder about you myself."

"Perfect."

I called the Chief of Staff of the Air Force, General Winters, as a courtesy. "I just want you to know, sir, that I am sending your people into harm's way."

There was a heartbeat of a pause before he replied.

"Well, President Jafari, that's what they're trained for," he said.

Six hours later, four fighter jets took off from the Grand Forks Air Force Base in North Dakota. The jets hugged the North Dakota border until they passed into Montana, then turned north toward the western portion of the pipeline.

Once over the pipeline, the jets let loose their cargo. One by one, the squeal of live pigs rent the air as each of the twelve animals crashed and splattered through the pipeline with unnerving accuracy. American Air Force pilots don't need high-tech gadgetry in their missiles to hit their targets. They manage quite well with live animals.

The screams of the soldiers stationed near the pipeline were so loud as to be picked up on the radar by an American special operations unit that had made its way a mile or so from the pipeline for reconnaissance.

Watching the scene unfold through satellite images broadcast into the Situation Room, I had to remind myself to breathe. I had no idea how fast Canada could scramble its air force. One false move and we would be at war, and despite China's assurances, I had no interest in testing the word of the Premier. China was a country with millions of young, unmarried men with nothing to lose. Such a war would surely encompass every country on the globe. The bloodshed would be unimaginable, and it would be my fault.

It took only minutes for news to reach the Canadian military that the pipeline in Alberta was under attack. This was unexpected news. Hunter had expected me to fold, and if an attack was to be launched, he assumed it would be aimed at Ontario, closer to Lake Superior. The news that live pigs were falling from the sky was so suspect that at first the report was dismissed by Hunter as a sick prank.

By the time the Canadians arrived, the pipeline lay in rubble, the soldiers stationed by the pipeline forever traumatized but physically uninjured, while the American fighter jets were back in the safety of the Montana sky.

I sent a message to Hunter: *Build another pipeline and you won't believe what I will rain down on you next.*

Thirty-six hours after Canada attempted to claim our water rights as their own, Rodney Hunter announced that transporting water from Lake Superior was no longer feasible, and his government would be seeking other solutions.

War was averted. Thousands of lives were saved. Animal-rights groups, however, never forgave me, and to this day picket every public appearance I make.

Chapter Thirty-Seven

Former President Richard M. Nixon called the Bohemian Club's encampment "the most faggy goddamn thing you can imagine," which probably offends a lot of the Republicans who look forward to it each year. Republican men get particularly offended when their sexual orientation is questioned, and Nixon's description perhaps explains why his fellow Republicans abandoned him when Watergate came to light, even though Nixon, who became a Club member in 1953, credited his speech to the 1967 encampment as the first step on his journey to the presidency.

The Bohemian Grove is a campground in Monte Rio, California, owned by a private men's club in San Francisco called the Bohemian Club. The Club's membership is all male, all Republican, all white, and all very, very wealthy. Members include top Republican politicians, financiers, military contractors, and journalists—as long as they are male, white, and wealthy.

High-ranking Republican women and men who are not white are sometimes invited as guests, provided they are rich enough or powerful enough, such as Arab oil sheiks. Members are occasionally allowed to bring their wives, but the wives are required to be off Grove property by nightfall.

Every summer, Club members gather for a three-week encampment, where they drink heavily and hold pagan ceremonies in front of a forty-foot owl shrine made of concrete, and run naked among the redwood trees. In fact, the Club's defense to a sexual discrimination claim in 1978, arising from the Club's refusal to hire women to work at the camp, was that the members preferred to urinate freely, in the open, and hiring women would infringe on their right to do so. The members of the Club are men at the height of their professions, and their legal defense was "we want to pee in the woods and we don't want women to see."

Most controversially, members make backroom business and political deals at the encampment. These backroom deals have been the subject of protests for years, after journalists infiltrated the Grove during an encampment in the 1980s. Today, if you accidentally wander onto Grove property, you will be escorted off the property by armed guards, even when no members are in residence.

When Jackson once again requested three weeks off in July of 2026, I knew darn well where he was going, and although I did not seriously expect an invitation from the Club, after three years as president I was still insulted by the slight, and disappointed in my fellow Republicans. History bears witness to why I was not invited, even for the daytime meetings. It is difficult to plot treason when the person you plan to overthrow is sitting across from you.

I knew they would complain about my gender, and my race, and my religion, but a coup? The signs seem obvious in retrospect, but I was not privy to all of that information until later, after the Freeborn Commission released its report. The most troubling aspect of the entire report is not the fact that Frank Kirsch and his cronies hated me so, but that they gave so little regard to the lives of American civilians, and the people under their command. Their definition of acceptable collateral damage differs greatly from mine, and they knew that I would not willingly place Americans, civilian or military, in danger.

The mistake they made was underestimating the measures I would take to protect the country. Putting men and women in harm's way was not my first choice, but it was a choice I was willing to make when interlopers decided to storm the castle.

Jackson, of course, was central to their plot. Once I was forcibly removed from office, he would be installed as president. All Jackson ever wanted was the White House, and here it was, being offered to him on a platter.

It was a humid, sunny day at the Bohemian Grove when Jackson learned of the plot to overthrow the government. Well, not the government exactly. Mostly, just me. The following conversation took place between Kirsch and Jackson. The content of this conversation was released following the treason investigation by the Freeborn Committee.

"She's in over her head. She needs someone to take all the worries and details off of her shoulders," said Kirsch as they sat under the redwood trees outside the Silverado Squatters tent, the sleeping quarters for Republicans from the business and defense sectors.

"She's doing fine," Jackson reassured him, unaware yet of Kirsch's ultimate motives. "She's not afraid to ask for help, and she usually takes the advice that's given to her. And when she doesn't, it turns out she's right."

"We need to save the capitalist system," Kirsch informed him, opening another beer. "She's not a real American. She doesn't understand our way of life."

"She was born here," Jackson reminded him.

"It's not in her blood," Kirsch protested. "We understand how the country works. We understand that the current setup needs to be changed a bit. She's changed the method of financing the government, and we cannot allow that to stand."

"So you are going to force her to change the taxation system?"

"Not at all. We are going to help her. She can go around and visit hospitals and garden shows or have a baby, and someone else can do the heavy lifting."

It amazes me even now how much time other people spent contemplating my reproductive system.

"You're talking about the President becoming a figurehead, and replacing the office with someone of your choosing. That goes against the whole nature of democracy," protested Jackson.

"It doesn't take any constitutional change to authorize another

Cabinet official to take over the details of the office. She could still be president, but the day-to-day details would be done by someone else. An assistant president, if you will."

"How would she explain that to the people?"

"She wouldn't have to explain it. That's the beauty of our plan. No one needs to know that the assistant president is pulling the strings," explained Kirsch.

"Suraiya is not going to go for that."

"She won't have a choice. We have five million members in the American Liberty League right now, and we're still under the radar. She'll be relieved to have someone save her from all the stress."

"Who did you have in mind?"

"You understand what America needs. How America works. Low-income people don't pay taxes. They don't drive the economy. We do. We can't move America forward if the commoners are dragging us down. And we will help you."

"Who do you mean by 'we'?"

"Advisors from the American Liberty League. A council of sorts. We would provide you with any support you might find helpful."

"Like the Cabinet."

"Better than the Cabinet. The Cabinet is political appointees. Your council would be made up of men who understand what's best for America. Who understand the vision of the Founding Fathers. America is a nation founded by civilized men for the benefit of civilized men."

"Perhaps you should go back to history class, Kirsch. White Christian men were not the first to walk these lands. Half the country was inhabited by Native Americans, and the other half was inhabited by the Mexicans, who were not yet under the influence of the Christian missionaries."

Kirsch waved Jackson's history lesson away as he would an errant gnat.

"They were savages before we came here. Those people should thank us."

The irony is that Kirsch's ancestors did not arrive on America's shores until 1840, from Ireland, during the great potato famine. He was descended from farmers, and rose to wealth by riding the stock market in the early 1980s.

"What you're proposing will take money," Jackson pointed out. "A lot of money. You're going to need a private army, and that doesn't come cheap."

"We have thirty million dollars to start with, in cash. We can get three hundred million if we need it, but I doubt we will. We'll use the nation's military to impose martial law."

"Only the Commander-In-Chief can order the military to do that kind of work."

"A technicality. We have influence everywhere."

"What about the 2028 election?" Jackson asked.

Kirsch shook his head. "There will be no more need for elections. We tried that for two hundred years and look where that got us. It's time to put the rightful leaders in charge and keep them there."

Kirsch's plan, ostentatiously nicknamed Operation Lincoln by the Liberty League, was to lure me to the Grove for the last day of encampment and hold me captive there until I agreed to step aside. This show of force was to frighten me enough to allow the League to take over the government peacefully. If I refused to agree, Kirsch would order a couple of the guards at the Grove to make me disappear permanently, and Kirsch's co-conspirators at the Pentagon would send troops into the nation's capital to declare martial law.

The League had plans for all sectors of what it considered the inferior classes. Take, for example, the League's plan to solve the veteran unemployment crisis. Kirsch said I had muffed the whole deal when I ordered that housing units on former military bases be remodeled to provide housing and assistance to homeless veterans and their families. The League wanted to put unemployed veterans in labor camps. The people in these camps would be put to work in exchange for provisions. That way, according to the League, they would have the enjoyment of working, and still get food and housing provided by the government.

"It would eliminate entitlement programs and solve unemployment overnight," Kirsch bragged. He failed to consider the cost of setting up and maintaining such a program, which would have cost twice as much as the plan I instituted. As I said, it all comes down to economics. America was not for sale.

Jackson must have been tempted.

"Never," he told me later.

"Your loyalty to me is that strong?" I asked.

He laughed. "My loyalty to my country is that strong. You, I merely respect."

That, I believe. Either way, Vice President Jackson Martin deserves credit for finally alerting me to the plot, and guiding us through the six days that followed. Six days. That's how long we had to undermine a plan that had been in the works for more than a year.

He disagreed with the armed occupation of the Grove, though he supported the initial invasion. He would have preferred to maintain the status quo, but it was time for a new America—one that allowed everyone, regardless of gender, race, or religion, to participate. Well, almost everyone. The Club is still off-limits to Democrats.

Chapter Thirty-Eight

Education reform nearly got me killed. Henry created a new education plan in 2025, the summer after we won reelection, which we called the Shaw Partnership. The Shaw Partnership brought together leaders from the education arena, nonprofit sector, and the private technology sector. The group created a curriculum for seventh through twelfth grades that taught the core subjects of English, math, history, and science by using precepts of technology. In an eight-week period, the teachers designed the concepts to be taught, the computer engineers found a cost-effective way to marry it with technology, and the nonprofit leaders created a way to get it into the schools.

Any student enrolled in the Shaw Partnership would graduate from high school with a bachelor's degree in computer science, information systems, or technology management. In short, the kids would leave high school with a college degree, ready to enter the workforce as taxpayers. It was a rigorous year-round program, leaving students with little time to get into trouble.

"We should name this thing after Abraham Lincoln or Martin Luther King, Jr.," Sam complained. "People love them. It's going to be tougher to market if we name it after Henry."

I insisted. "It is his idea. His research. His plan. He deserves the credit for this."

We were already looking ahead to the 2028 election. If we could get the Shaw Partnership in place quickly, we would be able to see initial results within three years. If we tried to get it through Congress, it would be stalled for months, if not years.

Not everyone agrees that better education is desirable. Several states make concerted efforts to underfund public education, ensuring an easily manipulated workforce that is uneducated, ill-prepared, and nearly illiterate. It is a shameful practice that continues to this day.

To get around politicians who would stand in our way, we offered the Shaw Partnership to any school district in the U.S. that wanted it. The cost was borne by grants from the Department of Education and the tech sector, which was alarmed at the dearth of qualified American job seekers. As soon as we announced the program, we were overrun by requests from hundreds of school districts hungry for resources. Greg joined the Shaw Partnership to help the task force manage the workload. He placed the poorest of the schools at the top of the list, and the group got to work.

The Shaw Partnership was criticized as devaluing the humanities and forcing students into an Indian cult of engineering. Art is great. I love art. But starving artists do not pay income taxes or real property taxes or sales taxes. To create revenue, we needed people with skills employers were willing to pay for, and that meant information.

In early 2027 we were beginning to see the early effects of this partnership. The first wave of Shaw graduates were entering the workforce. These were kids from some of the poorest and roughest areas of the country, and without Henry's program, many of them would not have finished high school, much less gone to college. We offered them a hand up and they grabbed on and did the rest.

The crime rate was ticking down. The teenage pregnancy rate was decreasing. Drug use was on the decline. Revenue was inching up.

"You are a genius," I told Henry when we went over the numbers.

"We haven't been able to keep up with demand," Henry reminded me. "There's a waiting list now, and that's going to be an issue in the election."

"We're making a dent, and I can work with that," I reassured him.

The American Liberty League was looking at the numbers, too, and they did not like what they were seeing. An underprivileged kid with a good job was bound to threaten their power in the future, and they were not about to let that happen.

Jackson confessed the traitors' plan to me a few days before the Bohemian Grove Encampment of 2027. He was to extend an invitation to me to attend encampment. I was not to know that the official encampment had ended forty-eight hours earlier. Once at the Grove I would be imprisoned until I agreed to step down and let Jackson take over as president, "guided" by a council led by Frank Kirsch. If I did not agree, I would be killed.

I could not contain my anger and disappointment in Jackson.

"This has been in the works for a year, and you're just telling me now!"

Jackson hung his head. "I swear, Suraiya, I thought it was all talk. I didn't think they would go through with it."

"Who is in on it?" I asked.

Jackson shook his head. "I don't know for sure. Frank has initiated all of the conversations with me, but there must be many others backing him. Governors, party officials, Secret Service agents, Cabinet members. Who knows?"

"What about Sam?"

Jackson thought about this. "It's possible. Anything is possible. My guess is that Sam will wait to see who comes out on top, and then declare his loyalties to the victor."

We were sitting in the First Family's private quarters, the only place in the White House where there are no Secret Service agents. Jackson did not want anyone to witness the conversation for fear of word getting back to Frank that I knew about the coup. He was right to be concerned. I was pacing the living room and waving my arms like a madwoman.

"That son of a ..." I picked up my teacup and threw it against the wall, shocking Jackson.

"If you don't go to the Grove, his plan fails," Jackson pointed out.

"And how long until they try again?" I shouted. Greg came running into the room. He scanned the living room, taking in the shards of teacup, Jackson's red eyes and pale face, and my agitation.

"What's happened?" He looked at my clenched fists and turned to Jackson.

"Tell me what's going on."

Jackson turned to me and shook his head. I've never taken a survey, but I'm pretty sure most wives are never forced to look closely at their husbands and wonder if he is in on a conspiracy to remove her from the Oval Office. I'm ashamed now to admit that I hesitated before telling Greg, if only for a second.

"There's a plot to kill me in six days," I told him.

"They won't kill you if you do what they want," Jackson interrupted.

I rolled my eyes. "Wake up, Jackson! They're going to kill me no matter what!"

Greg was staring at us.

"There are always plots to kill you," Greg said calmly. "There's been a plot uncovered every week since you took office. Isn't this what the Secret Service is for?"

"This is different," Jackson told him. "It's an inside job. There may be agents in on it. We don't know who to trust."

Greg opened his mouth to speak, then closed it. He left the room, and I heard the clank of a metal door being opened and shut, and I knew what he was doing. A moment later he returned, a loaded 9mm in each hand. He handed one to me, and I took it.

Greg met my eyes. "They'll have to get through me first."

I nodded. "Don't worry. I know who I can trust."

Thirty-six hours later there was a crowd in my White House living room. SSgt. Embers was studying a map of the Grove, along with Bussman, Clark, and Hernandez. Alim and Greg leaned in over the back of the sofa.

Jackson was pacing near the piano, stopping every now and then to chew an antacid tablet and answer questions about the Grove. Only Embers was still serving active duty. The others were on inactive status unless recalled by the military. They all had been in this room many times before with their families, celebrating birthdays or anniversaries or simply enjoying a quiet evening with us. This time we were all somber.

I was honest when I called each of them.

“I need your help. You can’t tell anyone where you are going when you leave, and it’s possible you may not be able to tell them where you’ve been when you get back.”

I rarely finished my little speech before each of them said, “I’m in.”

“They’ll be watching the shoreline and the main road,” said Embers, tapping the map. “There will be motion sensors and cameras in the trees. There is no way in or out undetected. We’ll need to disable the video feeds and the electronic signals to take them by surprise.”

“I can hack into their system and disrupt their communications. But you’ll only have a few seconds before they realize something is happening,” said Greg.

“If we can coordinate that disruption with sniper fire to take out the guards we can see, we’ll have enough of an advantage to overpower the ones we don’t know about,” said Embers.

“Give me some of those,” I said to Jackson, who poured a pile of fruit-flavored antacid tablets into my palm. My friends were planning an invasion on American soil to save the American presidency. They were planning to save me. If one of them died, I would never forgive myself.

“We’re going to need troops,” Embers said to me.

“The California Army National Guard is headquartered less than three hours away from the Grove,” I told him. “Tell me what you need. It will be ready.”

By the time we had finished planning the invasion, there were three days until Frank expected me to make an appearance. The plan was for Embers and the other men to lead the National Guard in storming the Grove the night before I was scheduled to arrive, thereby surprising Frank and his cohorts. In the meantime, we had to pretend that everything was normal. We didn't know who was watching or what side they were on. I was now carrying a weapon at all times, concealed under my blazer.

We had no idea who would be at the Grove, and whether the people there were part of the conspiracy or full-time security personnel simply doing their jobs. I did not want innocent people killed, but I knew the guards would not hesitate to open fire on my people. The National Guard troops would do what they had to do.

Two days before the invasion, SSgt. Embers left for California with Greg, Bussman, Clark, and Hernandez. The Secret Service was preparing for my official trip. They did not know yet that I would be staying in Washington. Henry, Grace, and Aaron were on vacation. I had sent Sam as my emissary to a fundraiser in Florida.

I called Alim into the Oval Office.

"You're going to visit the American embassy in London, tonight," I said.

Alim was not happy with this news.

"I should be with you now."

I ignored his protests.

"Take Hasna and the girls. Make sure you're seen by as many people as possible. Take the Muslim congressmen with you. And any high-ranking Muslim staffers. You all need to be far away from here when this happens."

"I am not afraid of what people will think, Suraiya."

I lost my patience.

"Then you are a fool, brother! We will be fending off conspiracy theories for generations. Do you not think that people will worry about my motives when they find out I ordered a military operation *on our own soil*?"

"You will tell them about the plot."

"And Frank will call me a liar. Then who will people believe? Do you really want to give our enemies fodder for their stories?"

Alim paced the floor a moment, then hugged me to him. "We will pray for your safety, Suraiya."

"When you get back, Alim, you must teach me some of your prayers. I find I need them more and more."

When Alim sent me a text that they had landed in London and were on their way to the embassy, I called the California governor, a Democrat by the name of Graham Strommer.

"This is a courtesy call, Governor. I mobilized your National Guard. They will be taking orders from my men for at least the next forty-eight hours."

Governor Strommer was silent.

"Governor?"

"Is there something I should know, President Jafari?"

"It is a matter of national security. If you leak news of it to the press early, you will look like a traitor. If you keep mum until I call again, you can use it in your next election. How's that?"

"There will be no leaks from me." Strommer kept his word, a fact he emphasized in all of his campaign materials in the next election, and I would have kept mine, if our plan had not gone wrong.

Chapter Thirty-Nine

The flaw in our plan was in thinking that Kirsch would play by his own script.

Embers had advised me to wait out the military takeover of the Grove in the Situation Room, which I did. We did not know whom to trust in those precarious days, and I put my faith in as few people as possible. I had given the White House staff—from the administrative assistants to the custodians—the day off. Only GeriAnne ignored my orders and was dutifully at her desk.

The PPD had refused my orders to give me space, until I threw what my mother used to call a "hissyfit." Frank would not have been so confident in his plan unless he had agents under his control, and it was unknown whether the PPD could be trusted. Later, the Secret Service director offered her resignation, blaming herself for the failure to detect the double agents. I refused to accept it. I knew she would leave no stone unturned in her quest to prevent something like that from happening again on her watch. From that day forward I was the safest person in all the world.

I stayed in the safety of the Situation Room until Greg called to tell me that the Grove was under Embers's command, and the Grove's surviving occupants in handcuffs. Greg estimated less than a dozen dead, and all of those were heavily armed Groves personnel. Certainly those men never knew the plan being perpetrated by the people they were protecting, and we took care that they not be labeled co-conspirators.

The intelligence unit of the National Guard was interrogating the people found at the Grove while Bussman observed the interrogations, separating those who were traitors from those who were merely employees. Clark and Hernandez were searching the Grove for evidence of the American Liberty League's involvement.

Jackson called a few minutes later.

"Kirsch isn't here," he said. "He's deviating from the plan."

"Any idea where we can find him?" I asked.

"Nope. And no one here is talking."

"He's probably in hiding," I said, thinking back to my days in Afghanistan, when insurgents disappeared into holes in the ground like rats. "Keep searching the compound."

"Suraiya..." He trailed off.

"What is it?"

"I'm not sure. My gut is telling me that something is off."

I learned a long time ago to trust my gut, but we were walking a perilous road, and quite frankly, my trust in Jackson in those hours was hanging by a thread. I'm ashamed to admit that now. If I had trusted him more, if I had paid more attention to what his gut was telling him, I would not have walked so blithely to my own assassination.

The hair on the back of my neck stood up as soon as I entered the Oval Office, although I did not see anyone in the room, except for Grace's stupid Santa doll perched on a pedestal where a bust of Thomas Jefferson was supposed to sit. The 9mm weighed heavily in its holster under my jacket, as though signaling that it was time for its White House appearance.

I looked around the room and saw nothing out of place, yet the very air was awry. Walking toward the center of the room, I removed my weapon from its holster.

"Put the gun down, Suraiya," said Kirsch, materializing from behind a silk curtain to my right. He held a revolver pointed straight at my chest.

"A traitor in the draperies," I said. "That sounds like an appropriate title for your autobiography, Kirsch."

He sneered. "I am saving this country. History will remember me as a hero. Now put the gun down."

I set my 9mm on the coffee table, then calmly sat down on the sofa.

"How do you see this playing out, Frank?"

"I was going to be generous with you. I was going to let you remain as the figurehead of the country. But you and that coward Martin ruined that plan. So now I think I'll kill you."

"Jackson will never be your puppet," I said.

"At least you will be out of office and things will return to normal."

"Normal. As in, a country run by old white men."

"Better than a country run by Muslim radicals."

"If you are going to kill me, at least let me enjoy one last cup of tea," I said.

"You're not going anywhere."

I raised my hands in defeat. "I did not ask to leave. I will face my death with dignity. I only want you to ring GeriAnne and ask her to bring in a tea tray."

"And let her alert the Secret Service? No way."

"The agents were dismissed from the White House interior until the takeover of the Grove was complete," I informed him. "There are no agents on this floor today. Only myself and GeriAnne. Surely you are not scared of an elderly secretary."

He looked uncertain. "Fine. Ask her for tea. But if you alert her in any way, I'll kill you both."

I walked to my desk, buzzed GeriAnne, and asked for the tea tray. "Earl Grey, GeriAnne, if you will. And two cups." It was a vague signal that all was not well, and I hoped she would pick up on it.

I returned to the sofa, and motioned Kirsch to sit at the Resolute desk. "You've spent months conspiring to sit in this office, you might as well take your opportunity."

"Jackson may come to his senses, yet," insisted Kirsch. He sat on the sofa across from me, where Jackson had sat only four years ago to accept the vice presidency, and we waited.

GeriAnne entered with the tea tray, setting it on the table between us. Kirsch held his revolver down by his thigh, out of her sight, but still pointing at me. Without speaking, she poured a cup of tea for Kirsch, then me. She left the room without so much as backward glance. So much for a signal for help.

I held my saucer in my left hand, lifting the cup with my right. "To the future," I toasted, "whatever that might be."

Kirsch sipped his tea absently, momentarily letting go of his revolver. I tried to calculate the odds of reaching my gun before he managed to get to his.

"Don't even think about it," he said, reading my mind.

"What did I do to you to deserve such animosity?" I asked.

He shrugged. "It's not personal. Someone like you has no place in the White House."

"Gee, how could I take that personally?" I muttered, my patience wearing thin. I took a deep breath, digging down inside to my military training.

No matter how much training a soldier goes through, the heart starts to pound when the battle gets dicey. The only way to cope is to tap into the anger at the enemy for trying to separate your body from your soul. In battle it is kill or be killed. If I was going to die, I was going to make sure I went down fighting, and I was definitely going to do my best to take Kirsch with me.

"There's still time to back out, Frank," I bargained. "Do you really want your family to live with the stain of your treason? Walk out now. Leave the country. Don't come back. No one will ever know your shame."

Kirsch chuckled, a little too loudly, I thought. I noticed a glaze moving across his eyes. He drank the rest of his tea, and I realized as he attempted to place his cup on the saucer, and the saucer on the table, that his hands were unsteady.

A fog was moving across my brain too. I had not drunk as much tea as Kirsch, so while my reflexes were diminished, I was not as impaired as was Kirsch. I mustered all my faculties, which were decreasing significantly as each second passed by, and lunged for my gun. My shin collided with the corner of the coffee table, sending me sprawling onto the floor while trying to get a grasp on my gun.

Kirsch was a fierce, albeit slightly incapacitated, adversary. He struggled to gain a hold on his revolver, and by the time I was in a standing position, we were facing off in what can only be described as a modern duel. There was no one there to count off twenty paces.

He fired his weapon.

I fired mine.

Mine missed.

His did not.

Chapter Forty

Greg hovered over me in a dream.

"She's waking up!" I heard him say.

My eyelids were too heavy to keep open. Fingers pried my eyelids apart and a light flashed into my pupils.

"Leave me alone," I ordered the light.

"Honey," Greg coaxed, "open your eyes, just for a little bit."

I did as he asked, squinting to bring him into focus.

"Somebody hand me her glasses," he commanded.

There was whispering and shuffling in the room as shadows moved about. He gently placed the plastic eyeglass frames on my face, and as my sight adjusted to the surroundings, I felt him release a sigh of relief.

"You're going to be fine," he told me.

"Am I sick?" I asked.

Greg exchanged looks with a shadow in a white coat that I began to realize was the White House physician, Dr. Fishman. Soon other shadows came into focus: Jackson, Junie, Alim, and even GeriAnne, were gathered about the room, wringing their hands with worry. A flash of memory bolted through my mind: the plot, the Grove, Kirsch in my office, guns going off.

"What was in that tea?" I growled at GeriAnne. I tried to use my arms to push myself into a sitting position, but a searing pain ripped through my left shoulder.

"Shhh," soothed Greg. "You've been shot. The doctors were able to remove the bullet, but they had to rebuild your shoulder. You're going to be out of commission for awhile."

Alim drifted in and out of focus over Greg's shoulder.

"You were right, brother."

He moved closer.

"You did well, Suraiya. You honored your people with your actions. All of your people. Your parents would be so proud to see you now."

"What about Kirsch?"

Jackson stepped forward. "In prison, charged with treason. He collapsed as you pulled the trigger and your bullet hit the Santa doll. Otherwise you would have gotten Kirsch right in the heart."

"I wish I had," I mumbled, embarrassed that my shot was off and the civilian Kirsch had hit its target.

I looked at Jackson. "Kirsch got his way. You're running the country now."

"Only until you get back on your feet," Jackson said. "We've got a reelection to plan."

"Do you think we can win?"

Jackson chuckled. "You shot Santa. It doesn't look good for us."

Junie stepped forward, and I noticed her eyes rimmed with red.

"Don't cry, Junie. Unless..." I struggled to process the facts, and grasped her hand, "Am I dying, Junie?"

"We were worried about you, that's all. The whole country is worried about you. Churches, mosques, synagogues—they've all been holding prayer vigils for you around the clock for three days. Even atheists are lighting candles for you outside the front gate." She turned to Jackson. "You need to reassure the people that Suraiya is going to be alright."

Another flash of memory: my brain growing foggy. Kirsch's

eyes glazing over. I pointed at GeriAnne. "She drugged me. Arrest her."

"She saved you, Suraiya," said Greg, stroking my hand. "She knew something was wrong when you asked for Earl Grey, so she put sedatives in it to disorient Kirsch. She tried to signal you by pouring you only half a cup. Didn't you notice?"

My brain tried to connect the flashes pinging around my mind, and failed. My eyelids grew heavy again.

"She needs to rest," said Dr. Fishman, ushering the Martins and Alim and GeriAnne to the door. A ping in my brain hit its mark.

"Wait! GeriAnne, why did you have sedatives in your desk at the White House?" I asked.

She shrugged. "When you became vice president, I thought I might need to use them on you someday." With that, she turned and walked out the door.

I never let GeriAnne prepare my tea again.

Chapter Forty-One

When the dust settled at the Grove, we had enough evidence to indict Kirsch and Claire Herrick, the Secretary of the Department of Homeland Security, for treason. We also had confirmation of the involvement of several prominent business people and two Republican governors.

"Proving what they knew and when they knew it will be difficult," Sam pointed out when he came to visit me in the hospital. "There are ways we can use this to our advantage."

"They're traitors, Sam. I'm not going to let the Attorney General negotiate plea bargains with them."

Jackson sat silently in the corner, nursing a cup of tea. I was worried about him. He hadn't been the same since we had sifted through the transcripts of Frank's texts and Jackson realized how expendable he had been considered by people he thought were his friends.

"Even if we could get these men to enter plea bargains, which I doubt, that would only put them in prison. They are much more useful to us if we hold this evidence over their heads," said Sam.

"That's extortion. Which is illegal."

Sam shook his head.

"It's negotiating. We'll let them know we have the evidence, and we are considering all of our options. Then we'll point out we are willing to believe that Kirsch and Herrick acted on their own, and we want to focus our attention on the upcoming election and we would appreciate their help in doing so."

"You want me to let them buy their way out."

Sam shrugged. "It's politics, Suraiya. You try to take them down and you'll spend the next decade fighting them in court. You let this slide, and they'll return the favor."

"Jackson? What's your take on this?"

Jackson sighed.

"He's right. It's a different game with these people, Suraiya. If you don't set the rules, you'll be forced to play by theirs, and they won't quit until they destroy you."

The deal was struck. Speculation has swirled ever since about exactly who was involved and how they escaped prosecution. That was the game we played. I will never reveal the names of the players. I will keep my word.

The executions were scheduled for a frigid Thursday morning in February. Kirsch and Herrick were to be given lethal injections at 10:00 a.m. in their respective prisons. Kirsch asked for death by firing squad, apparently deeming that a more noble death, and the court was only too happy to oblige.

The night before the executions, I gathered my most trusted advisors in the Oval Office for a meeting about whether to stop the executions and commute the sentences to life in prison. Alim, Sam, Vivian, Henry, Grace, and Aaron were all squeezed onto the new cream-colored sofas, replacements for the sofas that had been spattered with my blood when Kirsch shot me. Jackson and I sat in the wing chairs.

"Good riddance to bad rubbish," said Jackson, sipping his chai. The taste had grown on him, and he now drank more tea than I did. Jackson did a daily battle with bitterness at people with whom he still had to socialize and remain cordial.

"We may be making martyrs out of them," I said.

Jackson considered this. "You have to make an example of them."

"The country needs to heal," I said quietly. I wasn't sure that televised executions would accomplish that.

"The country needs to see you take a hard line against treason," said Sam.

"Life in prison would be no picnic," I replied.

"It would be no deterrent, either," said Henry.

"Show of hands: Who is in favor of execution?" I asked.

Jackson, Sam, and Vivian raised their hands immediately. After a moment, Henry, Grace, and Aaron raised their hands, followed by Alim.

The question I get asked more than any other is whether, knowing what I know now, I would again choose to commute their sentences. I honestly do not know. Kirsch railed against the commutation, requesting instead that the execution proceed as scheduled.

I refused.

He hanged himself in his prison cell in Florence, Colorado. He preferred to die rather than live in a world where I was president.

Chapter Forty-Two

I misjudged the anger of the American people. They wanted vengeance against the conspirators who so eagerly placed their country at risk for personal gain, and when I deprived them of that vengeance they turned on me.

On November 7, 2028, I lost my bid for reelection by the widest margin in history, carrying only two states, Minnesota and Texas. I won't pretend that I wasn't shocked, embarrassed, and hurt by this result. The American economy was in the best shape in three decades. Unemployment was at its lowest since the turn of the century. Crime was down. International trade was up.

The American people had everything—*everything*—they said they wanted. But it was not enough. The only thing they wanted more than their own well-being was the death of another, and that I could not in good conscience give them.

Greg was far more sanguine.

"I'll give you four days to grieve," he told me after my concession speech in November. "Then we're planning our next chapter."

For four days I refused to speak to anyone; to see anyone but

Greg, who would bring me a pint of Izzy's avocado ice cream and a spoon every afternoon. It was the only thing I could keep down.

On the morning of the fifth day after the election, I sat down at the breakfast table, showered and dressed and ready to face the world, to find a written invitation from Junie offering the use of their Hawaiian estate. She and Jackson would be dividing their time between their ranch in Texas and their penthouse apartment in Paris, she wrote. Would we consider keeping an eye on their Oahu property for a time?

"Did you finagle this?" I asked Greg.

"She approached me," he confessed. "She said that if you were anything like Jackson you would spend the next year pouting, and you might as well pout while overlooking the Pacific."

Normally, the new president arrives with his transition team in the middle of December. My successor showed up with his entourage at the end of November. I did my best to be civil to him until January, when it was time for my long walk down the red carpet to Marine One to leave Washington, D.C.

Marine One brought us to Air Force One at Andrews Air Force Base, where Greg and I boarded the plane to Hawaii. We watched the inauguration onboard on the television screen, and as soon as the swearing-in was over, I muted the video feed and pressed the button that would allow me to hear the pilot's transmissions from the cockpit.

"You don't always have to walk full blast into the fire," Greg said, taking my hand.

I didn't answer, choosing instead to stare out the window, clasping both my hands around his, and refusing to allow the tears to fall. We were passing over Kansas City at that time, and I listened to the captain radio the transmission tower to change the call sign, saying "Kansas City, please change our sign from Air Force One to SAM 2700."

The tower answered. "Roger 2700. Give our best to Ms. Jafari."

My time as president was done.

Sam spent the next eight years at posts within the Republican Party, assisting in party campaigns and biding his time until a new Republican, Kevin Gilbert, took the White House in 2036. Sam was once again the Chief of Staff, the power behind the power, a place he relished.

Alim went back to the State Department, building his network of contacts throughout the world, which finally paid off when he was offered the Secretary of State position in the new administration. Gilbert risked no accusations of being part of a Muslim conspiracy with the appointment. Alim, his girls grown, was willing to take on the challenge.

Olivia is rarely in one spot for more than a few weeks. She is now one of the most sought-after campaign managers in the country.

Henry returned to Minnesota and accepted a professorship at the Humphrey School of Public Policy. Academics suit him far better than the cutthroat world of Washington. Once a year I travel to Minnesota to speak to his students about our time in the White House. Greg and I crash in Henry's guest room for a few days, and Grace and Aaron come over and we all stay up late reminiscing about those heady days when we ran the world.

Grace and Aaron reopened the law office, this time in a high-rise building overlooking a lake in the western suburbs of Minneapolis. Grace argues cases before the state supreme court as an appellate lawyer. Aaron now specializes in acrimonious divorces among high-worth spouses. He once told me that no matter how bitter the divorce, it was still more cordial than dealing with politicians.

Daris and Neeta quietly divorced the year after I left office, and Daris moved in with his long-term partner, Alan, of whom I was not aware until they visited us in Hawaii. Hanging out with the two of them around the dinner table, listening to them finish each other's sentences, it finally occurred to me that in spite of religion and politics, sometimes two people just fall in love.

One sunny day, Alan, a former college quarterback, was tossing a football back and forth with Greg on the beach while Daris and I watched from the lanai.

I turned to Daris."Is he the one you want to be with forever?" I asked.

Daris stole a glance in my direction.

"He's my everything, Suraiya."

That was a sentiment that I could understand.

"Then, if you decide to marry, I would like to host the wedding for you here. Whenever you want. I just want to be a part of it."

It was a beautiful ceremony, and when Daris asked me to stand at his side while he and Alan exchanged vows, I knew he had finally forgiven me.

Jackson died in 2033. In his trust, he left the use of the Oahu estate to Greg and me for our lifetimes, writing "You had my back, now I have yours. Thanks, Suraiya." Jackson Martin, politician to the end.

Greg and I stayed in Hawaii for a year, until I felt emotionally ready to stop walking the beach and rejoin the world. Greg threw a dart at the map, where it landed on Morocco, and off we went.

Greg and I now divide our time between Hawaii, where Greg works as an IT consultant, and a cottage in the Alps that we bought on a whim while traveling through Switzerland in 2036. I spend my days reading, keeping in touch with our families and friends, and studying the Quran through a course I found online. I am working on building a closer relationship with God, and figuring out what my faith means to me.

Sometimes, when Greg and I are feeling nostalgic, we turn on music and we waltz. We rarely go back to the mainland, preferring instead the quiet of the island. We were the most coveted assignment in the Secret Service for ten years, until our protection tenure ran out.

I tell my story now for one reason only: because if I do not, someone else will. Much has been written about me and my presidency and much of it is wrong. All my life, others sought to define me.

With this memoir, I define myself.

Acknowledgments

A special thanks is owed to the Indian-Americans who shared their stories with me to create the Jafari family:

Savita Harjani, whose strength and elegance served as the basis for Suraiya's personality and integrity. Savita not only inspired the character of Suraiya, but named her as well.

Chux Madhav, who shared his family's background in Gujarat, India, and Mozambique, Africa, including his childhood memory of being in the internment camps.

J. Ashwin Madia, the political alter-ego for Suraiya, for his time and insight into the running of a Congressional campaign and being a Marine Corps lawyer.

Nirmala Rajasekar, the extraordinary musician, who shared her insights on bridging two cultures and introduced me to Carnatic music.

Thanks also to Professor David Larson of Hamline University School of Law in St. Paul, Minnesota, who helped me start a war over water rights.

I am so grateful to the friends who inspire me: Sue Johnson, Julie Loquai, Jane Carlson, Janine Fugate, Whitney Hanson, Sheila Emery, Ging Wiandt, Karen Utt, Carla Kilian, Cindy Perusse, and

Nicole Debevec. These are the people who lift my spirits on a daily basis.

My writing group is not only talented, but generous with their time and knowledge. These women—Miriam Queensen, Amber Stoner, Marnie Jorneby, and May Chaplin—have read countless drafts of various stories over the years, and always brought added dimension to the plots and characters.

Thank you to my editors, Amber Stoner, Carla Ewert, and Patti Frazee, for ensuring that Suraiya's story was readable.

My deepest gratitude to my parents, Wendel and Betty, for their years of dedication and support, and for teaching me that voting is a privilege never to be squandered.

A special thanks goes to The Sis, Amy DeBoer, who is also my best friend. If everyone had a sister like her, the world would be a better place.

A big shout-out goes to Kymberly MacFarlane for the fantastic cover design.

A heartfelt thank you to Michael, Molly, and Maya, for their patience and encouragement while Suraiya took over our lives.

And finally, thanks to the original "accidental" White House occupants, President Gerald Ford and First Lady Betty Ford, for giving me an example of tremendous grace under incredible pressure.

Made in the USA
Middletown, DE
14 January 2022